Wild SAINT

VICIOUS EMPIRE: THREE

LUNA KAYNE

Wild Saint is the third book in the Vicious Empire series. It is NOT recommended that the books in this series be read as standalones as there is an ongoing story that began in the first book, **CRUEL SAINT**, and will continue through the four books in this series.

You can't find your way if you don't know you're lost.

— LUNA KAYNE

DAGEN

The last time I saw Nyla, I was in the desert, naked and cuffed to a tree with my own handcuffs.

It wasn't one of my finer moments.

I didn't know her as Nyla at the time. When I met her, she introduced herself as Sierra.

I was all jacked up on residual adrenaline from a job I'd completed, and I needed an outlet.

I was stuck in the middle of nowhere and making my way along the northern edges of the Chihuahuan Desert, looking for the first city with an airport so I could get the hell out and collect my paycheck.

In my line of work, it doesn't pay to stay in one place too long. The longer a job takes, the greater the chance of something going wrong.

I'm a finder.

I find things, and people pay a lot of money for the things I find for them.

I'm known to my clients as Raguel, or bank account number 749-238-09.

They don't need to know anything beyond that, so long as I do my job and acquire what they want.

I make no friends; I have enough of those. I have my brothers, and I have my privacy, which keeps me safe.

Finders are essentially ghosts. We are never seen. We have no description, so no one needs to know I'm actually in the older age bracket for this line of work.

At thirty-two, I am literally getting too old for this shit.

I've been a finder since I turned eighteen, and I'm close to the going retirement age. The jobs pay well, and when you are at the top of the food chain, people pay even more to hire the best.

I first heard about finders through an associate of my father's. I overheard them talking one night at a party my parents were hosting. The guy was retiring, on his way out of the business, and the stories he told sucked me in.

I wanted to see the world, work for myself, and enjoy the finer things in life on my terms.

I didn't even wait for the ink to dry on my high school diploma before I was gone, shocking my brothers and father, who thought I was heading into the family business on the heels of my older brother Lennox.

It wasn't my thing.

I figured my father had enough sons to follow in his footsteps, so he surely wouldn't miss me.

I was wrong, but I didn't know how wrong until recently, when I was made horribly aware of what happened after I left.

This job isn't easy. It's definitely not legal at times, but it is lucrative.

Someone in my line of work can comfortably retire after ten years and live out their life stress free, basking in the sun on their own private island somewhere.

I would have been there already, except I've been

distracted for the last couple of years, lending my time and expertise to my brothers.

But now it's time to do something for myself, which brings me to my code name. I chose Raguel because he's the archangel of justice and fairness, which serves my finder reputation well.

He's also known as the archangel of vengeance, which brings me back to Nyla—or Sierra.

It doesn't matter.

I found out after my night with her that Sierra was just one of the many names she went by.

Looking back, as I have countless times over the last five years, everything about her seemed too perfect. She just happened to saunter into the local watering hole in a podunk town, looking like something from the cover of Playboy with just enough classy grace to make me want to pursue her.

I wanted her the second I saw her, and my dick overrode my common sense as soon as I heard the bartender call her by her name and hold up a drink just for her.

In my horny mind, a local knew her, so she checked out, and I was getting laid.

I only found out later that she'd paid him a hundred bucks five minutes earlier to say her fake name and make her a Jack and Coke—hold the Jack.

So while I continued to drink a few more doubles, she was just becoming highly caffeinated.

I had planned on grabbing one drink and getting back on the road, but as the night wore on, the rundown motel a mile back was looking better and better. Then she leaned into me with a naughty confession of her own that sounded like the best idea I've ever heard.

It turns out Sierra loved the outdoors, and she'd always wanted to fuck outside, but she never got the chance—and who would I be if I didn't help this deprived woman out?

It turns out Nyla is a finder too.

Looking over her past jobs, I'd say she's pretty close to the second-best finder around, after yours truly.

I always assumed the *guy* who was operating under the code name Satyr was just overcompensating for something. It never occurred to me that *he* was a *she*, and that mistake cost me just north of two million dollars.

The last time I saw Nyla, she ran off with my pants, which wasn't a big deal on its own, except that they carried the keys to my rental car, and she took that too. I'd normally chalk that up to poor judgment and a lesson learned, except sitting in the trunk was just over two million dollars, which belonged to a client of mine, and—you guessed it—she took that too.

The clients I work for don't accept failure, and they really wouldn't accept an excuse like I just had to put my dick in a honey-eyed hottie I just met at a dive bar in the middle of nowhere because the poor creature had never had sex under the stars and I was broadening her horizons.

A mistake like this could cost me my reputation or, worse, my life.

So I paid my buyer out of my own pocket and created a debt to sweet little Sierra, who I found out later had claimed her own paycheck under the name Satyr. Her payday came from her employer, who was the one I originally stole it from.

The fact I stole the money first is irrelevant.

What matters is she took from me.

And, as I stood there cuffed to a deceptively sturdy tree with my own handcuffs, wearing nothing but a stiff cock pointing in the direction of my rental's taillights as they disappeared into the night, I vowed vengeance.

Little did I know I would have to wait five years to find her again.

When I saw her face on the security video from the storage unit, I lost my shit.

I was beginning to believe I would never find her, and there she was, walking out of the building carrying the file we needed, and not more than forty feet away from my brothers sitting in their car.

She was right there.

My own team couldn't track her down in the five years they had, so I switched gears.

My younger brother Cole hooked me up with his tech guy, who hacked our contracts system, which is tantamount to treason in my line of work—if it was ever discovered I was behind it—but this information was too good to pass up.

He pulled all of the job's contract information, including the names of everyone who accepted it.

This is when I finally located the name she goes by, but that was all there was.

Any other morsel of Nyla was simply not there.

It's like she didn't exist until ten years ago.

But that isn't all Dark Webb found.

There is a new contract she's signed on for. It's paying out an unheard-of amount of money, and it's open to all of the finders who signed up to retrieve the microfiche that Ryder and Cole are looking for.

Nothing about this adds up.

I shouldn't care that Nyla is walking into what is most likely a trap, but I do, and this frustrates me even more.

I should want to recover what she took from me, take retribution for the money she owes me, and throw her to the wolves, but there is something holding me back.

I had Cole's guy get me a date and a location so I could intercept her.

The date is today, and this old hotel in the middle of Fairbanks, Alaska, is where she's going to be.

I am a finder.

I find things.

Nothing else has ever eluded me for this long.

And here we are.

It has been exactly five years, one month, and three days since I last saw Nyla, and those wide eyes staring back at me in utter fear tell me she isn't as excited about our reunion as I am.

Making my way across the crowded lobby, I'm locked on her as her gaze shoots around the room, no doubt looking for an escape.

She remembers, and she knows where she stands with me.

Good.

I hate explaining myself.

While her appearance has changed, she still moves with the same purpose and grace that sucked me in the first time. That tight little body of hers did the rest, and I can't help but flash back to her raw need as she rode me home on a little blanket in the moonlight.

I've replayed the moment I would finally see her again over and over in my mind, and it's true what they say: there really is nothing like the real thing.

I close in on her position, and I'm twenty feet away from having her when her hand shoots up in panic, causing me to slow my step as she continues to look around the room.

As I follow her line of sight, I realize she isn't looking for an escape; she's looking at all of the other faces in the lobby, and the hairs on the back of my neck stand up.

My chest tightens as I consider our situation.

Scanning the faces, I recognize one other person in the room, although it is from his photo only. He's a low-level finder, just starting out. As I step between Nyla and the person who goes by the code name Blue Dog, I get the impression this guy thinks he's the only one here in our line of work. The guy sits casually reading a newspaper, and he hasn't bothered to scan his surroundings to look for any possible threats.

Nyla's hand tells me to stay back as she puts her other hand to her ear. Her lips move without a voice, just like mine do when I communicate through my earpiece.

Remembering I went radio silent with my own team, I tap my earpiece on, and a voice crackles through before I start speaking.

"Man, am I happy to hear from you. Something's going on," Nigel says. "I'm trying to find out more, but I can't get in touch with your brothers."

While I listen to Nigel speak, I keep my eyes trained on Nyla.

Her face falls as she nods to herself, no doubt receiving some information from her team, and it's probably information I need.

"Look, by my count, four of *us* are in the lobby of this hotel at the same time." I wonder if Nyla noticed the guy dressed as a porter by the front desk. "That doesn't happen."

Nigel types away on his keyboard before telling me the location on their contract has just been updated. "The new information is that the item they need to retrieve is in the safe in room 339."

A contract is never changed once it is agreed upon.

Never.

"Hack in. I want to know who's in that room."

"On it."

Nyla braves a glance in my direction.

I furrow my brows, silently warning her to stay put. The bustle around the lobby becomes background noise to the sound of fingers rapidly tapping on a keyboard through my earpiece.

Then, suddenly, everything goes quiet.

"Shit," Nigel hisses.

"What?"

"There is no room 339," he answers. "At least, not in the system there isn't. If there's a room 339 in the building, and they are all heading for it at the same time, then it's—"

"A kill box."

Mistakes like this never occur in my line of work, and the reasons for wrong information are very few, starting with sabotage and ending with setup operations, and if I'm not the one doing the setup, I'm the one being set up.

Everyone on this contract is about to be sucked into a trap.

I know what's coming before Nigel says the words.

I thought I had more time to extract Nyla before whatever is about to happen happens, but my time just ran out, and I'm too close.

"You're out, Raguel. I've sent notice to the pilot; you'll be wheels up in twenty minutes. Get out of there. We'll figure this out later. I'll alert the rest of the team. We good?" Nigel asks.

"Almost," I answer and turn off my headset.

I have no time to listen to Nigel argue the finer points of leaving now.

I know our emergency procedures.

Leave everything behind, and get the hell out.

It's simple, really, except that it's not.

I have a score to settle, and there's no way I'm leaving *everything* behind.

After closing the last few feet between us, I grab Nyla's arm without hesitation and begin to move toward the exit.

She goes stiff in my grasp as she furiously looks around us.

She hasn't said anything yet, but I can practically see her gears working overtime to figure out her own plan of escape.

A group of camera-carrying, wide-eyed tourists files out of the large tour bus parked out front, and they begin to fill the lobby.

Everything swells and slows around us.

Nyla leans hard to the left, and I'm about to have it out with her when I notice a key in her hand, which is extended toward a row of temporary lockers.

I relent and allow her to open a cubby.

With her one free hand, she removes a duffel, slings it over her shoulder, then nods once.

She's being more agreeable than I thought she would be, so I can only assume she hasn't come up with a better plan yet.

I continue toward the exit.

A woman's voice echoes over the lobby intercom, announcing an urgent call for Mr. Carlisle. Nyla's body stiffens in my grasp, then she attempts to look back over her shoulder.

"Your signal?" I ask, keeping my eyes focused on our exit.

"I—yes." She whispers her response, and she sounds disoriented.

This will work in my favor.

Plastering on my nicest smile for the tourists in front of us, I continue to walk to the door, doling out excuse-me's along with my flirtiest smile to the older ladies blocking our way.

As we pass the seating area, Nyla watches as Blue Dog stands, folds his paper, and makes his way to the stairwell.

She must recognize him as well.

The woman does her homework. I'm impressed.

In examining the situation with Nyla, I know I have the upper hand right now. I have her, and she can't make a scene. There is also something else that has thrown her off her game.

I'll use this to my advantage.

She can try to fight me, but it would draw attention. I expect she'll make a move when we're clear from the building, and she doesn't disappoint me.

As soon as we're through the front doors and on the street, she pulls hard on her arm and tries her best to head east, farther into the city. The only problem is I'm heading west to my plane, which is fully fueled and waiting to leave.

Her attempts to free herself from my hold are beginning to frustrate me.

Her small frame is no match for mine, and I spin her around to speak directly to her for the first time in over five years. That's when I notice her eyes have become glossy.

I'm about to pull her hard in the direction I want when a shot cracks into the cold street. Instinctively ducking, we both scan our area, looking for the shot's origin, when a second and a third come from inside the hotel, and people begin rampaging through the door to escape the crowded lobby.

"What do you know?" I demand as I yank her hard to face me.

Judging by the panic in her eyes, it isn't me she is scared of.

She yanks her arm in short tugs, trying to get away. "I don't know anything."

Her eyes flit from me to the street to the hotel and back. She's cagey. She brings her free hand up, and her slender fingers pick at mine, trying to dislodge her arm from my grip.

"Really? You all just happen to have the exact same job, in Alaska, of all places. Tell me what you know." I hold her there with me in the street.

I know she wants to get out of the area as badly as I do, so she'll talk, or there's a good chance we'll both be shot at next.

"Fine. My team just got some information, and they sent it to me before—" Nyla pauses, and I sense there is more to her story.

"Before what? I don't have time for this. Whoever set you up must know you didn't show up by now. They'll be looking for you," I say urgently, tilting my head toward the hotel exit to remind her we aren't safe yet.

"Before my team evacuated. I—I'm on my own until I can get back and contact them," she answers with another pull.

"Why did your team abandon you?" I ask incredulously.

Radio silence is the last option in my team's emergency plans, and it's only implemented in the event of—*oh shit.*

"A contract hit was placed on me this morning. I just found out. I ordered the evac. I need to leave," she says with another futile tug of her arm. Then she continues, "Look we need to get out of here. The hit is—"

"And why would I care about a hit on you?" I cut her off, putting her in her place.

I definitely have the upper hand, and I'm keeping it until she repays her debt to me.

She turns slowly, and derision replaces the fear on her face. She knows something I don't, and I'm bothered all over again.

"Because, *Dagen Saint*"—so she remembers my name— "your name is listed on the same contract—right below mine."

2

NYLA

Zero.

Count them: zero things went to plan today.

I went from having a fully operational team, an easy payday, and my anonymity to losing it all.

Everything about the job fell apart as I waited in the lobby for my next instructions to come through my earpiece.

First, I recognized a second *finder*, a newcomer to the scene who goes by the name Blue Dog. Then my team called through my comms: a hit on me surfaced in our back channels, and my name isn't the only one on it.

I ordered the evacuation immediately.

The devastating piece to all of this is that the name listed on the hit is the name I've been going by for a decade: Nyla Jensen. Not my code name, Satyr, not one of the aliases everyone outside of my team knows me by, but my name.

It's not my real name, but it's close—too close.

As my teammate listed the other names on the hit, one made the blood drain from my face.

Dagen Saint.

It threw me into a tailspin for two reasons. The first is I still can't believe Raguel let his real name slip when I conned the big con just over five years ago. And the second is because, as she said his name, I looked up and locked eyes with the one and only as he stared me down from across the lobby.

Time slowed, and my entire body grew heavy.

My feet were frozen to the ground; I couldn't move as his smirk morphed into something entirely triumphant.

There's something primal in the way he stalked toward me, making me feel small and hunted, caught in a trap of his own making.

While we are both dressed to blend in with the tourists, my clothing is more tactical, to benefit me in the job I've been hired to complete.

His clothing is tailored.

It looks expensive.

I couldn't see him from behind, but the appreciative stares he got as he walked by a group of women made me think it was quite the sight. His shirt is fitted in places that make my breath hitch with memories of the last time I saw him.

I haven't stopped revisiting our time together in the desert, but a job is a job, and we were on opposite sides of that game. Only one of us could win, and, unfortunately for him, I had information he didn't.

I still have information he doesn't.

I've sacrificed so much to keep my secrets safe and myself off his radar.

Now, it seems this was never a contract. We were being lured into some kind of trap, and I'm guessing Blue Dog's real name is one of those I don't recognize on the same hit as ours.

My team has protocols in place for emergencies like this, and they are now scattered. I need to get back to make sure everyone else is okay and find out why someone wants me dead.

The crisp Alaskan air sobers me as we step into the street. His fingers feel like a vise around my upper arm.

My heart thuds into my chest, and it isn't just because there's a threat on my life.

Dagen's proximity is partially to blame, as I remember how good it felt to be close to him, even if it was mostly a lie.

He smells good too—really good.

Does he have cologne on?

He still hasn't said anything since I told him his name was listed right below mine, but I can tell he's agitated by the tension in his jaw as he scans the street while weighing the truth in my words.

His hold is firm, and a hot wave of worry sets in when he doesn't immediately start moving to get us out of here, since shots were just fired inside the hotel, and tourists are scattering.

We're on the sidewalk at the end of an alley and only partially blocked by a dumpster.

I attempt to head in the direction I want to go once more when a rusted door groans open on its hinges halfway down the alley.

We both freeze.

The van waiting in the alley faces away from us, and it's obvious by the size and shape of the bags being shoved into the back that there are bodies in there. Whether they're dead or drugged, I don't know.

I'm sure if they are still alive, they'll be wishing they weren't soon enough.

That would have been me.

My throat tightens at the thought as chills run the length of my spine.

How could I have been so careless?

This was it.

This was supposed to be my last job, and I was done.

Of course it was too good to be true.

I'm not ready to leave her. The thought brings a wave of guilt over the choices I've made.

Dagen meets my gaze before we return to watching the van in the alley, and I take a half step into Dagen's front to hide myself behind the corner of the dumpster.

He sucks in a deep breath.

In my line of work, I've become conditioned to listen for certain things, and I pick up the pitch of sirens still far off in the distance.

"We've gotta go." Dagen catches me off guard, and he makes it five steps down the block before I recover and hold firm.

"I've got my own way out." The tremble in my voice robs my tone of its confidence, and Dagen tilts his head to the side in curious consideration.

I just finished telling the guy I have no team and I'm on my own.

"No you don't." His eyes flit between my own and my lips. "I'm willing to bet you have a plane ticket, or you're planning on taking the bus. Both will be heavily watched until they get their hands on you."

I snarl my lip at him, and for the first time since I've seen him again, he smiles. It's more smug than anything. He knows he's right.

"I've got a plane." Dagen turns to walk again, as though his statement solves everything.

"Good for you, let go of me." I tug once more.

"No."

"No?"

"No."

I take a deep breath and try again. "We should split up. It's easier to get out on our own."

He squares himself on me and levels me with a glare. "Nice try. I'm your only shot at getting out of here alive, and you know it. You're with me."

"I'm better off without you." I wish I could mask the evident panic and doubt in my tone.

I'm not just talking about this moment.

As soon as I looked into him and learned what being a Saint meant, I kept myself far away from him and his family.

"Again, nice try. You weren't complaining the last time we saw each other. Or maybe you were; I couldn't see your face during that memorable reverse cowgirl move of yours." There is no mistaking his pompous chuckle.

Still, his comment sends me back to that night, and he takes advantage of my stupefied pause to pull me toward an alley across the street as two unmarked police vehicles race to the front of the hotel.

It's late morning now, and the commotion out front has settled into controlled chaos.

I don't fight Dagen as he enters the alley, but I glance around his solid frame to see an older car parked halfway down the back lane.

I'm still stunned. My body settles into some kind of numbed shock, and I shuffle my feet, kicking a rock. It echoes sharply down the alley as it hits the side of a metal trash can.

I'm the only one who falters at the jarring sound.

Dagen is focused on the vehicle in front of us.

My heart rate spikes as we get closer to the car, and Dagen loosens his grip on my upper arm.

I could run, but I'm sure all I'll manage to do is piss him off further, and it would be stupid to go out on my own. I know in my bones that I won't make it out of here on my own.

I'll have to take my chances with Dagen.

He glances at me out of the corner of his eye as I match his pace.

He thought I was going to run too.

When we reach the trunk of the car, I break away from him toward the passenger side to check the door: it's locked. He opens the driver's side, slides into the front seat, and reaches across, manually lifting the lock.

I swing my bag off my shoulder, sit down in my seat, and secure my belongings on my lap before drawing the seat belt across everything. Then I steal a glance at the man I thought I had figured out from afar.

I must have questions etched into my expression because he pauses, asking, "What?"

"Nothing. I just had you pegged as someone with a more expensive car," I mumble.

"Please." He sounds like I've insulted him.

He reaches into his pocket and pulls out a keychain with a multi-tool attached. He jams a small screwdriver into the ignition, turns it, and the car starts.

I was right after all.

The car isn't his.

Dagen's eyes lower to my midsection, stopping when he sees I've secured my seat belt, then he casually drives down the back lane.

I check the rearview mirror to see if anyone has noticed the car is gone yet, and the alley remains empty.

Once away from the area, he picks up speed, and the ten-minute drive to the airport is done in five. There is an awkward silence that I'm more than happy to sit through, and I use the time to mentally take stock of the items I have with me in my bag.

In our line of work, we carry everything we need to get out in case anything ever goes wrong.

I don't have much, just the necessities and some rations to get me through the next couple of days.

I wonder what type of things Dagen would have in his bag.

Both times I've seen him, he looked like he just walked off the pages of a magazine. I imagine he'd have expensive shampoo and some face masks. I snort at the thought, earning myself a side-eyed glare from the driver's seat.

We pass the airport and pull up to the hangars on the far side of the airfield.

I hate admitting it, but Dagen is right. There's no way I'd make it out on a commercial flight. If my name was listed on the hit, then they probably have a secondary list of all of my aliases, and I'm only traveling with two sets of IDs right now.

I can't revert back to my real identity, mostly because I don't have any proof of it with me, but also because, according to the outside world, she died ten years ago.

Dagen stops suddenly in the middle of the lot, taking no care to park properly. We don't have time for any of that.

"I'm not boarding your plane." I drop my bag at my feet, stretch out my arms, and look at Dagen over the roof of the car.

There are a few small planes on this side of the airfield. I can try hiring someone to get me to the next airport and go from there.

Dagen stills, sizing me up.

After what I did to him five years ago, I'm grateful to him for getting me out of the hotel today, but there's no way I'm going with him.

I knew he was Raguel five years ago.

He was a mark, and I enjoyed my job—a little too much.

I crossed a line.

I wanted him, and I had him.

There was something in his smile. Not the smile he shot at the waitress and the other women in the bar. It was in the way he smiled at me.

Or maybe it wasn't. Maybe his smile reflected everything I was missing.

Regardless, I stepped out of line, and it cost me in ways he doesn't know, but ways I am grateful for. I'll never give up, and I can't go with him.

Not because I don't want to—but because I do.

I want to get lost like I did that night, and that will cloud my judgment.

After we were together, and before I handcuffed him to a tree and took off with my payday, he told me his name. He really didn't know who I was, and, up until that minute, I didn't know he was Dagen Saint.

Months after I left him, I had to look him up.

My situation changed, and I needed to get in touch with him.

What I found out about his family conflicted with who I thought he was in the short time I knew him.

Dagen came across as someone who was fundamentally good and easygoing. I could tell he thrived under pressure and enjoyed the adventure of the hunt.

My team and I are thorough though, and a deeper dig uncovered what his family was really a part of. The businesses he and his brothers took over from their father are legal, but they are used to hide dark secrets, and none of them are to be messed with.

Learning this broke my heart for a number of reasons, so I stayed far away.

I remained hidden, and I didn't look for him again.

It was better this way—for everyone involved.

So that's why I can't get on his plane.

While I'm busy trying to talk my way out of leaving, a man runs over to us. Dagen greets him with his name: Nick.

"Sir, we need to leave now. We should have enough gas to get into Vancouver on fumes. I told ATC we're taking off with an emergency, and I have clearance to go within the next five minutes. Whatever happened at your hotel is on its way here." He talks at record speed then waits for his orders.

Dagen nods, then tilts his head in the direction of the Cessna waiting on the tarmac, and Nick turns and runs toward it.

That's not a plane, it's a jet.

"You heard that, right? You won't find another pilot to get you out of here now. You're getting on the plane." The decisive, authoritative tone in his voice makes my feet want to follow him, but my head keeps me in place.

"How do I know you aren't going to turn on me and hand me over to *them* to save yourself?"

He does a double take and levels me with his impatient eyes.

Fine, I was the one who double-crossed him first, and he has no reason to trust me either, but my mind goes back to those people in the body bags.

Are they alive or dead?

I can't afford to trust him with my life.

I have too much to lose.

"You don't. We have unfinished business, you and I. I can't believe I'm saving your ass just so I can punish my two million dollars out of it." His words hit me differently, and a shudder runs through me. "Now get on the fucking plane, or I'm going to carry you onto it."

I open my mouth to respond when the sound of tires screeching around the front of the hangar catches our attention.

There's no one else around. It's clear who they're coming for.

Dagen swears under his breath.

My fight-or-flight decision has been made.

Snapping my lips closed, I grab my bag from the ground and swing it over my shoulder. Then I run past Dagen and toward the plane, not bothering to look back to see how close they are. Dagen's footsteps sound on the pavement behind me, but he beats me to the jet and helps me up into it.

Dagen doesn't even have the door to the aircraft closed before he's yelling at the pilot to take off with or without final permission.

The little plane starts rolling in response as the door swings shut.

Dagen turns to me and wraps his hands around my upper arms, but this time, his touch is different.

"Sit down and buckle up. This is going to be rough." His eyes meet mine when he says the last word, and the pause between both of us is obvious.

I really shouldn't have gotten on this plane, but I had no other choice that would keep me alive.

I clear my throat and nod.

I don't trust my voice to sound as strong as it should, so I drop my eyes and scan the available seats.

I prefer to see what is coming for me, so I take a seat with a view of the car as it drives onto the tarmac. An airport vehicle with flashing lights on its roof follows close behind.

I'm not sure if they are after us or them.

The plane taxis down the runway, and I listen as the pilot talks with air traffic control. They're telling him they aren't ready and to turn back or face fines. Nick doesn't back down, responding that we are taking off due to an emergency and he already cleared it. Then he tells them they need to manage it on their end.

He doesn't wait for their response.

The engine roars as we continue then turn onto another strip.

I lose sight of the car behind us.

We're moving, so there's still a chance we'll make it.

"We're good; ATC already told me this runway is clear to use for the next five minutes. Take a seat," Nick yells over his shoulder.

I realize he's talking to Dagen, who is still standing in the aisle. He's busy securing items in the cabin. He steals a glance at me out of the corner of his eye but quickly turns away, sitting down and buckling himself in.

No sooner is he settled than my stomach drops as the front wheels leave the ground, and we're up.

I close my eyes and count slowly, willing my breathing to even out, pushing my panic away. I have no idea how high I should count, but I keep going because the sting of tears is starting to build behind my eyelids, and I won't cry here.

The rush of getting away seeps out of my system and is replaced by the sobering awareness of what just happened.

I've never come this close to biting it before, and images of my little girl steal my breath.

I'm done.

I'm out.

As soon as I get back on safe ground, I'm cashing in, and I am leaving everything behind.

I was on my own for so long, and I was killing it.

I had even surpassed the great Raguel, but then she came along and changed everything.

These last few years were for her, and I almost threw it all away today.

I must have stopped counting at some point because when I take a steady breath, I forget what number I was on.

"Hey. You're okay."

My eyes fly open at his gentle voice, and I squeak in surprise at Dagen's close proximity.

I didn't hear him unfasten his seat belt and close the distance between us to kneel in front of me.

This is very unlike me.

"Are you a nervous flier?" His question confuses me.

"What? No." I guffaw at him.

He breaks eye contact, lowering his gaze to my hands, and I follow only to see I'm gripping the armrests, my knuckles pale under the strain of my hold.

I release my fingers and fold them across my lap.

I hate that he noticed this, and I don't know why it bothers me.

He examines my face, lingering on my eyes and lips before his concern morphs into a mask of indifference.

"I'll be back in a minute. I'm going to check on Nick."

I nod, thankful for the space to breathe once again.

When he stands to his full height and turns, I make a soft sound to catch his attention.

"Look, um, Dagen, thank you."

He flashes the same smile he did the first night I met him, but his demeanor doesn't carry the same promise it did back then.

There's something darker there.

"Don't thank me yet."

3

DAGEN

The grateful expression falls from Nyla's face.

She's picked up on the warning in my words.

The plane rattles through some turbulence as I leave Nyla in her seat and make my way to the cockpit.

When Nick notices me, he flips a switch and shifts in his seat, turning his attention to me. I look out the front window. I guess it isn't like driving a car, where you need your eyes on the road at all times.

As if reading my thoughts, he offers, "Autopilot."

I lift a headset from the copilot's seat, hang it on the dash, and sit. The seat is small and uncomfortable.

"Have you heard from Nigel?" I ask, running my hand through my hair.

That was close—too close.

"Um, yeah. He told me to tell you to check in when you land." He glances out the little door and toward the back of the plane. "Is she okay?"

I can't see Nyla from where I'm sitting, but I glance back anyway.

I like the lull we're in now. There is no immediate threat, which means I have the momentary peace I need to reflect on our situation.

I have her.

I chastise and correct myself:

I have access to the information we need.

I shouldn't want to have her, but when I saw worry flash across her face, I felt something, and I didn't like it.

I nod, answering Nick's question.

Lennox was supposed to be here with me, but something wasn't sitting right with him in Seattle, so he called to tell me to make my own way up on a commercial flight, that he'd have his guy fly in and meet me at the airport to transport us back.

"Does she have the thing you're looking for?" Nick turns his attention to the dials in front of him.

I don't like the question.

If it were Lennox or one of my younger brothers, I'd be talking openly about it right now. But this isn't his business. Nick is Lennox's employee, not mine.

This is my first time meeting him, but if Lennox sent him, then I trust that much.

I don't know how much Lennox filled him in on, and it isn't something he needs to know.

"She destroyed it," I lie.

Nick shakes his head, unfazed by my answer. "That's tough luck, man."

I huff a bitter breath.

I need a few minutes to breathe.

I haven't stopped moving since I arrived in Alaska.

I look at the sea of switches and panels around us, taking in our altitude as well as an information sheet posted beside what would be the copilot's seat. It may as well be written in a foreign language.

After the first section, which covers the Cessna basics: size, weight, maximum flight time, distance on a full tank of fuel, and passenger capacity, the rest garbles together, and I return to my thoughts.

I wish Lennox were here. He'd know what to do, and he'd keep me in line.

My heart and my head went haywire the moment I saw Nyla again, and I went from seeking retribution to possessively removing her from a dangerous situation in order to protect her.

These past eight months have been an emotional roller coaster.

Ryder almost lost Amara, we almost lost Cole when Harlow took a bullet meant for him, and the secrets surfacing now are tearing us apart.

I began to doubt Lennox's innocence in all of this, and the guilt I feel for that and for abandoning all of my brothers is eating away at me.

Lennox and I were tight growing up.

We had each other's backs—always.

When I hit my teens, he began to pull away, and I didn't think anything of it at first. I was hurt, but I had my two younger brothers keeping me busy.

I didn't notice the separation.

I should have.

I hate myself for not paying attention. I should have pushed him. I should have supported him, but I let him go.

I took his strength for granted.

We all have a limit.

Then I abandoned him when I went out on my own. I abandoned all of them, and it weighs on me now.

I shouldn't have been so selfish.

Our own father sent someone to kill Cole because he

couldn't find me. Cole still wears the evidence of that carved deep into his back.

All of that is my cross to bear, and this is on me.

Nyla stole the file we need, and this is how I can make up for leaving them.

But is it the whole truth?

I shake off my thoughts and look over at Nick, who is staring out the window.

"Where are we?"

"I had to swing inland to avoid some weather. We crossed the US-Canada border a while ago. We're over British Columbia now, and we're heading straight down to Vancouver. Why don't you get some rest." Nick returns his focus to the front, flipping the same button and taking back control. "I'll let you know if anything changes."

I take another look at the landscape below.

It is stunning.

We're flying a little above the tallest peaks, and the rivers and valleys below us look untouched. It's the last place I would want to vacation, but it is pretty from up here.

Cole loves to joke around about my expensive tastes, but give me a five-star hotel with personal concierge service, and I'm a happy man.

I work hard for the things I enjoy, and I enjoy the shit out of them.

I stay, sitting with Nick in silence for another fifteen minutes before I return to the cabin to find Nyla's eyes closed. Her head is tilted to the side, resting on the bag she's clutching and using as a pillow.

I've thought about her for over five years. I've replayed our night together—mostly the sex parts—but I don't like to relive the bit where she beat me at my own game.

Watching her sleep is anticlimactic.

I don't know what I expected, but her snoring and drooling on a camouflage duffel isn't it.

Anxiety surges through me when I'm near her.

Am I so furious that I can't bear to look at her?

Or is it something else?

I take the seat across from her so I can watch her sleep. Resting my head against the backrest, I take her in.

Her adrenaline overload from earlier must have drained her.

As soon as the plane leveled out, I looked over to find her lost in a state of internal terror. I was kneeling in front of her before I realized I had unbuckled my seat belt.

It wasn't her strength that drew me to her the first night we met, although she had a lot of that. It was her vulnerability. I got the impression it was a state she didn't show to many, if at all.

She was quick to hide her worry away, and I let her. She was no good to me in a sheer state of panic, and she's no good to me in that state now.

Nyla shifts in the uncomfortable seat and hugs her bag, mumbling broken syllables before she settles.

Exhaustion tugs at my limbs.

I could close my eyes for a while myself, but I can't afford to lose any time. I'll question her about the microfiche when she wakes up.

The extra rest might make her amenable.

She doesn't irritate me as much when she's unconscious.

One of her hands drops away from the bag she uses as a pillow. I'm curious what she carries with her.

Does she have photos of her loved ones?

Does she have someone she loves?

I yank myself out of that thought and look around the cabin.

I have her with me, yet I can't get rid of the uneasy feeling prickling just below my skin.

No matter how much I check my gear and secure the cabin, there is something fundamentally off about our present situation.

It's unsettling because we just escaped literal death. I should be taking deep, cleansing breaths of relief, but I'm not.

Instead, a nagging thought in the back of my mind won't go away, but it won't come into focus either.

I tilt my head back and close my eyes, replaying the events of the day.

I pause when I remember the bodies being loaded into the back of the van behind the hotel. Neither of us were prepared for an extraction of that magnitude. There was nothing we could have done to save them, and I can live with that, but I wonder if Nyla can. She shouldn't have to.

If I hadn't intercepted Nyla and forced her out of the building, she would have been in her own bag along with them. That thought makes me want to burn shit down.

But she's here now, and we're in the air.

There are no other imminent threats, yet my tension refuses to let go.

I'm missing something.

I run the day through my head again. It's what I do, and it's why I'm the best in this business. I run the scenario until there is no room for error, then I execute my plan.

Most of the people in my line of work are serious adrenaline junkies. They don't think their jobs through; they don't plan. And planning is what makes me the best.

I close my eyes and review everything from the moment I first saw Nyla up until now. Then I go over it again.

I'm replaying our drive to the airport when a rogue thought about a tank of gas on the old beater I stole leads to a secondary memory, and my eyes fly open.

When I was in the cockpit, the docket listing the specs on this plane mentioned that this aircraft can fly five hundred miles on one full tank of fuel.

Vancouver has to be at least twice that far.

Our pilot would know this.

He would have made at least one stop on the way up.

That's not Nick.

There's no way Lennox would send someone he didn't trust to fly us back.

Whoever this guy is, he isn't on my brother's payroll. He intercepted the real Nick, either before he left to fly up or before I met him at the hangar.

I'm about to bet my life on it.

My math puts us close to that fork in the road, and I run scenarios.

Regardless of what happens, this plane is going to run out of fuel in the air. Glancing down the aisle, I take stock of our surroundings.

Nyla has her arms wrapped around her go bag, and I have mine. I left it here this morning when I met *Nick* to go over the plane and my timeline. I glance over to confirm it's still there.

If we've prepared properly, that's all we need. With that thought in my head, I reach across my stomach and quietly release my seat belt.

I stand and stretch, taking a few steps toward the plane's last seat, where I saw the two parachutes stored this morning.

There's only one here now.

Dread sinks deep into my stomach as I gather the second chute and quietly make my way toward the front, dropping it beside Nyla's still-slumbering form.

When I reach the cockpit, the sight before me confirms everything.

I've interrupted him.

We are on autopilot, and the second parachute is now sitting in the copilot's seat. Not-Nick must have stored it up here before we got on the plane.

We were never going to land anywhere.

This plane was always going to go down.

I was smart to hold my cards close to my chest.

If I had told this guy that I didn't know if Nyla still had what I was after, he probably would have killed me as soon as I turned my back on him, then set his sights on her. Instead, he waited until he thought we were asleep, and I wonder if he was going to kill me, then jump with her and let me go down with the plane.

My death would be easier to cover up if it looked like I ran out of fuel and crashed; it would be harder to explain if I were found with a bullet in my head.

Not-Nick startles when I step too close.

"Shit. I—I thought you were sleeping." His guilty eyes flit around the cockpit, and he turns to face the front in an attempt to act natural.

"Well, I—" I don't finish my sentence. I use the element of surprise to step behind him, slide my forearm under his jawline and around his neck, and squeeze.

He kicks his legs, and I lift him out of his seat and away from the buttons in front of him, spinning him to face the cabin so he can't undo anything he's already done.

He lurches for the chute. His hand slides underneath it and pulls out a large hunting knife, but he doesn't have a good grip on it, and it clatters to the ground.

He was planning on gutting me.

I lift my shoulders up and back and start counting in my

head. I get to three when his arms shoot up in panic to grip my own, then nine when they drop away.

With my hold still in place around his neck, I turn to face the front of the plane, blocking the view from the cabin with my body.

I continue counting until I reach fifteen, but I'm not done.

Glancing over my shoulder once more, I see Nyla is still asleep.

If I release this guy now, he'll regain consciousness before we can get off the plane. I'll have to fight him again, this time in front of Nyla, and for some reason I would prefer it if she didn't see this side of me yet.

I drop him to his knees, then adjust my stance and wrap my hands around his head, snapping his neck. His limp body falls at an angle behind the seat.

I scan the landscape for a good place to exit, but we are already dangerously close to the ground. I've never completed a jump this low.

A lake comes into view.

We'll pass over it shortly before we crash, and that is our point of exit.

I grab the chute from the seat and sling it over my shoulders before taking the knife with me.

I turn in the small space and make my way back to Nyla.

I envy the peace she feels at this moment.

We're in the middle of nowhere, on a plane that's going down, but her face rests in the most serene look I've ever seen on anyone.

I take the deepest breath I can before my lungs ache, then I exhale slowly.

My go bag sits on a seat across the aisle from her. I unzip it and secure the knife inside.

It's now or never, I tell myself as I reach out to wake Nyla from what is probably a dream and toss us both into our new nightmare.

4

NYLA

I'm jostling around in my seat as I open my eyes, and for a moment I think we've hit turbulence. I try to sit up. I'm stretching my arms and opening my eyes when I come face-to-face with Dagen, and I squeak in surprise again.

He unfastens my seat belt.

"So—hey—it's time to disembark." His tone is oddly matter-of-fact, and I stare dumbfounded at him with my mouth open.

I blink twice.

It feels like we're still in the air.

I look out the little window.

We are.

Dagen must not get the response he's looking for because he tries again, this time with more urgency.

"The plane is going down. We're getting off." He reaches to the floor beside me and lifts a parachute, and it's just then I realize he's wearing one too.

My stomach fills with butterflies as the plane hits a bumpy patch then corrects itself.

"Shit." I jump up from my seat, fisting Dagen's shirt over his pecs. "What happened?"

"No time—here." He spins me around and fidgets with the chute. Once it's on, I hook my arms through the straps of my duffel so it's sitting on my chest. I don't carry much, but I'm not leaving this behind. "Have you skydived before?"

"Yes." I lean forward, glancing out the window to see the mountaintops getting closer. My hands instinctively roam over the straps of my parachute, double-checking it is secure. "Where are we?"

"Somewhere over northern BC. We're going to land on Canadian soil. This is going to be an extremely low jump, but it's doable, and these are low-level chutes. When we jump, keep your eyes on me, and deploy your chute as soon as you see me open mine. We have a small window."

I nod dumbly.

"I need to do something before we jump." He doesn't wait for me to answer, he just turns and rushes toward the cockpit.

My mouth is open, ready to ask about Nick, when Dagen steps over something on the floor.

Feet.

What happened?

I cautiously approach Nick's lifeless body.

The sight before me is surreal.

Dagen's back is turned as he pulls the headset's cord out of its plug and flips a switch.

Nothing happens.

"He disabled communication somehow," Dagen murmurs to himself before turning to face me. "You ready?"

He doesn't wait for my answer. He takes a step toward me, and I back into the cabin and let him lead me to the door.

This is it.

We're not safe yet.

We're going down.

With one hand on the door, Dagen speaks quickly, scanning my eyes closely to make sure I hear all of his orders.

"You're jumping first. Level out quickly, and I'll catch up to you. We need to clear the plane before we deploy. Eyes on me, always—do what I do. Aim for the water. Less chance of scrapes and broken bones. Got it?" His eyes meet mine, and the grave look on his face tells me he doesn't entirely believe we're going to live through this.

"Got it," I bark back, catching him off guard, and before I get another word out, he reaches past me and pulls the side door open, then turns me to face the open sky.

"Good. After you, Nyla Jensen," he says as I glance at him one last time. I watch his lips stretch wolfishly across his face.

Before I realize he knows my real name, he nudges me out of the plane. Gravity and air pressure do the rest.

I knew I was jumping, but the force of the pull temporarily distorts my line of sight, and I scramble to determine up from down and locate Dagen. As I catch a good look at the bright sky, sunspots blot out my vision.

I blink the tears out of my eyes, and a black shadow registers above me. I keep my focus on it as I level myself out.

Dagen was right: this is an extremely low jump, and there isn't room for any error.

Morbid curiosity almost gets the better of me. I want to look at the plane and watch it crash, but I keep my eyes locked on Dagen as he opens his parachute.

The moment the fabric explodes from his back, I pull my cord. My heart pounds hard into my chest. I'm waiting for the familiar pull, and it's almost too late, but my chute opens and tugs me up before the water rises fast to meet me.

The distant sound of a crash catches my attention before I

go under, and I whip my head around, looking for the point of impact.

As beautiful as the clear blue water looks from above, it is deceivingly frigid, and the shock stops my breath as my head goes under. I struggle with the weight of my bag as I fight to get back to the surface and free myself from my harness.

Dagen landed farther out than I did, but we make it to shore at the same time due to the added difficulty of pulling our parachutes in with us.

"We need to get to the crash and salvage anything we can use to stay alive out here. The plane went over those trees." Dagen's shirt clings to his hard muscles, and I follow the ripples on his chest before snapping myself out of my daydream and back to our plan.

I nod, then add, "First, we need to get these chutes hidden. If they're seen from above, anyone looking for us will be able to track us better. The plane should have sent out an ELT signal. It started transmitting the plane's location as soon as the nose hit the ground. The good news is it means help is on the way, but the bad news is they aren't going to be the only ones looking for us."

Dagen takes a long look at me, considering my words before agreeing with a nod of his own.

A low bush hovers along the water's edge, and I scramble to grab some extra branches on the shore while Dagen secures each parachute under the foliage and out of sight.

"We need to start moving." Dagen lifts his pack as I do the same.

My little duffel is waterproof, and, short of a few drops of water, most of my stuff in the bag is dry. It's extremely compact and easy to carry, so I can move easily in a hurry. However, that meant I had to sacrifice additional space, and what I don't have is a change of dry clothes.

As Dagen unzips his bag, he exhales a frustrated sigh and mutters to himself, "At least my phone case is waterproof, but what good is a phone without a cell tower?"

I check my own case. It should have been waterproof, but the screen has cracked, and it won't power on.

"Mine is dead." I hold it up to Dagen before setting it in my bag. "Turn yours off for now. Don't drain the battery. We'll turn it on periodically to check for bars."

I step out of my boots, then unzip my pants and push them down to my ankles.

"What are you doing?" The pitch in his voice increases as he asks his question with wide eyes, and I notice a slight chatter in his teeth.

"I'm taking off my clothes. It's sunny right now, and we'll be hiking. My body will warm up faster, and the clothes will dry quicker if they are hanging in the warm breeze while we hike to the plane. It looks like an easy walk. Your lips are turning a little purple; you should do this too. Once night falls, we won't be able to dry them. A fire will be too noticeable, and we'll freeze out here in wet clothes." I remove my shirt and clip my clothes to the back of my bag, then put my wet shoes back on.

Dagen sizes me up hard, and I get the sense he's fighting to maintain eye contact. I smirk at the thought that I'm tempting his gaze away from my face.

My smug smile vanishes when Dagen does exactly as I suggest. I'm not prepared for the muscles the guy is packing under his wet clothes.

I've seen the guy before, but damn he's fine.

I turn to give him some privacy.

At least, that's what I'm telling myself as my skin flushes with warmth and I shiver for an entirely different reason.

"So who was he?" I ask the tree standing in front of me.

"Who was who?"

"The guy on the plane. If he wasn't this Nick person you thought he was."

"I don't know. Nick was one of my brother's men. I had no idea it wasn't him." He zips up his bag. "How do you know about all of this...outdoorsy shit?"

My chest swells with pride.

I like that I've impressed him.

I turn to find him taking me in.

The sight of him in only his shoes and trunks reignites the memory of me riding him, and I swallow hard.

"I was outdoors a lot as a kid. It's just how I grew up." Goosebumps prickle along my exposed skin.

"Which was where?" Dagen pushes for more.

"None of your business." I raise my brow at him, shutting down any talk of my personal life. The less he knows about me the better, and I end with, "We should go. We need to make bread while the sun shines."

Dagen pauses mid-step. "Don't you mean *hay*? It's, 'We need to make hay while the sun shines.'" He looks at me with confusion wrinkling his forehead.

I pause, crossing my arms. "You don't make hay. Hay makes itself. That's ridiculous," I retort incredulously.

"But why do you need to make bread while the sun shines?"

I level him with a look that says I can't believe I'm even explaining myself right now. "Because—you need to see what you're doing," I answer matter-of-factly and start walking in the direction of our downed plane.

The snapping of twigs underfoot behind me tells me Dagen is close behind.

I don't bother to make small talk. It looks like we'll have a lot of time to talk later, and I want silence so I can listen to our surroundings for anything that will help us get out of here and back to—

My daughter's beautiful face dances into my head.

Vaughn.

I've been missing her a lot lately.

I used to spread out my jobs so I could be there for her, but things started feeling off about four months ago. First, our home was broken into. Then someone contacted her school, pretending to be a relative and asking for information.

I moved us out of state the next day, and she's been in hiding with my cousin ever since.

That was when I decided to up my game and retire early.

I thought if I worked back-to-back jobs for the next few months that I'd have enough to permanently remove us and start over. I could give her the life every little girl should have.

But I've screwed up somewhere along the way, and I can't figure out where that is so I can try to correct it, and we are literally running out of time.

"You didn't say why the plane went down." I look over my shoulder at Dagen.

"It ran out of fuel. We were never going to make it to our destination."

I return to the landscape in front of us to consider what he's saying.

The guy was planning on getting off here, but he's in the middle of nowhere. He would be just as lost as we are...unless—

"Someone will be coming for him," I muse to myself, and Dagen confirms my theory.

"I agree. I think he was going to deal with us, then meet up for an extraction. I think they're coming here regardless. When they find his body, they'll start searching for us."

Shit.

We're about to be hunted.

They'll definitely find us before anyone else has the chance to, and we can't afford to waste any time.

We need to keep moving, and I need to keep plotting. Dagen and I need to stick together—for now. Going our own ways is the worst thing either of us could do, but I need to be smart about this.

I can't mistake Dagen's cooperation for kindness. As far as he is concerned, we have a history, and I owe him a debt.

As soon as we're in the clear, I'll need to start planning my exit.

I can't allow him to cloud my judgment.

I have too much to lose. That thought takes me back to my daughter.

When I stop at a clearing and turn to him, I'm met with a sight I'm not ready for.

Dagen's deep, soulful look holds my own, and I'm temporarily grounded in place by one thought: she has his eyes.

5

DAGEN

Hiking the mountains of Northern Canada in my underwear wasn't something I thought I'd be doing when I woke up this morning, yet here we are.

With each step, water squeezes through my shoes, but I have to admit, I like the view from back here. I could follow Nyla's ass in those black boy shorts for hours.

It's a challenge to keep my dick from showing how much he likes it, so it's a good thing she's in the lead.

We haven't spoken for twenty minutes, and I'm thankful for the break. It gives me time to think.

When we reach the crash site, we'll have to move fast to get any extra supplies and get gone before anyone else shows up.

I know Lennox won't find us first.

Any rescue teams are already on their way—so is whoever else is after us. My brother probably hasn't been notified yet that the plane went down.

My mind wanders to Nigel.

He'll probably be getting the information by now, but he still needs to organize and contact my family.

Out of habit, I check my watch—I wince. I wore my favorite piece, and it wasn't cheap. It wasn't waterproof either.

Then a nagging question gives me pause.

Why did I wear this watch?

I wasn't on a date. I was on a mission of vengeance and retribution. I wasn't trying to impress anyone, yet I wore a watch that costs more than most cars do. Subconsciously, the way I looked when Nyla first saw me again after all of this time must have mattered more to me than I wanted to believe it did.

I'm so deep in thought that I don't notice Nyla has stopped walking, and I almost run into her.

When I steady myself, the look on her face makes my stomach knot.

I don't know her well enough, but I'd say she looks regretful, and the sight of her tugs at my heart.

Before I ask her what's wrong, she schools her features and clears her throat.

"It looks like the plane is down there." She turns and looks into the distance in front of us.

I try to see what she sees, but there's nothing. "I don't see anything."

"Wait for it." She points at a spot between the trees and pauses. A small swirl of smoke wafts up on the breeze, and she continues walking toward it, speaking over her shoulder. "You said we were flying on fumes. There won't be a lot to burn, and the wreckage won't be easily spotted from the sky. If we get down there quickly, we can probably dry the last of our things by the heat."

As I bring up her rear—I mean *the* rear, I can't help but be impressed with how she is handling herself out here.

I've got to hand it to Nyla: so far, she's been the one with all of the great ideas. We'll need to rely on each other if we're going to make it out of here alive.

The descent to the bottom of the shallow ravine is easy enough. We clear the trees and step onto the dried riverbed floor. Pieces of the Cessna are scattered everywhere. Knowing our plane went down and seeing the wreckage are two different things.

The severity of our situation sinks in as we move quickly to where the cockpit should be, but the front of the aircraft is split open.

"He's not in the plane," I say, glancing around the area. I wish I had the chance to search him for any information he might have been carrying before we had to jump.

Nyla stretches her hand toward me. "Give me your clothes. I'm going to lay them out and dry them while we search the area."

I drop my pack on the ground for her as I begin to explore the site.

Starting at the center of the crash, I circle around the wreckage, expanding my search on each pass. I make note of some of the supplies I see and gather others, but there's still no sign of our dead pilot.

I hit the outer rim of the ravine on my last pass, and there's still no body.

"Dagen. I don't think we're going to find him if we haven't already." Nyla's voice startles me as she comes up behind me. "Come back to the plane; you need to dry your shoes. We can't stay here too long. Sit with me and we'll talk some of this out."

I turn to tell her no, but my drive leaves as soon as I see the look on her face. These are all new sides of Nyla I haven't seen yet.

Worry is clearly defined in the lines across her forehead, but it isn't what stops me from looking for our dead body. In spite of how uneasy she is, there is a survival instinct ingrained in that little heart of hers. It's her determination to keep going until we can't that pulls me back to the plane and makes me take off my shoes and sit still long enough to work out a plan.

Nyla sets my shoes beside hers next to a small fire burning on the bedrock. It takes me a moment to realize she's made a separate fire with some wood and twigs.

I watch in awe as she uses pieces of scrap metal to lift some hot rocks out of the fire and set them into my shoes, no doubt to dry them from the inside out.

Where did she learn to survive like this?

Then she leans over the fire, close enough to warm her hands, and I join her.

"We need to figure out which way is south. I'll check the cabin to see if we have a compass." I straighten to search for it, but she stops me.

"I have a compass in my duffel, but we don't need it. That way is south." Nyla lifts her chin, nodding just past me, and I turn to look across the ravine before looking back at her.

"How do you know that?"

She offers me a soft smile.

I think it looks like pity.

"It was lunchtime when our plane went down. The sun is moving west. That way is west." She points. "And that way is south." She points again, raising her brow like I should have known that.

I probably should have known that.

"We can't stay here much longer. We don't know if whoever is after us is closing in," I start, and she answers again.

"We're okay right now."

I glare at her, silently asking her to share her wisdom, and she pauses before she smiles.

She's obviously enjoying her smug self right now.

"We've been sitting here quietly for a while. We're no threat to our surroundings." She lifts her head. "Listen to the birds," she says, and I'm starting to think she hit her head on the way down as she rolls her eyes and continues, "They're singing. Birds make a different sound when there is danger or something new to them, to warn each other. Their chirping will change when we stand to collect our things and head out." She looks back at the fire for a long minute. "Do you want my theory?"

"Theory?"

"About why we're being hunted, why we have a hit on us," she responds, and I nod for her to continue because I want to see how close she is to the mark. "I think someone found or saw something they shouldn't have."

The only difference between us is I know why those names are on that hit—at least, why everyone else's is but mine.

I play along. "Why do you say that?"

"I think everyone listed in the contract does what we do." She points between the two of us. "I saw a couple of *others* in the lobby today. I just don't know why so many of us are listed. It feels like someone is trying to clean up a mess."

"So of all of us listed in the contract, one of us is carrying something, or we know something," I bait her.

She nods in agreement as she turns to look at me. She's starting to figure out where I'm going with this, and she adds her thoughts.

"We can assume, by those gunshots, at least one and probably all of the other names have been eliminated. Yet they are still after us. So that means they didn't get what they were looking for and—" Her sentence trails off as I begin nodding my head, and I answer her silent question.

"It's one of us."

Her face falls at my conclusion. "Is it you?" she asks outright.

"No. It's not me. I think it's you." I throw it right back at her, and she stands tall, crossing her arms as if to block my claim.

"It's not me," she answers defensively, and I realize we could go back and forth all day.

"Fine." I raise my hands in mock defeat. Then I grab my clothes and begin to put them back on. "So either one of us is lying, or one of us has no idea what they have."

She considers my olive branch for a moment before deciding to accept it.

Then she freezes in place.

"Shh!" Nyla tilts her head to the side. "Hear that?"

I strain to listen against the sound of the birds, and at first I don't hear anything else.

Then I hear a faint sound in the distance, echoing off the mountains. Something is in the air. It's still pretty far away, but it won't be for long.

Nyla reaches over, gathering her clothes and getting dressed as she speaks. "We need to gather supplies and get moving. We only have a couple of daylight hours left, then we'll have to find a safe spot for the night."

I step beside her, pulling my pants on, and they are toasty warm. Then I reach for my shirt. When my head pops through the neck of the shirt, I catch Nyla watching me...only she's not meeting my gaze.

Her eyes are lowered.

She sucks her lower lip between her teeth and nibbles while she drinks in my chest. Pulling my shirt down, I cover my pecs and abs, and her eyes slowly travel up to meet mine, then widen when she realizes I just caught her gawking.

Her gaze drops to the ground, and she looks around our area—she looks everywhere but back at me, as though she's trying to erase what we both know just happened.

She just checked me out.

She can act like she's unaffected all she wants, but we both know that isn't true.

I tip the rocks out of my shoes, and it worked: they're warm and almost dry.

Grabbing my pack, I make my way through the wreckage, gathering a medical kit, food, and anything else I can carry.

Nyla does the same.

She finds a sleeping bag, unrolls it, and shoves a tarp from the plane inside.

I make my way to what is left of the cockpit. Everything has died down, and I find a flashlight and store it in my backpack.

"Are you ready?" Nyla pokes her head into the cockpit, catching me off guard, and I startle as she continues, "Why so jumpy? Did I miss something?"

"No. Just on edge. You ready?" I ask, in an attempt to deflect my nerves.

Nodding, she turns to leave, and I follow her out of the wreckage to a pile of supplies she's gathered in a clearing. I pull out the additional supplies I found and add them.

"So these are all of the things that will help us survive out here." She waves her hand over the items, and I nod in agreement as she continues, "By my estimate, both of us— together—can carry a quarter of this pile along with our bags and still make good time."

I'd say we can carry more, but we are being hunted. We need to travel light and not leave a trail.

We circle the outskirts of our pile, staring at our necessities for a few silent minutes. Choosing the wrong items could hold us back, but leaving the wrong supplies behind could mean our end.

"I've packed a blanket and some food I found in the cabin in here." Nyla lifts the sleeping bag off the ground. "We'll need the sleeping bag. The nights will get cold, but I only found one, so we'll have to share. Do you have a water bottle?" she asks, and I shake my head. "I have one we'll share. We'll fill it the first chance we get."

I take one last look around the crumpled pieces of the plane we sat on a couple of hours ago.

"Let's go, it'll be dark soon." I walk toward the tree line.

"South is this way." She points off to the side.

I can tell she's biting her cheek to try and hold back her smirk.

"I know that," I say derisively. "We need to head east for a bit first. It's just a matter of time before they locate this site. They'll be expecting us to go either south or west. This will give us some distance."

Nyla pauses to consider my words, then begins to walk in my direction, and I can't help myself.

"You're not the only one with mad survival skills," I say smugly.

Her face distorts as she mumbles, repeating what I just said mockingly as she walks by.

Her sass goes straight to my cock, and I wish I was in a position to bend her over a rock. The image alone makes me strain against my freshly dried pants.

She rips me out of my fantasy when she says, "Whatever, Robinson Crusoe. Just keep your eyes peeled for the poisonous Canadian Maple Spider. They drop out of the trees around here, and their bite will kill you instantly."

Suddenly, I no longer feel safe or horny as I pick up my pace behind Nyla, scanning the trees as we disappear into them.

Silence hangs between us for five minutes before my curiosity gets the better of me.

"So is it a certain type of tree, or are they in any of them?" I ask to a fit of giggles from the jackass leading the way.

6

NYLA

We've been walking east along a shallow stream for the last half an hour.

As the tree line breaks into a small open field, I pause to look at the dusky sky as Dagen stops behind me.

"The sun is setting, we need to find shelter for the night." He voices my thoughts, and I nod in agreement as he continues, "We don't have a lot of cover here, but it isn't the worst option. We found a tarp and some rope on the plane." He pats his bag.

"Let's set up just inside the tree line. The cover of the trees should hide us. We'll use the tarp to tie our supplies up and off the ground," I add, and we both walk closer to the bushes to look for a spot.

We drop our supplies into a pile then dig around for the items we need. I notice both Dagen and I are keeping our own bags close to our person. I know what I'm hiding, and I wonder if he's hiding something of his own.

I dig in my bag for the one extra piece of clothing I have: a lightweight, thermal long sleeve shirt. My oldest brother once taught me on a camping trip to save your fresh clothes for bed.

Unworn clothes are supposed to keep you warmer during the night.

Huh. I haven't thought about my family in a long time.

I share my knowledge with Dagen.

"If you have extra clothing, put it on. The temperature is going to drop, and I don't think it's a good idea to start a fire tonight." I reach into the sleeping bag and pull out a package of trail mix and crackers I found in the plane's cabin.

I hand Dagen his share, and as I eat the small snack, my stomach grumbles its thanks.

"There's only one sleeping bag," Dagen says, as though I'm bad at math, and I nod silently. I know where he's going with this.

"We'll need to share it," I remind him.

"You mean take turns while the other is on watch?" he asks, and I shake my head.

"No. If anyone is after us, they'll need to sleep too. We'll be well hidden. We need to wedge ourselves together in that bag and sleep," I answer, and he smirks at me. "What?"

"I was just remembering something." Setting the sleeping bag on a soft patch of grass, he smiles to himself, and my curiosity gets the better of me.

"What is it?"

"Well, I'd just like to point out, we're in the great outdoors. You know, in case you want a do-over." He punctuates his comment with a wink, and my eyes roll into my head so hard I think they're going to stay there.

Warmth floods my face, and I'm sure I'm blushing, but I try to mask it behind my crossed arms and attitude. The evening shadows hide the rest.

"Please. If I remember correctly, it didn't end well for you." I do a double hard wink back, wiping the smirk off his face.

Dagen takes a long look at me, then tosses his head back

and laughs. It's genuine, and it catches me off guard. I've never heard him laugh like this, not even the first night I met him.

"Are you sure about that? If my memory serves me correctly, you already had me, hook, line, and sinker, before we had sex. You could have cuffed me to that tree at any time." He speaks as he sorts through our supplies, then stands and turns toward me, his face growing serious.

He takes a few steady steps in my direction, dropping his tone low and sucking the humor out of the conversation. "But you didn't take the first chance to leave. You took the first chance to fuck me. Why?"

His question gives me pause.

The truth is, I don't know why I didn't just leave.

It went against everything I planned for when I chose to stay. Staying changed many things for me, and cost me more than he knows.

"I—um..." I shrug, looking around the ground for something to work with. We were just joking a second ago, but it's turned into something different, and I'm not prepared.

Grabbing the last of the food we took from the plane, I change the subject. "There's not much food left, but there are a bunch of berries near the creek, and I noticed a few edible plants along the way. We will need to hunt or fish in the next day or two, for strength, but we can forage as we walk. We should finish this up, so we don't attract any wildlife."

I hold the food out in Dagen's direction, and he takes a long look at it. His eyes shift between mine and the food, and I get the feeling he wants to go back to what we were just talking about, so I keep talking.

"We should eat and settle in quickly. We probably won't get much sleep tonight." Dagen smiles at my words, and I realize, a little too late, that they sound like an invitation, so I quickly correct myself. "What I mean is, when we wake up, it'll be cold. We'll need to move out because we won't get back to sleep. We should hurry while we both still have a lot of our body heat."

Dagen stays still. He looks like he's assessing where he wants this conversation to go.

I hold out my hand with his rations, and he gives me the space I was hoping for when he takes his share.

I open my duffel and begin to search through its pockets, taking inventory of what we can work with and being careful to avoid pulling some items out by mistake.

"So what do you carry?" Dagen asks over my shoulder. He swats his neck, wincing in irritation.

"Pardon?"

"What do you carry with you? On your jobs. We all have our essentials. What are yours? Lipstick?" He tries to make his question sound nonchalant, but I sense he's fishing.

The fact that one of us still has something we are being hunted for is not lost on either of us.

Trying to settle his curiosity, I decide to answer as best as I can while still hiding what I need to keep secret.

Opening the top of my duffel wide, I start pulling out my supplies. First I show him my wallet and my fake passport. Then I smirk when I pull out my ChapStick, adding, "It's for dry lips, not my appearance."

He chuckles softly.

I go through the rest of the items. They are mostly survival items I learned to carry from experience, including multi-tools, a small amount of cash, some sealable plastic baggies, and one plastic bag carrying an extra bra and panties.

Dagen's expression darkens when I handle the little white cotton undies in the bag.

I quickly pack everything away, conveniently staying away from the item I don't want to draw attention to.

"We need to wrap this up and get some sleep in the next half hour. We should be quiet and still, so we don't attract anything we don't want to," I suggest, and Dagen grabs the sleeping bag to unload the remaining supplies so we can get in.

He unfolds the tarp and spreads it out on the ground. It would have been too small to use as a tent, but it is perfect for getting our bags and the little food we have left off the ground for the night. Once we've packed everything away, he ties it and throws the rope over the branch of a tree, looking self-satisfied as he hoists it up.

"Don't be so shocked. My brother, Lennox, and I used to make forts in our yard all the time when we were kids." His eyes drift away, and he goes somewhere with his last sentence before somberly adding, "That was a long time ago."

I sense he doesn't want to share any more of his memory with me.

I don't blame him.

I don't want to talk about my family either.

A soft glow from Dagen's palms draws my attention, and I turn as he mutters, "Still no service," before turning off his phone.

I reach into my bag for my own phone and slip it into my pocket.

"I'm going to find a bathroom spot, then we should turn in." I call over my shoulder as I put some distance between myself and our little camp.

I find a small, covered area far enough away from our camp and pull out my phone. It still doesn't power on, but power isn't what I'm looking for.

Sliding out a little compartment on the case, I remove a

photo and lift it up, turning my body until enough light from the sky illuminates the happy little face staring back at me.

She'll be getting ready for bed right now, lining her teddy bears up in a row along her wall and picking out which one she wants to sleep with before kissing all of the rest goodnight.

The light is fading fast, and I angle the photo a few more times to make out the outline of her beautiful face before kissing it and storing it away.

I wanted to contact Dagen when I first found out I was pregnant, but it all changed when I looked into who he was—more importantly, who his family was.

The Saints only look good on paper.

In reality, their legal businesses hide the awful things they are involved in.

I didn't want to believe Dagen could be a part of that, but what I want and feel don't matter when it comes to my daughter—*our daughter*. What matters is her happiness and safety, and I will protect both with every fiber of my being, even if it means freezing him out of his daughter's life.

A sick pit forms deep in my gut.

When I return to our site, I take a long, quiet listen for anything out of place. It's dusk now, and the birds are singing loudly. It's the perfect time to get to sleep so we're nice and quiet when everything else settles.

Dagen steps into the clearing from his own spot, and the only thing left is to get both of us into one sleeping bag and go to sleep.

It sounds simple enough.

"We'll need to take our shoes off." I kneel down, untying my laces and slipping out of my hikers before removing my socks as well. I make a mental note to add a clean pair of socks to my go bag for next time—if we make it out of this.

Dagen looks at me in confusion, so I clarify, "We won't be able to settle into the sleeping bag with them on."

Dagen toes his heel and slides his boots off. Then he unzips the bag halfway and slides in, waiting for me to join him.

We struggle against ourselves and each other as we try to find a position that will suit us both.

Dagen has gone quiet, his words replaced with a grunt here and a sigh there as his frustration builds.

I know this isn't going to be ideal, but dying out here isn't an option either.

I'm exerting way more energy than I need to on this, and the close proximity, coupled with our restricted movement, is working away at my patience.

I flop into a pile of deadweight to catch my breath and preserve my energy, which is fading fast.

"This isn't working. Let's try again." I shimmy myself out of our fluffy prison, and we both stand, the sleeping bag twisted into disarray at our feet.

Dagen swats at his neck again, cursing the insect that just bit him, and I feel a little bite of my own.

Now that the sun has set, the bugs will be out, and a renewed determination to be sealed up tight in a sleeping bag pushes me on.

I unzip the bag completely and spread it out, then tilt my head toward the ground. Dagen understands the gesture and lies in the middle of it. He shifts as he gets comfortable, then gently looks at me with a sultry wink and taps the fabric beside him in invitation.

I pick up a small blanket and roll it up. Kneeling by his side, I lift his head from an awkward angle and slide the blanket underneath, so he won't have a sore neck in the morning.

His expression shifts into something I can't place, and he

watches me with wide eyes, swallowing hard before he says, "Thank you."

It's then I realize what I did without thinking.

Clearing my throat, I mutter that it's no big deal, but the way his eyes follow me around as I get ready to join him tells me it matters to him.

Whatever is passing between us can't continue, and I turn my front away from him when I lie down and reach for the zipper.

"Face me, Nyla." His tone is heady.

There's a heavy double meaning in his words.

I take a deep breath to calm myself before turning over, but I can't quite meet his eyes.

Reaching behind me, I slide the zipper up as far as it will go, and Dagen zips it the rest of the way.

The sleeping bag fits both of us, and it closes just above our heads, cocooning us together.

He moves slowly with me to wedge ourselves into place for the evening, and my forehead lines up with his chest.

Slowly, cautiously, he stretches his arms around me, wrapping them together at my back, and my ear rests on his bicep, his lips grazing my hairline.

My brain immediately tries to settle, and I tell myself this is the best position to sleep in to share our body heat as his musky scent fills my nose.

"That's not so bad, is it?" he asks, nuzzling his face into my hair.

I want to nod and say yes, it is so, so bad, because I shouldn't want him.

I don't trust myself to answer, so I simply shake my head and hope he shuts up.

He gives up waiting for a verbal response after a couple of minutes.

I release a steady breath when the muscles in his arm relax under my head.

I'm almost completely settled and drifting off to sleep when he whispers, "I know it's you they're after."

Keeping my head buried into his shoulder, I do my best to feign indifference. "How do you know that?" I ask into his solid chest.

"Because I'm after the same thing."

I feel his lips curl into that annoying smirk of his against my scalp.

My eyes fly open under the covers, and I freeze in his arms for half a second before I startle and try to jump up.

But Dagen tightens his grip around me, holding me against him.

"Now, now. We just got in here, and I am not going through that again."

Bastard.

He waited until I got into a spot I couldn't get out of to drop this on me.

We are literally wrapped tight, like two sausages in a sock.

I climbed right into this.

I stop pushing against him and go limp in his arms.

The air between us suddenly feels suffocating.

His strong arms around me are both a comfort and a threat.

"What are you after?"

His chest rumbles with a dark chuckle. "Many things, *Sierra.*" I swallow hard at his use of the name I gave him when we first met. I am in deep shit. "But let's deal with the most pressing matter first. You stole something about four months ago, and I need it."

He allows me to sit in silence with him while I search my brain for what he could possibly be talking about.

I purposefully avoided contracts that would put me on any

Saint's radar, but he didn't say I stole from him. He's simply looking for what I was able to get.

"Which is?" I slow the conversation down. I get the feeling I'm going to need to tread lightly, as Dagen is mentally circling me.

"I'm looking for a document"—I start listing off all the jobs I've completed in my head when Dagen fills in the blank—"on microfiche."

My lips pinch together as I recall everything about that job. It's like it happened yesterday. It was an easy in and out, but I haven't had time to hand it over to my buyer. They didn't seem like they were in a rush to get it, only that it would not be handed over to anyone else.

"I don't know what you're talking about." I'm thankful my face is hidden from him.

I wasn't expecting this, and I know I'm not hiding my lie well.

My mind goes back to the photo of my daughter hidden in the slide-out section of my phone case. That isn't the only thing I'm hiding in there. Between the case and my phone lies the little piece of microfiche, preserved between two pieces of packing tape.

Dagen's fingers trail listlessly, drawing circles on my back through my clothing. The vibrations from his chuckle rattle along my skin, and I shiver in his arms even though I'm not cold.

"So be it. Get some rest, Nyla. You're going to need it."

"What is that supposed to mean?"

"If you think I'm going to allow you to lie to me, you are *sorely* mistaken." He draws out "sorely," like proving it is something he's going to enjoy.

I'm just now realizing how outmanned I am.

Dagen is a master at presentation.

Everyone sees what he wants them to see until it is too late.

He hides his true nature well.

Like the prey I am, I feel the weight of his eyes on me in the dark. He's waiting, just outside of my comfort zone, for the perfect moment to strike.

There is no way I'm getting any sleep tonight.

7

DAGEN

I've never enjoyed the moment between being asleep and being awake.

The flurry of seconds when consciousness returns, and your brain scrambles to ascertain if you're safe or in danger.

I don't imagine this happens to most people.

I think a regular person wakes up, rolls around in the comfort and safety of the world they built for themselves. Then they stretch their limbs as they decide if they're going to have their coffee before or after they let the dog out to take a piss.

I envy that sometimes.

Take right now, for example.

I already know I'm not in my bed.

A faint reminder of when I went to summer camp registers as I smell what can only be described as wet dirt and fish.

I try to inhale a cleansing breath, but the air is thick and hot. My first instinct is to push out of the fabric I'm cocooned in and remove myself before I suffocate.

I swallow my exhalation as a faint moan catches my attention.

As I open my eyes to find a layer of soft fabric over my face, yesterday's events become clear in my memory once again.

Nyla's breath is still deep, and I weigh my options.

With the sleeping bag over our heads, I can't tell if it's morning yet, and stretching to check could wake both of us up too soon.

She'll no doubt wake up guarded.

I couldn't help dropping my bombshell on her before we fell asleep.

I'd been biding my time, waiting to get her into a position she couldn't get out of since she defiantly announced that whoever is after us couldn't possibly be after her.

I can't describe the feeling I get when I catch her off guard.

I crave her vulnerability, and I got it in spades last night when I knew something she didn't.

Her fight erupted from her like an inferno, but when she tried to get out of the sleeping bag I was ready for her, holding her against me until she surrendered and settled.

Her survival instinct is on point, and it will serve both of us well out here.

I won't admit it to her—at least not yet—but she impresses me.

With the odds currently against us, I wouldn't blame anyone for cracking and entertaining their fear, but Nyla moves with determination, as though she's moving toward something rather than running away.

As if sensing my thoughts, she stirs.

Her fingers stretch out along my midsection, affecting me in ways I don't want to think about.

It's been a long time since I allowed anyone to spend the night in my arms.

Trusting someone enough to sleep next to them is not a luxury I can afford, and I'm sure the same is true for her.

I was willing to try it once—with Nyla, actually—and it blew up in my face.

I've searched for her for five years to claim my retribution, and I will. But first we need to get out of this alive, and for that, temporary trust needs to be put in place. If we don't work together, then we are both as good as dead.

This is why I started coming clean with her last night. I can't keep any secrets from her. If she finds out later that I knew why we were being chased all along, then I'll lose what little trust I'm building. She already looks at me like she's sizing up her opponent, and this can't continue.

I decide to give sleep another chance, and I close my eyes when a poke to my temple through the sleeping bag freezes me in place.

My mind races with thoughts of what it could be as I try to even out my breathing. If we've been found already, we're going to have to start fighting from a serious disadvantage.

Nyla whispers as though reading my mind, and she startles me out of my thoughts. "It's not them."

"Then who is it?" I lower my voice to match her level.

"Not who, *what*. Don't move. Do you have a weapon?"

I flex my fingers just above my head. They brush along the hilt of the hunting knife, and I tell her I do.

She whispers as the poking continues. "Okay. I'm going to move my feet. If it's a predator, it'll pounce down there, then we'll need to make ourselves look like a threat to scare it off. If it's not dangerous, it should run away. Are you ready?"

"I'm good," I answer, but I know in my bones, if I come face-to-face with anything bigger than a fox, I'm going to shit myself.

My heart hammers wildly into my chest. Fighting a cougar for my life is not how I wanted to start this morning. It's never how I want to start any morning, but we have no choice today.

Nyla's fingers clench the fabric of my shirt against my chest. She begins to wriggle, and we hear a rustle followed by silence.

She goes for a more forceful kick the second time, and I swear my heart stops as her feet thud against something solid.

Whatever she kicked scatters wildly around the area.

Nyla scrambles to locate the zipper from over our heads. When she finds it, she peeks her eyes out of the sleeping bag.

I suck in a deep breath of the fresh air I've been needing.

The sheer tension and stress of the situation are causing me to overheat in this flannel inferno, and my patience is wearing thin.

"Well?" I ask, hoping to mask my anxiety with impatient curiosity.

"It's leaving. I think we were lucky. It looks like a wolverine."

"Wolverine?" I startle, confused, and my mind fills with images as I gawk at her.

Nyla stills, then turns to take me in at my question.

Cocking her head quizzically to the side, she keeps her thoughts to herself for a few seconds. Then she releases a ridiculous snort, and I just want her to get her ass out of my space so I can breathe and compose myself.

"A wolverine. Not *Wolverine*. Please tell me you weren't picturing a ruggedly handsome bloke with metal fingernails," she pleads as she mock-claws the air between us and barely tries to hold back an incessant giggle.

"What? No. Get out of the sleeping bag." I haven't even had my coffee yet, and this woman is already making me crave something stronger.

Coffee...right. There'll be no coffee today.

How easily I forget we are being hunted.

We're on our own, and we have no coffee.

Nyla crawls out of our sleeping bag and stretches, then I do the same.

The sky is an illuminated shade of midnight blue against an almost full moon.

It looks like we've still got a couple of hours of darkness to walk in, but it's hard to tell in the mountains.

"What do you mean *we were lucky?*" I ask, hoping she'll just answer my question and hold the sass.

"If there was something in our camp the wolverine wanted, or if it was hungry, it would have been a brawl. They are fierce when they're motivated. It was a good thing we ate the open food we had and slung up our bags. The fact you stink probably helped too." She winks then turns to look around our area, arching her back and stretching her arms over her head, giving me a great view of her midsection before bending over and putting her shoes on.

I stretch too and look around our camp.

Nothing is missing.

I walk a few steps to release the tarp from the trees, talking over my shoulder. "Okay. Let's pack up and get some water from the stream before we head out."

Nyla steps to my side, holding out her hand. "Agreed. I'll fill the bottle. We should stay at each other's sides until it's light. If we walk together, we'll look like a larger animal, and it should deter most predators."

A shiver runs down my spine when she says "most." I don't want to think about the ones that won't be afraid of us.

I do a half-assed job of packing everything up. I'll repack everything once the sun rises and I can see better.

I follow Nyla to the side of the stream. She fills the bottle, and I drop our things to kneel down and splash some water over my head. The freezing bite wakes me up instantly.

Nyla's features are muted under the cloak of darkness. I use the shadows to stare at her openly as she fills the bottle with water. Then she reaches her hands into the stream, splashing some onto her face and inhaling sharply at the cold rush.

She stills in a moment of silence, and I take the time to appreciate that, after all of this time, she's really here with me.

For the longest time, she was a big mystery.

She still is.

Now I have her real name, but I still know nothing about her.

Whatever she's protecting, she's doing a great job of it.

We start walking in the direction we noted was south before we fell asleep, and we spend the first five minutes of our walk shifting our bags and the items we're carrying until we're comfortable.

The conversation between Nyla and me was relaxed yesterday. When she didn't know why we were being hunted, her guard was down; not by much, but more than it is right now.

The farther we walk, the more our eyes adjust to the dark, and our pace increases.

I search my mind for anything to break the ice.

"Tell me about your family." Nyla is quiet for a long time before I try again. "You don't need to give me specifics: no names or places. Just give me something."

She takes another minute to consider my words. "My parents are retired. They're both actually in a care home. They —um, had me when they were older. I was—kind of...a mistake." I can't make out her features to see if my hunch is right, but she sounds dejected when she admits that last part. She clears her throat, and her tone changes. "I see them when I can, but my mom has Alzheimer's, and she doesn't recognize me much anymore. She thinks I'm the help when I visit."

I don't say anything for a full minute.

I'm mostly surprised she shared this much with me. I was fully prepared for a smart-ass response along the lines of, *I was born and now I'm here. The end.*

"My mom was recently diagnosed with Alzheimer's." I don't know why I offer this private piece about myself. I haven't even told anyone on my team about her situation yet.

Nyla is quiet for a long time before she says, "I'm sorry."

I wish I could see her face.

Her tone is pensive, and I wish I could read the room. Instead I mutter my appreciation for her concern and add, "You weren't a mistake."

She trips in her step but recovers quickly.

I don't know why, but I don't like that she referred to herself as something someone would have chosen not to have. While my life would have been infinitely more carefree without having met her, I don't regret that she passed through it.

She bested me at my own game, and that hasn't happened to me before.

If anything, I've become more ruthless at my job because of her.

So, for better or for worse, I've evolved because of Nyla.

We walk a few more minutes in silence, then I try to change the tone by asking another question. "Do you have any siblings?"

She sighs. "Yes. I have two older brothers. I don't talk to either of them."

I'm hitting all of the wrong nails on the head today.

I decide to table that discussion for another time.

This morning started on an awkward note, and it's just gone south from there.

I try one more time. "Is there someone waiting for you?"

I take two more steps before I realize she's stopped dead in her tracks.

Her voice is just above a whisper. "What do you mean?" I can't make out much, but I see the whites in her wide eyes as she stares me down.

"A partner? A spouse?" The tension hits a fever pitch, so I resort to my charm to diffuse the situation. "Do you have some fresh sucker tied to a tree waiting for you to come back and release him?"

There's no mistaking her soft chuckle when she says, "No. You're the only one who meant that much to me."

She closes the distance between us, and I decide to ease off the small talk for now. I hook my arm in hers, and we continue to hike through the woods at a fast pace until the sun comes up.

There's more I want to say, but I want to have a clear view of Nyla's face when I ask her some of the tougher questions.

8

NYLA

When the sun rises, it becomes easier to classify the plants and bushes as we pass them. I step in front of Dagen, pointing out the edible berries and telling him stories about the ones that are not.

One time I went camping with my family, and my two older brothers ate some berries they thought were fine. They spent the whole night crouched over in the bushes, praying for death to take them. I'm halfway through telling Dagen this story when I realize he's listening with an odd smile on his face.

What is even more out of place is that I've started to ramble and overshare, which are both foreign for me.

"Anyway. That was a long time ago." My cheeks warm, and I suddenly feel shy, which is also very unlike me.

"Why don't you talk to your brothers?" When Dagen asks the question, it doesn't feel like an interrogation.

I almost wish it did, because then I would know how to deflect it.

Even more disconcerting is that I want to answer him.

"I was young when they left, and my parents didn't talk

about what happened. From what I know, they fell into the wrong crowd, and they visited less and less. Finally, my father told them they couldn't come around anymore." I stop to pick some raspberries and hand some back to Dagen.

Then I return to the bush, pick my own handful of the berries, and shove them into my mouth to signal I am done with talking.

I bite down as I turn to face Dagen, and a squirt of juice dribbles out of the corner of my mouth.

Dagen is on me in two steps, lifting his hand to my face and wiping the red liquid off my chin before the expression on his face slips. He runs his finger along my lower lip.

The atmosphere around us shifts as his gaze follows his touch.

Without a thought in my head, I open my mouth and stick my tongue out to lick the sweetness off the tip of his finger.

It mixes with the saltiness of him.

"Why?" Dagen lowers his voice, his question just above a whisper.

He pulls his hand back.

His fingers, now wet with my spit and what is left of the juices, catch my attention before he lifts the same hand to his mouth and sucks everything off.

I gawk openly at his lips. I'm panting and swallowing hard.

He asked a question.

"Why what?"

I can't pull my eyes away from him, but my gaze relaxes, held by him in a heady fixation. His image blurs, splitting into two as I slip willingly into a trance.

"Tell me why you fucked me. I didn't see you coming. You could have completed your contract long before we left the bar. Long before we..." He drags his teeth over his lower lip. His eyes turn hungry, and I wonder if he's imagining the same thing I've been imagining over and over again for the last five years.

I had him.

He was an easy target.

No one could have seen me coming.

Everything about that job was perfect, and I was the perfect storm.

I know what he remembers.

He remembers letting his guard down.

He remembers the times—not once, but twice—when he excused himself to use the washroom and left his car keys on the table.

They were right there.

I could have taken them and been nothing more than a memory by the time he returned.

Yet I didn't.

Something changed for me, and I deviated from my flawless plan.

In a moment of weakness, I wanted to be that woman he just met in a bar. I was young, free, unattached, and married to my job.

I was missing something, and the moment I saw him, I felt it was him.

"I—wanted…more."

I wanted more than parents with ailing health who barely remembered me. I wanted more than two brothers who chose a life of crime over their own family. I wanted more than the empty apartment I returned to day after day.

I desperately wanted the temporary connection he was offering me.

When Dagen looked at me that night, it felt like he really saw me, and I never wanted him to look away.

I hate my answer as soon as I hear myself say it.

I hate it because it's the truth, and I hate it because I wasn't supposed to expose myself to him. Doing so opens a door, and if he steps through it, the others become easier and easier to kick down.

Dagen knows how to size people up.

He stalks just beyond my boundaries, waiting for my guard to drop, then he tests my walls until he finds a soft spot he can push through.

Is he able to do this with everyone, or is it just me?

When I meet his gaze, his eyes soften as he regards me with what feels like sadness or regret. Or is it understanding?

"And what about now? Do you still want—more?"

Yes—but no.

"I—can't."

He wrinkles his forehead as he considers my answer before tilting his head into my space and drawing his eyebrows together to ask his next question.

"Is there someone else?"

This is the very definition of a loaded question, and, unfortunately for Dagen, he worded it just right.

"Yes. There's someone else." I lower my eyes to the ground because I'm well aware that withholding information is the same thing as lying, and deceiving Dagen makes me feel nauseous.

He glances at my left hand before he takes a half step back, and I'm both relieved and upset at the space created between us.

"We should keep moving." Dagen's tone sours as he shuts the conversation down and steps around me to take the lead.

I'm taken aback by his reaction to my answer.

I had convinced myself that I was simply nothing more than a fun distraction for him.

It was easier to let him go that way.

Dagen walks at a fast pace, and I wait about fifteen minutes for the aftermath of our conversation to fade away before I speak again.

"Tell me about your family. You have three brothers?"

I wince as soon as the words leave my mouth.

I should have let him tell me that.

Dagen stops walking and side-eyes me over his shoulder before turning away, but not before the start of a smirk tugs at the corner of his lips.

"I do. I have one older brother and two younger."

"Oh." I try to sound as though his response is news to me, but I fall short.

I sound like an idiot.

Dagen shakes his head as he continues to walk in front of me, and I know he's not buying my ignorance.

He knows I've looked into him, and, considering he was the one after me in Alaska, I would have no reason to investigate him if I wasn't interested in him for some reason.

What he doesn't know is how thorough I was and why.

A quick internet search of his name gave me all the members of his family right away. At first, I found an eligible bachelor—one of four, apparently. The media loves them, so it wasn't hard to find photos of all four of them at the most popular events along the Eastern Seaboard, sometimes with a beautiful woman hanging off an arm, but never the same one twice.

Flags started popping up when I dug deeper into their family dealings, revealing connections with criminal organizations. At first, it seemed like they walked a fine line in the company they chose to keep. Many of their businesses, while questionable by some standards, were aboveboard and legal.

It wasn't until I followed a carrot down a rabbit hole that I found their seedy underbelly.

Just thinking about it is enough to sober me against Dagen.

I will never allow my daughter—*our daughter*—to be exposed to any of that.

"You're close with your family?" I hover around the edge of the questions I want to ask.

"I am with my brothers."

The distinction gives me pause, but I'm not ready to open that can of worms. I also don't want him to know just how pathetically I stalked him.

Dagen slows his pace and stops beside a large bush. I follow his line of sight up to—

"Those are poisonous." His gaze jumps to me before returning to the bright red berries that look good enough to eat. I step to his side and pick a few from the bush. "This is red elderberry. The whole thing is toxic, except for the pulp of the berry." He takes a berry from my hand and opens his mouth. Urgently, I add, "That includes the seeds that are still in the berry."

Chucking the berry over his shoulder, Dagen turns to continue walking south.

"I'm happy you're here." His tone is so hushed, I barely make out the words.

I don't acknowledge I heard him.

I'm pretty sure I wasn't meant to.

I look up to the sky to determine the approximate time.

"We should stop and eat soon. I have some granola bars and dried fruit we can share. Then I'll forage for dinner while we walk this afternoon."

We hike for a while longer before we break out along the side of a body of water. Its size places it somewhere between a pond and a lake.

I'm ready to sit down for a rest when Dagen points to the southern side of the water.

"Let's rest over there. We'll be able to see anyone coming from the north, and it'll give us more time to get away."

I look over my shoulder.

He is right.

I nod my agreement, and he smiles.

When he turns to head toward our stop, my face falls.

I almost forgot we are being pursued. Then I wonder if we really are. Maybe we aren't worth the effort, and they've decided to let Mother Nature deal with us.

Or maybe they'll meet up with us once we find our way back to civilization.

My stomach growls as we arrive at a good spot, and Dagen drops his bag and the sleeping bag of supplies he was carrying.

A large rock slopes gently into the water nearby, and I join him on it. I pull a blanket out of the bag and spread it out before settling myself on it.

It's a hot day, and I remove my shoes and socks before laying them flat in the sun to air out.

Then, pulling my duffel to my side, I search through it until I find our lunch: a two-pack of granola bars and an airtight bag of dried apricots.

Dagen fills the water bottle and rejoins me, sitting on a corner of the blanket. He pulls out his phone, checking for bars —there are none.

I pull my own phone out and try to power it on, it still doesn't work at all.

Abandoning our tech, he hands me the bottle to take the first sip.

It's all very polite and cozy.

But below the surface lie the questions Dagen hasn't asked me yet.

He hasn't mentioned the microfiche since last night. I'm not sure if he's waiting for me to bring it up, but I won't. I came into its possession because of a job I was hired to do, and I'm bound to the secrecy of the contract.

Dagen knows this better than anyone. Maybe that's why he hasn't asked about it again.

Still, I'm curious how he knows, without a doubt, that it's me who has it.

The rest of lunch is a line of awkward starters that go nowhere accompanied by stolen glances at each other.

If we weren't being hunted and Dagen wasn't here to take me in, then this would almost feel like a romantic first date: a picnic by the lake.

I close my eyes and turn my face toward the sun. Its rays create a bright orange glow behind my eyelids. It is going to be a hot afternoon.

I'm distantly aware of Dagen getting up from the blanket, but I stay where I am for a while longer.

My thoughts drift to my team.

We have procedures in place for this type of situation, but there's no way of knowing if our plans are flawed until we execute them. This will tell us if we did the right thing. Unfortunately, if we didn't, some or all of us will pay for those mistakes with our lives.

I'm safe right now, I remind myself, *and no matter what, even if they know my name, they won't find her.*

When I lower my head and open my eyes, everything looks like it's been touched by the heavens. The scenery is brighter, kissed by the same sunlight that touched my face, and standing in front of me, just by the water's edge, is Dagen.

He looks like an angel, with a warm glow glistening off the ridges of his muscles all the way down to his—

"Where are your pants?"

9

———

DAGEN

I never saw the appeal of being in the great outdoors.

My younger brother, Cole, would eat this up.

I'm half convinced he'd pay good money to be here.

Me? The only roughing it I'm all for comes with hair pulling and dirty talk.

I'd take sitting by the pool drinking margaritas with Nyla over trekking around these backwoods any day.

Why did I include her?

I've been asking myself questions like this ever since I saw her again.

There's someone else. Her words spread through me like a disease.

There's no ring on her finger.

When she opened up about herself earlier, she spoke about her brothers and parents, not a significant other.

Was that on purpose? Is she protecting him? Or has she simply not thought about him since I pulled her out of that hotel?

Then I remember the look on her face when the plane first took off. She was rattled right down to her core. There is no mistaking that level of panic.

Was she thinking about him?

I have to stop obsessing over this.

I haven't been able to think clearly since I laid eyes on her, and here we are sharing food and drink like we're a couple on an afternoon hike.

I rise from the blanket and put some distance between us.

Stepping to the edge of the water, I scan the trees we walked through at the far end of the lake. If anyone is coming after us, they'll be coming from that direction.

I don't know how much longer we have on our own, but we have right now, and this water looks cool, clear, and inviting.

I step out of my shoes and socks, then flex my toes against the ground as I peel off my shirt and drop it on the grass. When I turn to see where it lands, Nyla's relaxed position catches me off guard.

Her head is tilted back, catching her face in a ray of sunlight, and she looks serene. Her lip twitches ever so slightly into a smile, and I wonder what she's thinking about—or who.

Pushing my thoughts out of my head, I decide it's time to cool off. I unbutton my pants, step out of them, and take my underwear down with them.

It's nothing she hasn't seen before, and her thoughts are on some other guy anyway, so it doesn't matter.

I toss everything behind me and take another step closer to the water. The rock sloping into the lake is warm under the sun.

It's peaceful here.

I prop my knuckles on my hips and take in my surroundings like I own everything I see.

I'm starting to see the appeal of this place.

Or maybe it's because she's here with me.

"Where are your pants?" Nyla's shocked squeak startles me, and without thinking, I turn to face her.

Her eyes lower, then go wide as her jaw drops, and it is more than a solid second before she reacts, snapping her lips closed and attempting to cover her salacious gawking while she blushes a bright shade of red.

Interesting.

If she had reacted differently, I might have turned away, but something about the look in her eyes and the way she's timidly trying to cover her response tells me to stay the course.

I hold an indifferent expression on my face as I answer her.

"I'm going for a swim. We might not get another chance." Then I lower my voice and go for a direct approach, leaving any misunderstandings off the table. "You should join me."

Her eyes drift past me toward the water as her hand clutches her shirt near her neckline.

She's considering it.

I don't like that the thought makes me happy, but right now I want her in that lake with me more than I want to get out of this place, and that says a lot.

I really want to know how badly she misses this significant other of hers.

"Um, okay." She hesitantly stands on the blanket and looks down at herself before looking around the area—she looks everywhere but at me.

I turn toward the water.

I tell myself I'm doing it to grant her the mercy of a small reprieve, but I know my benevolence is all for me. If I watch her undress in front of me, even though we are both on the run, I will be as stiff as a metal rod before her pants are off.

I take a few steps into the lake. It isn't as cold as I thought it would be. Before I realize it, the water is up to my abs.

Splashing behind me draws my eyes back to her.

I steal a glance at her to see if she's decided to join me completely naked. If she has, I'll wait until she's underwater before returning to look at her fully.

She's wearing her bra and black boy shorts from yesterday.

I turn to face her and push myself backward into the water, swimming out on my back while I watch her lower herself and swim toward me.

I dip my head back into the water. The cool seeping onto my heated scalp is refreshing.

She does the same, and we both stand to wring out the excess water. The lake laps against her midsection, and a wave of heady lust hits me as I take in her curves through the thin fabric of her mismatched white sports bra. The water has now soaked the dried fibers that once kept her hidden from me, but it's all on display in front of me now.

It's all mine.

I'm lost in the vision of her, and it isn't until she lowers herself into the water, hiding herself away from me, that I snap out of my trance.

Nyla stares at me in silence, biting her lower lip as her hands lazily tread the water around her.

Fuck it.

I don't care if there's someone waiting for her.

She's here with me now.

I've never taken another man's woman, but this is different —Nyla is different.

For starters, she's mine, and she was mine first.

My thinking is illogical. I know this, but I don't care. I'll convince myself the sky is pink if it'll put Nyla back within my reach.

I test the literal and figurative water between us and swim closer. Her breath deepens, but she doesn't ask me to stop, so I don't.

By the time I swim directly in front of her, she's looking down at the water around us.

Humble and tentative.

I like this side of her. I saw it briefly the first night we met. Out of every expression that graces her beautiful face, this is the most honest version of her. The one she gave to me before she gave herself to me.

I wrap my arm around her waist and pull her into the water with me, swimming out a little farther. She braces herself against my chest with nervous fingers as her eyes travel too close to my gaze, and I lock her into my sights.

With my height advantage, I can stand in deeper water than she can, and I'll use it to get what I want.

After a minute, she slides her hands up from my chest to my shoulders, holding herself against me.

I sense the same connection we had that night. Even now that I know who she is, my heart beats just as furiously against my chest.

"We should—" She abandons her thoughts when I lick my lips, and I take advantage of her delay.

With my free hand, I cup my fingers along her jaw and tilt her face up to mine. Her pupils constrict in the sun.

I scan her round eyes before dropping to her full lips, then I lean in, smash my mouth against hers, and taste what I've missed for over five years.

Nyla melts into my body, lifting her legs and wrapping herself around me like she remembers where her home is, and I welcome her there, cupping her ass in my hands.

Our connection is natural, inevitable. There is something about this woman in my arms that I can't get enough of. Every kiss demands another. Every time I smell her, I want her that much more.

Nyla is the very definition of addiction.

As we continue to desperately kiss and taste each other, neither of us backing off, I'm hit with the knowledge that she feels the same, but she fights it.

I fought it too.

It was easier when I didn't know who or where she was. I could tell myself she owed me a debt, that finding her would allow me the retribution I was owed, but it was all bullshit.

Breaking our kiss, I stand panting and staring at her with her legs wrapped around me in the middle of the lake. Our breaths come out hot on each other's faces.

"Tell me there's someone else again," I challenge her, and her eyes shift left to right between my own.

"There's no one—like that."

I don't know what she means, and I don't care. All that matters now is the green light she's giving me to continue.

I kiss her again, and she relaxes her body for me, allowing me to tilt her and shift her as I want.

My mind swims with everything I want to say to her, all of the dirty things I want to do, but I stay silent. Words will only lessen this moment.

The sound of her panting, the way her chest rises and falls, her hard nipples breaking the surface of the water as she inhales and exhales, breaks my control. My cock strains against her pelvis. I lift her, sliding myself along the cotton between the apex of her thighs, and Nyla rolls her eyes up, tilting her head back, readying herself for me with a whimper.

I glide one hand under her, teasing my fingers along the seam of her panties between her legs before pulling the fabric aside. I reposition my free hand at the back of her head, guiding her to me.

When my mouth crashes down on hers again, I sink my finger deep inside of her, earning myself a desperate mewl.

I love that sound.

"Fuck." My hips thrust forward, shamelessly grinding my cock against her center, and her nails scratch along my back as she tries to climb up and position herself on my tip.

I drop my head, nuzzling my face into her neck as I continue to slide my fingers through her heat before circling her sensitive clit.

As if talking to herself more than me, Nyla tenses and says, "We shouldn't."

Oh hell yes we should.

"Why not?" I'm not a weak man. I'll let her go if this isn't what she wants, but I do want her to tell me the reason she's trying to run away, since her actions betray her words.

Nyla inhales deeply at my question, and I suddenly get the feeling her fight is with herself as something stirs behind her brown eyes.

She has an answer, and judging by the solemn look on her face, it's one I need to hear.

Was there a reason she hid herself away so well these last five years? I had assumed she just didn't want to be found in general, but did she not want to be found by me?

What could I have possibly done to her to break the connection I was sure we both felt?

"Nyla, we're the only ones here. What's holding you back?"

I don't get an answer.

Nyla releases her legs from my hips and hangs off me, biting her bottom lip as though she's pondering the repercussions of her answer.

Finally, she comes to an internal decision. She nods to herself and meets my eyes.

Relief floods me. She looks like she's decided to trust me with whatever weighs her down.

"There's something we need to talk abou—"

The rest of her sentence is cut off when a gunshot breaks the silence around us.

1 0

NYLA

’ve always trusted my gut, and it's been right my entire life—until Dagen Saint.

Five years ago, I accepted a closed contract for an "intercept and collect."

It's rare that a second job against the successful finder of a current contract is posted, because most people aren't expecting to be duped in the first place, but my buyer saw it coming.

That it was a closed contract meant that no one else had access to the details, and, considering it almost never happens, *Raguel* didn't expect to cross anyone who knew what he was doing out there in the desert.

This was also my chance to go up against one of the best finders on the books, and I knew, if I could complete my orders, it would kick me up to a higher pay grade.

I could demand more and retire earlier.

And so I settled into my role for the night.

Except it quickly transformed into something I wasn't ready for.

It became real.

The truth is, the first time he excused himself to the men's room, it had slipped my mind to leave. I sat there with a warm feeling, happy with our conversation and content to get to know more about him. It wasn't until he was walking back to the table that I snapped out of my daze and realized I was supposed to be a few minutes up the road by then.

Our conversation turned intimate, and by the second time he left the table, I knew I was going to stay. Rationality had left the building. I wanted him.

I've thought about him every day since I left him cuffed to that tree.

I knew he'd be pissed.

Every now and then I thought about how he would also be disappointed, and I didn't like the feelings that conjured.

When I found out I was pregnant, my first instinct was to reach out to him.

Our jobs are one thing, but a baby?

I had every intention of telling him.

I was so sure he was a good soul.

I couldn't be attracted to him if he wasn't, but I was wrong.

Or was I?

I can't deny how I feel in my heart when I'm near him.

When he called me in to join him in the water, that pull was there. It's the same pull I feel when I think about our daughter. It's like a beacon guiding me home.

It pushes everything I've learned about him aside and whispers that there's something else, something stronger than what I've learned about his family.

Maybe it's time to ask him some hard questions and either listen to this voice or silence it forever.

So when Dagen asks me what's holding me back, I decide that I have to talk to him. At the very least for the sake of our daughter, who should know her father if it turns out I'm wrong.

"There's something we need to talk abou—"

My stomach surges into my throat at the unmistakable sound of a gunshot echoing off the mountains around us, and I instinctively look for wounds.

It takes me a moment to realize that I checked Dagen's body first, rubbing my hands over his chest and back and holding my hands up to look for blood.

Scanning the area around us, I see no one approaching or moving along the trees. "Do you think it's hunters?" I ask.

Dagen tightens his grip around my midsection and spins around in the water. "It's not hunting season."

He takes a few steps toward the shore, and I let go of him to swim on my own so we can get out of the water faster.

"How do you know?" I never pictured Dagen as one who enjoyed the outdoors.

"I have a father who enjoys the pain and suffering of helpless creatures. He's an avid hunter." Then he mutters to himself, "I should have known."

The way he talks about his dad sinks its talons into my mind. This thought is going to stay with me for a while.

We reach the shore, and I toss the blanket to Dagen so he can dry himself as I gather everything we removed from the bags. I start shoving random things in without organizing them.

Dagen drops the blanket for me to use and takes over packing everything away.

I notice too late that I left my phone out. As his fingers graze the case, panic surges from my heart.

"That's mine. Give it to me."

Shit.

Dagen freezes, his eyes slowly lifting to meet mine. His tone is cautious. "I know. I don't want you to lose it."

His fingers tighten around it for a fraction of a second before he loosens his grip and hands it over.

The damage is done. There's no recovering from how I reacted to a phone that doesn't even power on, so I don't try. I just offer a lame excuse and pack it away, tilting my head toward the tree line. "I'm sorry. I'm on edge."

Dagen is already dressed, and I turn my front away from him. There's no time for modesty. I rub the blanket over my body, drying away our moment in the water, and remove my panties and bra. My other set is dry, and I'll be more comfortable.

When I turn back around. Dagen has his back to me. He's positioned himself to give me the privacy I couldn't afford to seek.

He looks out over the water as he speaks. "It sounded far off. We have time to get away."

I agree with him.

In my assessment, whoever these people are, they are not survivalists or hunters in the truest sense. They are amateur killers, and they were probably caught off guard by a predator and had to fire their weapon to scare it off.

Lucky for us—now we know for sure we are being hunted.

I hang my wet underwear from the straps on my bag so they'll dry while we run away. I finish dressing and get my shoes on, then retrieve the sealable plastic bags from the bottom of my duffel and secure them near the top so I can use them later.

We take one last look around the area to make sure our presence here will go unnoticed. I crouch down, brushing my fingers along the ground to revive the grass we crushed under the blanket.

The first couple of hours of our afternoon journey are split between hiking at a fast pace and jogging when we get to open terrain.

There's no doubt in my mind that whoever is attempting to track us has also increased their speed, since they've given themselves away by firing their weapon.

I slow us down when we come to a particularly lush area as soon as I see some plants I recognize, also known as dinner.

I kneel, lowering my bag off my back. I open it and hand Dagen one of the plastic bags, taking another for myself.

"Those are thimbleberries. We can eat them." I point to a section of viny bushes just past Dagen. Without further direction, he turns, picks a berry, and pops it in his mouth.

He stands, looking at me for half a minute before deciding to pick a small handful. Then he returns to me to trade them for the bag.

When he turns away and starts picking the fruit, I'm struck by a foreign feeling. It hits me that not only did Dagen trust me when I told him the berry was edible, but he tried one first before he gathered some for me, to make sure I would be okay eating them.

The lump forming in my throat is hard to swallow as I stand to look for more food we can forage.

"There's poison ivy at the base. Don't get too close." I lean over, holding my finger a few feet away so Dagen can get a good look at the plant at the base of the thimbleberries. He smiles his appreciation and returns to gathering.

There aren't many berries left on the bush. I didn't think there would be this late into August, but it will get us through today if I can find a few more plants.

"We're going to have to pass on all of the mushrooms we find. I don't know enough to tell which ones are poisonous," I admit before stepping up to my own thimbleberry vine and gathering some in my hand before adding them to his bag.

I'm saving my bag for plants, and as soon as I turn around, I find the first one I'm going to add to it.

Not even a couple of minutes later, Dagen joins me. "This is all there was. We should keep moving."

Slinging my duffel across my body, I hold the plastic bag as I follow Dagen into a dense patch of trees.

After about fifteen minutes of Dagen walking ahead of me, and me falling behind when I stop to forage, Dagen steps to the side. He's asking me to lead so he doesn't lose me.

What started out as a sunny day turned overcast quickly, and the distant rumble booming behind the ominous clouds indicates a storm is on the way.

Our hike returns to a jog as we fight to lay down as much distance as we can before we are forced to hunker down and wait it out.

We make it another hour at a fast clip as the winds whip around us before we run out of time.

A sudden change in air pressure chills everything around us.

Dagen notices it too.

As we continue to move forward, our focus shifts to our surroundings. We need to find the best place to stop. I'm five minutes away from calling it when I see the spot I was hoping to find.

It's located in the thick of the forest, surrounded by high trees, and there's a section at the base of the trunks where a group of bushes hang, hovering a few feet above the ground. I run to the edge, scanning the ground underneath, thankful nothing noxious is growing and it isn't sunken in, so water won't pool.

"We need to get the tarp over these bushes, then we'll set the sleeping bag up underneath and push the bags under with us." I raise my voice to speak over the wind and stretch my hand out for Dagen's bag of berries.

He hands it to me and starts on the tarp while I drop to my knees and frantically dump out the contents of my freezer bag. We have a full bottle of water, but I need it to last, so I set it aside and start pulling at the leaves and stems of the plants.

Once the bag is half full of the best-looking plants, I pour a small amount of water in to rinse them off. We're in nature, so I'm not worried about pesticides, but I would rather not pick bugs and dirt out of my teeth.

I drain the water, then reach into the bag of berries and toss a handful of them in with my salad before tearing at the peppergrass seeds to add them in. They aren't much, but they'll give the plants a peppery-berry taste.

"What are you doing?" I look up at the sound of Dagen's voice.

He has the tarp secured over the bushes, and he's on his knees, sliding everything underneath.

"You need to eat."

I mean to say *we* need to eat. We do. However, it isn't lost on me that Dagen is bigger than I am. He's the strongest of the two of us. He needs more sustenance. He really does need to eat before the storm rolls in, or he'll be ill in the morning, and we should hold on to the last of our rations until we absolutely need them.

I smash the berries in the salad bag and mix everything together just as lightning flashes across the sky, followed too closely by a deafening crack of thunder I feel in the pit of my stomach.

We might only have seconds.

Then I freeze.

My blood runs cold as soon as I hear the rain through the trees.

This isn't a shower. It's going to be a torrential downpour.

We lock eyes at the same time.

A combination of fury and worry mars Dagen's features. "Get your ass over here. NOW, NYLA!"

Fisting the bag, I gather the second bag full of berries and the water and scramble to the base of the bushes. Dagen pushes himself back as far as he can, to give me room to slide under with him, when the sky opens up and washes the outside world away in a steady shower.

Everything around us disappears into a light monotone blur as the heavy droplets rain down in a wall, blocking out everything around us.

"Jesus," I mutter under my breath as I place my cheek to the ground to view the spot where I just sat trying to prepare our meal.

Speaking of which. I pull the bag up between us. "We need to eat this. It's not going to taste good, but it's edible, and we need food. Then we can have the berries for dessert."

Although the clouds have blocked out much of the light, it's still daytime, and it isn't totally dark yet.

Dagen's eyes settle on the bag in my hands.

"Take off your shoes and get your feet in here, and we'll sort it out." He lifts up the edge of the sleeping bag.

I do as he says, toeing the heel of my first shoe, then my second. I slip them off but keep them nearby and shimmy close to him, lying on my stomach as I open the bag to smell it.

I crinkle my nose. "Whoof! This is going to suck."

Dagen's chest vibrates as he chuckles, and I smile.

Take life's blessings when they come your way, my mother used to tell me. And right now, it's a blessing that we're alive and settled—*and together.*

It is also a blessing that no one can be out in this weather, which means that whoever is after us has been forced to take shelter as well or perish.

Reaching into the bag, Dagen pinches the plants between his fingers, lifting a bite to his mouth before making a muffled sound. He swallows his bite down before he says, "You don't give yourself credit. This isn't so bad."

Even though I'm sure he can't quite make it out, I roll my eyes. "You don't need to be nice about it." I reach in to scoop some out for myself when he stops me.

"I wouldn't go ordering this in a restaurant, but you did good, Jensen."

Now I'm glad he can't make out any color among the grays of this dreary storm, or he'd see the bright flush filling my cheeks at the use of my last name.

"Thanks, Saint."

I stuff the plants into my mouth and chew. He's right: it isn't good by any culinary standards, but it isn't bad, considering we could eat this or we could eat nothing.

We eat the rest of the bag in silence.

I take a few handfuls at first, but then I spend the rest of the time putting my hand in the bag and coming away empty-handed, then putting my fingers to my mouth so he thinks I'm eating along with him.

There's still something deep inside of me that tells me Dagen would make sure we each get our fair share of the food, maybe even sacrificing his share so I had more, and he would suffer for it later.

I know my body, and I'm positive I'll be fine in the morning. We still have the rest of the berries to go.

When the bag is empty, Dagen rolls his body over with a groan that I feel in my own sore limbs, and I stretch myself out.

My thoughts drift to the photo in my phone. I won't be able to slide out her picture to say goodnight this time.

"What are you thinking about?" Dagen takes a thimbleberry and pops it into his mouth as he hands me the bag.

I can't tell him what I'm really thinking about, so I scramble for a good substitute. "I was just listing some things I should probably add to my go bag."

He pauses for a moment, and I wonder if he's thinking the same.

"Like a bathing suit?" There's a flirtatious hint to his tone, and I wonder if he's trying to circle back to where we were before we were interrupted.

"Among other things. Like a travel canteen and a dry pair of socks."

"Or a change of clothes," Dagen adds, stretching his limbs beside me.

We spend the rest of dessert eating in silence, and I don't force a conversation. I'm not ready to mentally return to the lake.

Dagen seems content to enjoy the break as well.

Once the berries are gone, I pull my bag close so we have a pillow, and we shuffle around each other until we are comfortable enough in the sleeping bag to close our eyes.

The fuzzy edge of sleep creeps in, and I'm about to drift off to the sound of the rain when Dagen's question cuts through the white noise.

"What would you be doing right now if you were at home?"

Home.

I don't move.

I pretend I'm already asleep because this is a question I can't answer.

After a minute, he relaxes around me. His lips brush against the hair at the top of my head, crushing my heart a little more.

If I were at home, I would be playing with the daughter he doesn't know he has, the daughter I'm starting to think he needs to know about the longer I'm here with him.

11

DAGEN

J jolt awake in the middle of the night.

The air in the sleeping bag has gone stale and heavy. Pulling the opening down over my head, I exchange it for a fresh breath. The humid cold sinks into the bones of my face.

The shushing sound of the rain has lost some of its strength, but there is no sign of it stopping any time soon. If there were, we'd probably be waking up and getting ready to put some space between us and whoever fired that gun yesterday.

When my consciousness fully returns, I realize it isn't the heavy pour of the rain that is causing the vibrations around me.

Beside me, Nyla shivers, and I run my hands over her arms to check on her. She's frozen to the touch and curled in on herself, and she's shaking like a leaf in her sleep.

"Nyla. Hey, baby. Wake up." I inadvertently use the term of endearment out of worry. She is dangerously cold, and she's slow to open her eyes.

I jostle her, and she starts to come around.

"Hey." She draws the word into a slur, and she sounds disoriented.

When she attempts to stretch and flattens her palm against my shirt, a frigid ache forms where she rests her hand.

"Dammit. Why didn't you tell me you were cold?"

"What?"

Her confusion is another red flag.

Did she just start losing body heat until she passed out? Did she even know her temperature was dropping?

What if I hadn't woken up? Would she have—

Nope.

Not going there.

We weren't prepared for the temperature to drop this much.

This is going to suck for a long minute, but it needs to be done because I'm still warm. My body temperature has always run hot. I'm sure I have some egotistical comment lurking in my head about that, but I'll have to share it with Nyla another time.

I unzip the sleeping bag, and she groans when the cold air hits her, which is a good sign. It means she still has some body heat left to lose, or save.

I go to work, lifting her top up to her neck and leaving only her bra between us before I open the buttons on my own shirt.

Then, tucking her limbs close to my body, I cocoon the both of us. I zip up the sleeping bag and furiously rub her arms as I drape my leg over both of hers and wrap myself around her body. Bringing her cold fingers up to my chest, I hold her to me tightly, her forehead level with my chin.

"You're hot." She sounds surprised.

"I'll remind you that you said that in the morning."

She tucks her head under my chin and laughs softly against my chest. Her arm wraps around my midsection, embracing me back.

The chill of her body against mine has a bite to it, but it feels good.

Nyla is strong.

She's a fighter, but holding her, taking care of her, and protecting her—it feels right.

I lift her and roll her partially on top of me, then hug her against my body.

"What are you doing?" She makes no move to get away from me.

"I'm getting you off the ground." I adjust my head against her duffel bag so I don't wake up with a sore neck.

Her trembling has already subsided.

Her body shudders with a chill then settles.

"Tell me something. Anything." She speaks her request against my flesh, and my skin swells with goosebumps where her warm breath hits me.

Although I can't see anything, my eyes are wide open.

Nyla smells nice.

It's an odd thought to have because I'm sure neither of us has any toiletries with us, but she fills my nostrils with something pleasing—which is strange because she washed her hair in a lake today.

I search my mind for what I should tell her.

I have a long list of things I want to say and tons of conflicting thoughts about this whole situation.

I take a deep, cleansing breath.

We're going to have to start opening up about the hard stuff soon, so now is a good time to start. This will definitely get Nyla's mind off the cold.

"My father is not a good man. My brothers and I need the microfiche you stole to take him down."

That's about as much of a nutshell as I can get everything

into, and saying the words out loud like this makes me angry. It's a combination of disappointment and fury, and it bleeds through me like poison.

I can't fathom a father hurting his children. Having kids of my own is still far off, but one thing I was taught is to put them above all else. Only now I realize the lessons I learned about being a good man came from Lennox, not our dad.

Nyla hasn't moved, but I know she's awake because her hand flexes around my upper arm. She clears her throat to speak, but my patience is thin, and I don't want her to have to lie about anything to adhere to her contract, so I cut her off.

"Just don't say anything. I know the rules." She nods against my chest. I pull the cover of the sleeping bag back over my head and speak into the dark, as though it will somehow swallow my confession whole.

"I replay everything again and again in my head. I didn't see it. It is literally my job to recognize dangers and see threats before they happen, and I grew up with the biggest threat of them all right under my own roof." She probably thinks I'm losing my mind, but now that I've started talking, I can't stop. Darkness wraps around us like a blanket, and not being able to see the look on Nyla's face frees my demons.

"The piece I can't wrap my head around is how disappointed I am in myself. Because of my ignorance, I let my brothers down. Now I need the microfiche to place the four of us on the right side of a war."

She's quiet for a long time before she asks her first question. "And the four of you had a falling out with your father? I thought you all owned your family business together."

A muscle at the corner of my mouth ticks up.

She has looked into me.

"We do, but what we own and what we thought we

operated are actually two different things. My father was trying to groom us into taking over something none of us have agreed to, and he's been methodically trying to remove us in secret for a while now, to keep his version of our family empire going. It's placed us on the wrong side of a turf war with our closest allies."

"And the microfiche?"

"Holds information our associates need, to tip the scales in their favor. It's the only remaining evidence that will lead them to Elia Lucciano's missing male heir and the next in line to take over. It's a long story."

"Elia Lucciano," she whispers to herself before turning her next question back to me. "Why are you telling me this?"

"Because I know you were the one who got the microfiche. I saw you on the video feed."

She lies on top of me in silence while she considers what I'm sharing, and I notice she's stopped shivering, which is a step in the right direction.

"I had the video from the warehouse scrubbed" is all she offers, but it is more than I hoped for.

She's confirming her job, and we're getting somewhere in the mutual trust department.

"I assumed you did, Jensen. I saw it in real time."

Nyla is impressive.

I don't offer praise lightly.

There is an extremely short list of people who are able to get under my skin, and she blew them all out of the water the first day we met.

"So you saw me walking out of the building with the file you needed—while it was happening?" There's a hint of amusement in her tone.

"Not only that, you were mere feet from two of my brothers, who were waiting in their car in the parking lot, but the video feed was on a delay, so by the time I told them to stop you—"

"I was already gone."

Yep. She's enjoying this immensely.

It is the second time she's gotten the better of me and got away with it.

Her fingers tap gently against my skin. "And this is why people are after us?"

It sounds more like a conclusion than a question.

"Elia Lucciano's heir will decide everything. Once he's named, the organization will follow the side who has his support. They want either the microfiche or, if it was destroyed, the name of who hired you."

I stop short of asking her if she has the microfiche. It's been months, and I see no reason why she would hold on to it. I am hoping she will have an idea of who hired her to steal it, but interrogating her now, when I'm bringing her back from hypothermia, won't win me any trust points.

"Are we going to make it out of this?" The smile I imagined she had on her face earlier is probably gone. Fear subdues Nyla's voice.

I listen to the rain around us as I consider her question and our situation.

Whether she believes it or not, Nyla is probably the strongest one out here. Not physically, but in survival smarts. I take comfort in knowing that, whatever we are going through, whoever is hunting us is going through worse because they don't have her on their team.

"I think we have a good chance if we stick together. We need to start looking for larger meals though. We are running out of rations, and forest leaves are only going to get us so far."

"Yeah." Her tone is casual yet hesitant.

I don't really want to be hunting bunnies and squirrels out

here either, but we've only got a day, maybe two, before we start to lose the strength we started with.

"Hopefully we'll come across a road first." I offer a sliver of hope, and she echoes her last response:

"Yeah."

She sounds defeated.

Our minds are crazy things.

Our internal thoughts can embolden or sabotage our efforts. Nyla is cold and tired. Her fight has taken a hit, but she doesn't strike me as the type to be down for long.

She needs to rest because I need her at her best tomorrow.

"We're going to make it out of here, Nyla. I don't accept failure. Besides, you owe me a debt, and I intend to collect—one way or another."

I give her a squeeze and kiss the top of her head gently, to show her my words are meant as a comfort and not entirely a threat.

"Um, I'm warm. I think I can give you some space." She braces her palms on either side of me and tries to push herself up.

I hold her tight.

"No. You'll stay here. I've got you. Now close your eyes."

"Okay." This time, she sounds distant.

An odd awareness slinks its way into my head. "Are you okay?"

She doesn't answer for a couple of minutes. It's still too dark to see, but I'm sure I feel something wet against my chest.

Is she crying?

I'm about to ask when I hear her sniffle against my skin.

Then she whispers, "I made a mistake."

Pushing my face into her hair, I shush her against her scalp.

Wallowing in the things we should have done will not serve us out here.

"It doesn't matter. I've got you. No matter what, we're in this together, and we'll get out of it together. Get some rest. We'll deal with tomorrow in the morning."

She sobs softly against my chest for a minute longer before her breathing evens out and her limbs relax around me.

12

NYLA

The next time I open my eyes, I'm warm.

My body rises and falls with Dagen's steady breathing.

When I turn my head to face his chest, only the tip of my nose is cold against the warmth of his skin, and I push my face in, inhaling his scent.

He smells a little like the forest around us, but there is something headier there that makes me want to take a second deep breath.

This time, when I set my hands on the sleeping bag on either side of his body to lift my weight off him, he doesn't hold me tight.

Spreading my legs on either side of his torso, I reach for the zipper.

The rain has slowed to a trickle now, and I hover a foot above Dagen under the overhang of the bushes when his eyes meet mine.

"Now this is the kind of good morning I can get behind—or

should I say under." His eyes glint in the light as he smirks before lowering his gaze.

I look down to see what he's getting at, then I yelp at the sight of my shirt lifted up to my neck and my girls pouring out of my bra. I cover myself before sliding off him.

I vaguely remember Dagen rolling me on top of him to heat me up. I wasn't aware I had become cold in the night.

The part that is crystal clear is what he said when he opened up about his family.

I'm in this a lot deeper than I initially thought.

I'm distracted by last night's conversation when Dagen reaches his hand to the hair covering my face and brushes it behind my ear.

"Why do you think you made a mistake?"

I stare at him blankly. Did I just say my thoughts out loud?

Dagen clarifies, "Last night, before you fell asleep, you said you made a mistake."

Wrinkles crease his forehead the longer I take to answer him.

I don't want to keep things from him, I'm just not sure right now is a good time to tell him he has a daughter. There probably isn't a good time to tell him I've knowingly kept him away from her because I found out some things I thought were true, but I was wrong.

I decide I'm going to tell him tonight when we settle in for the evening. Hopefully the rain will stop, and I'll be able to sit him down and say it to his face.

"I—I shouldn't have taken that job." I lower my voice and my eyes.

I've crossed a line with Dagen. At some point yesterday, my conscience decided that we no longer feel good about keeping things from him.

A mask covers Dagen's face as I speak, and I don't bother to clarify that my regret isn't because of him. Dagen recovers and props himself up on his forearm, looking out from the bush we are hiding under. "We need to keep our lead. We should head out."

I show my agreement by reaching down to put my shoes on. One of them slipped out from under the tarp in the night, so I'll be walking with one soaker.

The ground immediately around us didn't flood, but the bottoms of our bags are soaked.

I feel weak and hungry, and I don't want to carry as much as we did yesterday, but I crawl out from our hiding spot, stretch, and start to pull everything down.

We can't afford to leave any of this behind. First because we don't want to leave a trail, but also because we don't know if or when we'll find another shelter, so a tarp and sleeping bag is all we have for now.

We share the last of the water and don't bother with our rations. The chill has quickly set into my bones, and I need to warm up more than I need to eat.

We break to use our own spots in the forest to relieve ourselves, then gather our things and start walking.

Before long, the only part of me still cold is my one foot. The sensation of water seeping into my sock with every step is starting to drive me nuts, but there's nothing I can do about it.

After an hour of walking with our heads down, the rain subsides, and I step into a ray of light before I look up to see the clouds are starting to break apart.

It's another small mercy, but what is a good thing for us is also a good thing for the people who are hunting us.

I reach into my duffel for granola bars and pass one up to Dagen, telling him, "This is the last of my bars, but I have some dried fruit."

He answers by letting me know he still has some food of his own to share.

I'm drawn back to our conversation from the night before, when Dagen talked about needing to find more food. I'm not a vegetarian by any means, but the thought of catching and killing an animal out here makes my stomach turn.

When we pass a bush with brightly colored berries, I pull out the plastic bag from my pocket and begin to fill it.

"Is this lunch?" Dagen asks.

"No. This is western yew. It's poisonous, but the berries might come in handy later if we—um, need to trap an animal. The pulp tastes good, but the seeds are deadly. So don't eat it. Not even one."

Dagen takes a closer look at the bush, no doubt trying to add it to his mental list of things not to put in our mouths while we're out here.

"So granola bars it is then." He holds up the bar I passed him, and I close the bag of berries before stuffing it into the top of my duffel. We slow our step but continue to walk while we eat, and eventually we come across a stream alongside a hill.

The water is ice cold. It's probably running from way up on the top, weaving its way down and through the mountainside.

Beggars can't be choosers.

We take turns drinking before we fill the bottle and store it away. Then we decide to power hike for twenty minutes until our food settles before breaking out in our afternoon combination of running and jogging to put ground between us and whoever's after us.

The farther south we travel, the more the pit in my stomach grows. My guilt is eating away at me. I'm keeping this big secret from Dagen, but, more importantly, I've been keeping Vaughn's father away from her.

I've denied them both.

By the time Dagen slows down, I'm so lost in my thoughts and sick with worry that I almost barrel into his back.

His arms brace against me as he stops me from taking us both down, and I grip his shirt to steady myself.

"You look like you're running from a ghost." He examines my face.

"I'm okay. Just getting tired."

"Well, it might be our lucky day then. Look." He turns to point in front of him.

"A lake?" I'm happy we'll be able to get some more water when Dagen interrupts my thoughts.

"No. *Look!*" I follow his finger more closely to see something floating along the edge.

"Is that—a boat?"

"It looks like it."

We exchange a glance and take off running around the side, knowing what this means: we might be closer to a road than we think.

Neither of us says a thing until we hit the shore. The boat is tied to a tree. It bobs along with the gentle waves, its back end sunken under the water's surface and resting on the bottom. The whole thing is rusted out, and there are no supplies or nets inside that could help us fish for our next meal rather than hunt for it.

This boat hasn't been used in at least a decade, probably more.

Dagen mutters his disappointment under his breath, but I feel a burst of hope.

"We need to search the area. This boat was left here, which means it might have been used seasonally. We might be near an unregistered cabin."

"I don't know what that means." Dagen takes a step into the water to fill our bottle.

"There are a lot of unclaimed, hidden shacks out here that are sitting illegally on Crown land. Most were used by trappers and fishers, even miners during the gold rush. If there is one still standing, it might have something useful. At the very least, we'll have an actual place to stay tonight."

"Fine. We look, but we stay on the south side. If we don't find anything in half an hour, we head out."

I agree and turn to look away from the boat, scanning for anything that might look like a hiking trail. There are a couple of options, but one of them circles back in the direction we came from. Judging by gaps in the trees and some tags set up to mark a path, we choose the second option and walk south for five minutes before we come to a deep ravine directly to our right.

It's a dangerous path, but it is a path, and that says something.

"Should we turn back and try a different way?" Dagen takes one step, then bends at his hip to look over the edge.

"No. I really think there may be something this way. If it is an unclaimed shack, then it is going to be small. If we don't walk directly to it, we might miss it entirely."

Dagen doesn't challenge my theory, so I continue walking, but I slow my step.

After ten minutes along the ravine, the path leads inward, and I make out a mound of something in the distance. It isn't easy to see; it's like a shadow lurking through the trees, but its mass doesn't match its surroundings.

"There it is." I point toward the old building.

Dagen looks both relieved and shocked. "What if someone's there?"

I scan the area. "It's probably empty. You said it's not hunting season. Hopefully it isn't completely abandoned, or animals will have moved in."

Dagen reaches into his pocket, pulls out his phone, and turns it on, checking for bars. He holds it up for a minute, turning around where he stands, then shakes his head at me before turning it off.

The log cabin looks like it is only going to have one room. It's no more than fifteen feet wide and deep. It's clear it was built a long time ago, by someone using their bare hands and not much else.

Four large stumps circle a makeshift pit surrounded by large rocks in front of the cabin. Weathered plywood has been laid down along the front of the shack to create a small porch, but it has since rotted out, making it more of a hindrance than help at this point. The only two windows are sealed with one pane of glass, and neither one looks like it will open.

The plywood bows as Dagen steps onto it and opens the flimsy screen door: its mesh is stapled to the inner side of the door and ripped in two places. Otherwise, the place looks secure to the elements.

There are no locks, and the inside door opens easily. The place is most likely used by whoever finds it first come hunting season. There's probably nothing of value inside.

"We could stay here tonight." I'm so desperate for a good night's sleep that the words slip out.

In my head, I justify that it is getting close to dinnertime, and we made good time when we ran today. Then I look toward the back of the room, and my eyes land on the answer to our prayers.

A handmade wooden bed frame sits in the corner. There is no mattress, but we could spread out the sleeping bag and sleep off the ground for a night.

A wash basin sits in the corner, and there's a rusted metal folding table and three chairs in the middle of the room. A few tools, some utensils, two pots, a cast-iron skillet, and a broken plate are scattered around the room, along with a few other items no one cared enough about to take with them.

Then my heart skips a beat.

"You have got to be kidding me." I push past Dagen and crouch in front of the tackle box on the floor. I'm sure I sound like a kid on Christmas morning when I say, "There are fishing hooks in here!"

Dagen joins me at my side, looking over our newfound treasure.

I'm elated.

Mostly because I was pretty sure we wouldn't be trapping a little woodland animal any time soon.

I didn't even want to think about how I would get its fur off, and it's not like there are featherless chickens running around out here all prepared to just sit on the fire.

I love the outdoors, but I have my limits.

As if reading my thoughts, Dagen jumps to his feet and takes a couple of steps away from me toward one of the corners.

"Here's a fishing rod. It's broken, but I'm sure we can fix it. Look what else I found." He holds up a hatchet, and his grin lights up the whole room. Or maybe I notice it because it is the same look our daughter gets when she's proud of herself.

There is no good time.

I need to tell him.

"Dagen, I—"

"I know. I'll get on it. We don't have much daylight left. We can head back to the water and fish. I'll chop some wood with this, and we can start a fire to cook our dinner, but we'll have to keep it low. We'll leave early in the morning to make up time."

My heart sinks.

There will never be a good time to tell him, but now really isn't it.

We're going to lose ground by staying here tonight, and if I tell him here, it could eat up the time we have left.

Dagen's chuckle seems out of place.

"What's so funny?" I busy myself in the tackle box, sorting the line, weights, and hooks we'll need. Then I find a pair of needle-nose pliers and start setting them up.

"I wish Cole could see me now." He sees I don't understand the meaning behind his words, and he sits back on his heels for a moment, waving his hand around the room. "This is more in my brother's wheelhouse than mine." We share a smile, then he adds, "Although I am seeing the appeal."

He makes no effort to hide the fact that his comment is aimed at me.

My cheeks heat, but I don't push it. If I don't have time to tell him we have a daughter, I shouldn't have time to enjoy his compliments.

I smile and return to the items in my hand.

Instinctively, I want to flatten the barbed hook like my brother showed me a long time ago, but we're not fishing for fun —we need to eat.

"Did your dad teach you how to fish?" Dagen joins me with the items he's found, and I look over the rod and reel in his hands.

We have everything we need to fish, although a net would be nice, but I haven't found one.

"Kind of. He taught my brothers, and my oldest brother, Jonah, taught me. There was a big gap between our ages, and our dad thought if we did things together, it would bring us closer." *Then he sent them away.*

I don't voice the last part because I don't blame my father.

I blame Elia Lucciano.

I took the microfiche job because I let curiosity get the better of me.

I was curious about Elia Lucciano's organization.

After all, he is the man who took my brothers away from my family. He is the reason my father banned them from ever coming home.

After Jonah and Carson left, my parents never spoke about them in front of me again. I went from having siblings to being an only child overnight.

I would listen in on my parents' conversations when they thought I was asleep. It was Elia's name they spoke, and it was often followed by my mother's tears.

When the contract came up, I was driven to accept it.

I had become obsessed.

I needed to see what Elia was all about. I was hoping I would find out where my brothers were—if they were still alive —but all it ended up being was a dying man's wish to find his own kid.

The bastard took my family away from me, and now he wants his own back?

And I hold the answer in my hands—sometimes literally.

It gives me an odd sense of power, knowing I have something Elia Lucciano wants so desperately, because he has my brothers, and I want them back just as much.

My buyer is in no rush to get the microfiche back, but they do want to see it before it is destroyed, to make sure I recovered the correct document.

I got the impression they also didn't want Elia to have it, so I was happy to hold on to it.

I don't like that I take a perverse joy in knowing that I'm the one who is keeping this away from Elia, but it's the only thing that gives me any power over the void Jonah and Carson created when they left.

Now this power feels bittersweet.

Dagen needs this microfiche to help his brothers. I need it

to complete my contract and soothe my childhood broken heart.

"You ready?" I startle at Dagen's voice.

When I look up at him, he is carefully watching me, and I mask my anger behind a smile.

I take stock of everything we have before answering, "I am. Have you fished before?"

Dagen's brazen smirk contradicts his answer. "Never. I have no idea what I'm doing. This should be fun."

13

DAGEN

I'm quietly contemplating my conversation with Nyla while we hike along the ravine back to the lake.

She shared her brothers' names with me. I'm not sure if she meant to, or if she's falling into a welcome complacency.

Nyla struggles with something deep inside whenever she recalls her family. Sometimes I think she's being secretive. Other times, I wonder if reliving the memory is painful.

She carries so much emotion in her features at times. I wish I knew why, but she's hidden her past away from the world.

"This looks like a good spot." Nyla steps onto a group of boulders at the water's edge.

These rocks are large enough to fit both of us comfortably and act as a dock.

She sets the tackle box and a plastic bucket on the ground and reaches her hand toward me, silently asking for the rod in my hand.

Bending the section where the break was, she pinches her lips together and nods her approval at my handiwork.

I like that I've impressed her, but I look down and away from her so she doesn't see the pride stretching its way across my face in what is probably a ridiculous smile. Instead, I take a step to the water as it laps gently against the rock.

When I turn back, she's wrapped her hand around the string. She tugs it, and it snaps.

"The line is brittle," she murmurs. She bends down and pulls out a section of the tackle box to reveal a hidden compartment underneath.

Her eyes light up when she pulls out a new line, still in the package. Then she sits cross-legged on the rock and takes apart the rod.

This isn't my strength, and I won't pretend that it is.

I take a deep breath of fresh air. It's different out here. It feels real, as though the air in the city is manufactured. Still, I could do without the bug bites and lack of water pressure for a decent shower.

"Do you think your brothers have any idea what's happening now?" Nyla looks at me while she talks, but her hands continue their work.

I do the math in my head, considering how much time has passed versus how determined my brothers can be when they want something.

By now, they should have heard about the plane going down. They will have been in touch with Nigel and the local authorities.

If Nyla is right, and the plane transmitted our coordinates upon impact, then the authorities should be close to locating the crash site, if they haven't found it already.

Lennox owns the plane that went down, so he'll be one of the main contacts for information.

When my brothers discover there are no bodies on board, they should realize what I've done, and hopefully they'll stay put and wait for me to get in touch. I don't want any of them to cross paths with whoever is after us.

"I think so, but they'll give me some time to check in before they come running out here. They're probably trying to find out who is responsible, and they'll work back that way. What about your team? What happens now?"

Nyla glances briefly toward the sun. It's still fairly high in the sky, but our window for getting dinner is closing. She continues working as she answers me.

"They'll be lying low. We have a way of getting in touch, but I won't be able to check our channels until I have access to the internet."

She stands and tries the line once more.

It doesn't snap, and she looks at me. "Want to learn how to fish?"

"I don't know, maybe you should just—" I point to the water. I don't want her to waste precious time trying to teach me.

"Whether I cast it or you do, it's the same. We just need the hook in the water. Come on. I'll show you."

I'm not convinced it's the same, but if Nyla bonded with her brother over this, then I'm up for anything that might knock down some of the walls standing between us.

She hands me the rod. A hook dangles off the end, attached to a small weight. I take my spot on the boulder by the water, and she closes the distance and steps up behind me, wrapping her arms around my body to move me around.

I wish the roles were reversed, but then we wouldn't get any fishing done, and we still need to eat.

Nyla patiently names all the parts of the rod. Then she compresses a button and moves my arm behind us before flicking it forward and letting the button go at the same time.

The hook creates a small splash when it goes in the water,

and a surge of excitement floods my chest before I realize it landed only a foot away from the shore.

She shows me how to reel it in.

The rod is old and clunky, and the line gets stuck twice, but I'm able to reel the hook all the way in. She tells me to practice a few more times while she closes the tackle box.

On my third try, it lands farther out. Nyla's praise hits me like a sucker punch in the gut.

She steps beside me and shows me how to set the hook.

And now we wait.

We fall into a comfortable silence. I jerk gently on the rod, just like Nyla showed me, while we listen to the birds and the insects chirping.

The sound of her smacking a bug off her skin does dirty things to my thoughts. I have come to crave the sound of her skin being spanked—I mean—nope, I totally meant spanked.

Nyla sighs beside me. It sounds like a wistful moan. It's close to a whisper, but it reverberates through me, and it draws my attention to her.

Her eyes are closed, and she takes another deep breath, exhaling with that sinful sigh again. I swallow hard.

When she opens her eyes, she smiles at me before looking past me, and surprise replaces her serene expression.

She points at the water. "You—you caught a fish!"

I snap out of my daydream and suddenly feel the tugging on the rod in my hands. I lift the rod straight up, wrapping my fingers around the weak part of the rod, and the little tugs become a full-on brawl.

"What do I do?" Apparently I've completely forgotten the five minutes of basic fishing Nyla taught me.

"Don't let go. Keep the line tight. Don't let it go slack."

Okay. I can do this. It's no big deal.

"Slowly reel it in before the fish snaps the line."

I look at her like she's joking. "It can do that?"

Nyla bursts into laughter as she nods, and panic sets in as I realize I'm going to have to work for our dinner.

I only manage five turns of the reel before the line gets stuck again, and the jovial expression falls from Nyla's face.

This is our dinner we're talking about here.

"No. No no no no no no. We're going to lose it." Nyla gives the line a steady pull.

My stomach grumbles at the mere thought of defeat.

"Not on my watch, Jensen!"

I step off the rocks while keeping the line taut, then start running inland. I will drag this damn thing to Vancouver if I have to.

"What are you doing?" Nyla yells from behind me, and I turn to see her rolling up her pant legs with her shoes on the ground at the shoreline.

"We're eating this fish tonight!"

I'm not sure if the next growl comes from me or my stomach, but I revel in my determination. I embrace the fire it's lit under me.

A splash in the lake draws my attention, and I turn back just in time to see the tail of a fish go under. I trip over my step at the sight, but I manage to keep going.

Nyla waits by the edge of the water, and I wonder if she's actually going to jump in and wrestle the fish if it comes to that.

Damn, I crave her perseverance.

Seeing her own determined drive sends me into a primal state, and being out here in nature amplifies everything.

I'm almost into the trees when Nyla yells at me to stop.

I stay still, holding the rod up and away from the water, creating a tense bend. Nyla wraps her hand around the line and steps one foot into the lake.

The water splashes furiously around her for a few seconds.

Then she bends down, hooks her hand under the belly of the fish, and scoops it up. She tosses it onto the shore, yelling, "YOU DID IT!"

I run, gathering up the line as I return to Nyla at the lake.

Her smile is unrestrained, and she's laughing through tears and clutching her stomach. "That was crazy! You just started running." She points in the direction I ran to emphasize how funny this is to her, then wipes a tear from her eye and takes a cleansing breath. "Phew. I needed that."

She looks like she really did.

She bounces between her feet, energized by what just happened, before she catches herself and shifts self-consciously.

In a normal situation, we would hug out our victory, to work off some of the adrenaline that we built up, because that is what friends do. But we aren't friends. The lines that form our dynamic haven't been removed, so a heavy hesitation lingers between us.

We are two people who should be at odds with each other. She is my rival, and I'm her captor, even though we are working together to get away from a larger threat.

"I'll—um..." She looks down at the fish flopping on the ground, then around the area. "I'll get the hook out, and we'll fix the reel. Maybe we can catch some more."

She's quick to discard the moment that passed between us. She turns to rifle through the tackle box, returning with some pliers and something that looks like thick plastic rope.

"I'll get this one on the stringer. Try to see if you can free the line and reel it in."

Our moment has passed, and we spend the next five minutes in awkward silence while we complete our tasks.

We drop the line into the water for another half an hour. We manage to catch two more fish before Nyla reminds me it's getting late, and we pack up. Nyla fills the bucket with some lake water, then we divide the things we need to carry and make our way up the trail.

It's no secret among my brothers that I do not like the outdoors, but there's something about walking back to our little shack for the night with our dinner—which we worked damn hard for—hanging on a string that makes me feel like we crushed today.

Nyla has been noticeably quiet, only speaking to point out a dangerous step along the ravine.

The silence follows us all of the way back to camp, and we fall into an easy routine as we gather firewood. Nyla shows me how she was taught to filet a fish using my hunting knife and the bucket of water she carried from the lake.

Nyla's stomach growls when we set the fish on one of the old pans we found in the cabin, and she smiles sheepishly at the sound.

Once the fish is cooked, I set the pan on one of the stumps beside the fire, and we move two of the remaining stumps closer to make a dining spot.

Using my hunting knife, we take turns cutting pieces away until the pan cools enough that we both resort to using our fingers. Hunger gets the better of us, and we eat quickly.

As soon as we're done, Nyla pours water from the bucket into the pot, then dumps everything back into the bucket before adding the carcass and bones.

It's only when she tells me we need to hike our garbage away from the cabin that I notice how much it smells like an invitation to wild animals everywhere.

Nyla joins me on a trek to the ravine, where I toss the bucket and its contents over the side to the ground far below. It's got to be at least a fifty-foot drop, and it should be far enough away to keep us hidden from predators, at least until we head out in the morning.

A full moon sits low on the horizon, and it looks like it's going to be a clear night.

Nyla is still deep in thought when we return, and I ache to recover the distance building between us.

"Listen, Nyla, I—"

I'm not entirely sure I know what I was going to say, but it doesn't matter.

We're just through the front door of the cabin when Nyla spins, squaring herself on me. Then she pounces. Fisting my shirt into her hands, she pulls me down to meet her mouth in a frenzied kiss.

How long has she wanted to do this?

My mind swirls, and I'm getting on board when she breaks away and attempts to step back.

"I'm sorry. I—"

I won't let her run away from her actions.

I wrap my fingers around her throat and spin her, pushing her up against the wall and pinning her with my weight, my building erection pushing into her pelvis through our clothes.

It's my turn.

Lowering my head, I smash my mouth into hers, and she kisses me back with a whimper.

Cupping her hip with my free hand, I grind myself against her, aching to return to how I had her the first night we met.

When I break away this time, we pant hard and in unison.

Her wide eyes are filled with a combination of heady lust and need, and I want to bury the hatchet. I want to bury something else too, but I want to make sure this is what she wants.

"You can have this, Nyla. Just say the word."

14

NYLA

Something took hold of me when Dagen ran away from the lake and up the riverbank, dragging that poor fish behind him. It dug its claws into my heart and tore it open, and I didn't know what to do with myself.

This infuriatingly confident man just doesn't stop inching his way into my head and my heart.

I've wondered over and over again how things would be if we didn't have this history between us—or these secrets.

I didn't realize how much I had immersed myself in the moment with him until he asked how my team was.

I've barely thought about them.

I've thought only about getting back to Vaughn. And him.

There's no denying the chemistry we started out with. It was there when I saw him again in the hotel after five years, and if it wasn't for the gunshot, we would have acted on it yesterday, when we took our afternoon swim in the pond.

Now it's evolving into something beyond desire. It's becoming a force I don't want to deny.

But I have to tell him about our daughter, and I'm starting

to wonder if I'm putting it off because I'm scared he won't want anything to do with either of us. Or maybe he won't want anything to do with me once he learns I've kept this from him.

I can't lose her, but this isn't about me. I'm keeping them from knowing each other, and that can't continue.

I promise myself on the walk back from the lake that I'll tell him during dinner. Then I promise myself during dinner that I'll tell him as soon as we've eaten. Then I replay how I'm going to tell him on the walk back from the ravine, and I promise myself I'll tell him as soon as we walk through the door.

Then the screen door closes behind us, and Dagen turns to look at me. The dusky sky illuminates his features, and there's a fire burning in his eyes that matches my own.

"Listen, Nyla, I—"

I break all of my promises.

I don't want to talk.

We'll need to do enough of that soon.

I want to remember how he felt.

I'm selfish for taking this before I've come clean, but I don't care.

I make the first move when I lunge at him, pulling him into me by his shirt, and I kiss him to settle the storm that has been snaking its way through me.

It takes a moment for him to react, and I slip into a moment of uncertainty.

Have I misread the room?

I force myself to break the kiss and take a step away. Embarrassment warms my face.

"I'm sorry. I—"

Dagen doesn't let me finish my apology.

He furrows his brows and sets his eyes on me.

He looks angry, possessive.

Before I make sense of the situation, he spins me and

pushes me back against the wall. His fingers tighten around my throat as he presses his cock into me through our clothes, and I groan at the sensation.

Dagen lowers his head, getting his face close to mine and commanding all of my attention. His eyes devour my own, and he licks his lips before flashing his teeth in a wicked grin.

With a hot breath on my face, he says, "You can have this, Nyla. Just say the word."

It's a challenge.

The way his eyes narrow on mine and how he pins me to the wall makes me dizzy.

Frantic need bubbles up in my chest. It reflects in my tone when I answer, "I'll say any word you—"

The rest of my sentence is swallowed up with a claiming kiss that steals the air from my lungs.

And I let him take me.

His fingers are hot against my cool skin. They sink under my shirt and skim up my torso, leaving a trail of goosebumps in their wake.

His kiss is rough but his touch is gentle, and the contradiction between the two sends me into a frenzy.

I push off the wall and lift my leg to his waist, opening myself to him. Dagen drops his hands to my ass and lifts me, wrapping me around him and walking us over to the wooden platform where he laid our sleeping bag down earlier.

Cupping my head, he lowers us to the hard surface, and the voices in my head that were urging me to talk go silent as I tug his shirt out of his pants and over his head.

Dagen mirrors my actions, removing my shirt before lowering his body onto mine. His fingers comb into my hair at the base of my skull, and he nudges my head with his own until I turn my face to the side, exposing my neck to his mouth.

His mouth, licking and biting along the length of my throat, makes me shiver, and the sensation sends a shockwave straight to my core.

He shudders as he lifts himself off me to look me in the eyes.

The light in the room has dimmed, and the colors around us are fading into various shades of gray. We have a flashlight with us, but, like Dagen's phone, we won't use it unless we absolutely need to for fear of draining our precious batteries.

The moonlight is bright enough that I can still see his features. Concern creates shadows along his creased forehead.

"Nyla. I—I don't have—I didn't think we would be—" His tone is a mixture of regret and disappointment.

"I'm on birth control. I'm clean." I don't go further into the details of my IUD.

Neither of us brought up the subject of birth control the first time we were together, obviously, but both of us have grown wiser since then.

A tug on the button of my pants is the only indication that he is happy with my answer, and he returns his lips to my neck before trailing kisses down my body. Skimming over my breasts, he leaves my bra alone and draws lines with his fingers over my stomach while his lips and tongue follow.

I twist my fingers into his hair to ground myself as my body reacts in jolts and shivers at the contact.

Once he settles himself between my legs, he sits up, escaping my hold. Pulling my boots off first, he tosses them over his shoulder before pulling my pants and underwear down and throwing them onto the floor.

His gaze bores into my own through the dim room, and he holds his attention on me as he unfastens his belt before pulling it from the loops on his pants.

"Last time, we fucked on your terms. This time, we fuck on

mine." His voice is low, a warning, and little bumps prickle across my skin in response to his dominance.

He circles my wrists with the belt before sliding it through the buckle and tightening my hands together.

This is a lesson in trust. He allowed me to cuff him to a tree, and I took advantage of the control he granted me.

This is his retribution.

I'm to be the one who offers my power up to him this time.

I let my legs fall open around him and still, waiting for his lead.

He withholds his touch, instead devouring my body with his eyes. When his gaze settles on my core, a nervous tension begins to sneak its way into my mind.

My anxiety builds further when he doesn't look away or make any effort to touch me.

"Stay still, Nyla. I won't tell you again."

I shudder at his tone, but I don't move.

Slowly, he stands at the foot of our bed, unbuttoning his pants and sliding everything down.

His eyes never leave mine.

Dagen stands to his full height looking down at me, and I break our stare to look at his thick erection.

I clench my core to ease the pressure building inside of me.

When he returns to the bed, he's not gentle. He pushes my leg up and out, his fingers immediately grazing my shaved mound before sliding into my folds.

I flex my fingers in response, desperately wanting to touch him, to create my own connection, but he doesn't allow it.

Grabbing his belt, he lifts my hands above my head, then returns to rubbing circles around my clit and through my slick. He lets go of the belt, but the command remains: I'm to keep my hands above my head as his hand kneads my breast, pinching my nipple between his fingers.

He breaches my pussy, sliding two fingers deep inside me and curling them deliciously against my sensitive spot. I arch my body in response, and he groans at my reaction.

"Such a good girl for me."

Biting my lower lip, I moan at the praise in his words, drawing a sinful smirk from his lips when I open my legs further for him.

Shifting his weight, he lowers his mouth to my pussy, and I jerk my hips when he flattens his tongue over my clit. He braces his arm across my midsection to hold me against the bed.

The need to touch him overwhelms me and sends me into space. Without thought, I lower my arms, trying to run my fingers through his hair once more.

Dagen stops, and the space he creates when he pulls away makes me greedily stretch my fingers out.

Sliding his body up alongside my own, he grips the leather of his belt in his hand and jerks my hands back to their place above my head.

He drops his head to mine, and his lips tease along the shell of my ear, his breath scorching against my skin.

"Bad girl. You must be made to understand when you are not in charge—and, baby, you are not in charge here."

He makes his point by sliding three fingers through my wetness and into my pussy while holding his belt around my wrists high above my head.

The control I tried to claw back devolves into desperation as Dagen works his fingers inside of me, relentlessly drawing wanton mewls from my lips.

He brings me close to the edge, then eases me back again and again, until my whimpers are the only sounds in the quiet cabin around us.

He savors every sound I make. His lips rain kisses along my breast, which has now warmed to a fever pitch.

I break. "Please—"

Speaking was the wrong thing to do.

Dagen pushes his fingers, covered in my arousal, into my mouth while whispering a shush into my ears. I shudder as I quiet and suck myself off him.

He shifts his weight between my legs, the tip of his erection pressing against my entrance.

Keeping my mouth wrapped around his fingers, Dagen grips my chin with his thumb, turning my face to meet his predatory eyes.

"I recall you moaning while I fucked you. You were so needy, so loud, baby. Any animal within a five-hundred-yard radius heard you yelling that you were mine in the desert, and I don't remember giving you back." He growls his words into my face at the same time he lifts the belt higher and slides his thick cock all the way in.

My eyes roll up, and I groan in surrender as spittle coats my chin around his fingers, which are still shoved in my mouth. The taste of my need is evident on my tongue as I struggle to take his girth along with all of the dirty things he's saying to me.

"There's my kitten. I've missed my pussy. I love it when your body purrs for me."

His words slither into my head and take purchase as he pulls out, then thrusts in, forcing the air out of my lungs in a shameless gasp.

There's something about the way he talks to me. I thought maybe I had gotten off on dirty talk, but I tried it once with someone else, and it ended quickly when I couldn't stop giggling.

It wasn't dirty talk, it was Dagen.

It's the way he claims me and possesses me that I crave.

He removes his fingers, coated with my spit, and wraps his hand around my throat. His other hand remains around his belt as he pounds wildly into me. His face hovers inches away from my own as he stares deep into my soul, watching for the moment I break apart for him.

When I try to turn my head away, he uses his hold on my neck to demand I return to him, and my lower stomach tightens as my impending orgasm builds.

This isn't gentle; it's pure need, carnal desire, and primal possession. He fucks me as though he's consuming me whole, and I give myself over to him.

Tears roll out of the corners of my eyes when I close them. A firm pressure on my throat pulls me back into his commanding stare, and I blink rapidly while he watches my descent.

When he tells me he wants to feel me come all over his cock, I do, bucking wildly against him and screaming his name, my arms now limp in his hold above my head.

He rides me ferociously through my orgasm, telling me I'm still his, and his claim takes me higher.

As I soar on waves of weightlessness, he growls my name, stiffening as he releases himself inside of me.

There's no remorse when he pulls out and brushes the hair out of my face before kissing my forehead. There's no shame when he cups my breast and teases my hard nipple with his fingers. He releases the belt, but I keep my arms where he left them, and he lowers his mouth to my chest and sucks me into his lips before nipping my sensitive nipple between his teeth.

Exhaustion creeps in, and I curl into his side when he lowers my arms for me.

"I want you to sleep naked beside me, but you can't." There's a hint of remorse in his tone. "We'll lose body heat overnight if we don't get dressed before we close our eyes."

I nod against his chest and stand to gather my clothes when

he suggests we go out together to use the washroom before we close the door and go to sleep for the night.

Since we cooked the fish so close to the shack, I have to agree with him. The smell may still be lingering in the air, and we'll need to be careful outside now.

We waste no time running outside and back. Then we shut the door and prop an old chair against it to act as a flimsy reinforcement before settling into the sleeping bag to share our body heat.

I had plans to clean the spiderwebs out of this room before we fell asleep, but now it doesn't seem to matter.

Dagen circles his arms around me and pulls me into the warmth of his body.

This connection is different. It's evolved, and I nuzzle my body close to him, enjoying this brief moment of peace, but it's fleeting.

The morning will come, and when it does, I may lose him forever.

15

DAGEN

I'm vaguely aware of the creak in the screen door as it shuts when I open my eyes to the blinding morning sun.

The first thing I notice is that we slept longer than we should have.

The second is that Nyla is gone from our bed, but I don't feel alone. I sense a presence in the room with me.

The floor creaks, and I roll over to find a disheveled man pointing a gun at me, his hand trembling.

"Where's the girl?"

I have no idea.

I shut down the idea that she's left me here, even though she's done it once before.

"She left to gather some berries."

His expensive clothes are worn and torn from the elements. He obviously wasn't expecting to be out here for long.

He looks hungry.

Remembering my previous conversation with Nyla, I steal a glance at the yew berries sitting on the old table in the middle of the room. I snap my gaze back to my intruder in an obvious attempt to draw his attention to the *food* on the table.

He buys it.

Stepping toward the table, he licks his dry lips at the sight of the bright berries sitting in their bag. *The same berries we were going to use to lure an animal into a trap*, I muse to myself.

If the shoe fits.

Keeping his gun trained on me, he lifts a berry from the bag and sniffs it as though his superior senses can smell poison. When he doesn't detect anything, he nibbles a piece of the pulp away, and I briefly wonder if they taste good.

They must, because he tosses the whole berry down his gullet, then reaches for a handful from the bag and shoves them into his mouth, chewing and groaning.

He obviously has not been as good about securing food as we have. Judging by the way he shovels the berries down, I'd say he hasn't eaten much for a couple of days.

A shadow moves by the window, and my stomach drops. This guy just ate all of the poisonous berries, so I'm going to have to fight the next guy who comes in through the door.

"When will she be back?" The berries slop around as he asks with his mouth full.

The shadow hovers for a moment longer before slipping away.

"It shouldn't be long now." I watch him with wide eyes.

Nyla said these were poisonous, but she failed to tell me how toxic or fast-acting they are.

The guy looks at the watch on his wrist and presses something on the face. He's not checking the time. It looks like some sort of tracker, which means the rest of his team is probably moving toward this location as I sit here wasting time.

Nyla isn't back yet. I'm both relieved and irritated when the thought hits me again.

If this guy gets his hands on her, I'm dead. I'm dead soon either way. He's probably just waiting for confirmation from his team before he kills me.

But if she isn't back yet, it means I've fallen into a repeat of five years ago, and I willingly walked into her betrayal this time.

The guy groans, pulling me from my destructive thoughts, and I look up to see him rubbing his stomach with his free hand.

"Maybe you ate them too fast," I suggest, and he nods at the possibility and licks his lips, looking for water. Our bottle is empty. Then I go in for the kill, so to speak. "Or maybe it's because you just shoved a lethal amount of poisonous berries down your throat."

He freezes, narrowing his eyes on me, and I casually slip my feet off the bed and onto the floor. My shoes are too far away to get to.

For a few seconds, he looks like he doesn't believe me. Then he doubles over. One hand goes to the ground, and he fights to keep his gun trained on me.

If my assumption that he hasn't eaten in a couple of days is right, then the poison should work fast. That, and the fact he was an absolute pig and ate everything in the bag.

He seems to decide his own mortality trumps his need to capture me, and he pushes himself off the floor and runs to the door with his finger already shoved down his throat.

He makes it one step out when a loud crack makes me jump, and he stumbles back into the room and lands on his back.

Nyla follows him in, and she's holding the frying pan we used to cook the fish last night.

"Time to go." I barrel off the bed and push the both of us out of the cabin.

Nyla tenses in my arms, and I sense her thoughts as if they are my own.

She doesn't want to leave our supplies behind, but there's no time.

After a couple of steps, she starts to run toward the trees, and I stop her.

"Go to the lake. I'm right behind you. DO IT!"

I have no time to tell her I want her to stick to a path we already know. A new path might lead us to an open field, and this guy could easily shoot us there. The path back to the lake is not an easy one, nor are there many straight breaks, so we should be covered until I can think of a better plan.

She changes her course and heads for the path we took to go fishing, and I trail after her. If I had my shoes on, I could probably outrun her, but the pine needles and rocks digging into my bare feet are slowing me down.

Just as I clear the open space in front of the cabin, a gunshot rings out as the guy pushes his way out of the cabin, yelling obscenities at us as we go.

My feet burn and ache as I pound over the dirt, and I come up along the ravine. I hear the man in the trees behind me and Nyla pushing through some of the bushes in front of me.

There was another reason why I wanted Nyla to run this way.

I hurry along the edge until I get to a nook behind a group of trees, then I sink myself into the woods and stand still, waiting.

Nyla is still up ahead, and she's making enough of a sound that she draws him closer.

Fifteen seconds later, I hear his clumsy approach.

I lean into a stance, bracing one bare foot against the earth.

Muttering under his breath, he grunts and groans as he runs, resembling a rabid animal.

When he comes into view, I push off the ground and run straight for him from my hiding spot in the trees, catching him by surprise. He squeals in shock, but he's not quick enough to point the gun at me. I lower myself and go in for the hit, tackling him and pushing him as hard as I can to the side. The impact sends him flying, and he goes over the edge and into the ravine with a blood-curdling howl.

I don't bother to watch him hit the ground below, but I hear the thud just the same.

Half a minute passes before Nyla calls my name under a hushed breath.

She must have heard the scream and doubled back.

"I'm here. He's gone." I point into the depths of the ravine.

The first thing I notice when I look at her is the pure relief on her face, and I wonder if she's happy because he's no longer after her or—

Her eyes are brimming with unshed tears. "I was scared it was you." She hiccups between her words. "Dagen, I need to tell you—"

I close the distance between us.

"We're not safe yet. He was wearing a tracker. That means there are others. We need to get our things."

Her eyes dance between mine. Then she nods in agreement, and we hurry to the cabin, where I clean my feet and get my shoes on.

We take only what we need: our go bags, the sleeping bag, and the tarp. We add the hatchet, rod, and tackle box to our supplies, then leave all of our garbage behind.

Picking up the empty water bottle, Nyla eyes the bag that held the yew berries before shaking her head, and we leave, heading south in the direction she initially wanted to run in.

After twenty minutes of a fast jog, my feet ache, and we slow to a brisk hike.

My curiosity gets the better of me. "You came back for me." I mean it as a question, but it sounds more like a confused statement.

Nyla huffs and smiles at me with those wicked lips.

"I never left you. I needed to pee." She takes a few more steps before stopping and turning to me. "We're getting out of here—together."

A lump forms in my throat, rendering me speechless. I cough to clear it, but it doesn't help, so I nod once, then point in the direction we were headed, prompting Nyla to continue walking.

We walk for most of the day, stopping only to relieve ourselves and fill our bottle when we come across fresh water. Even our lunch, consisting of a pack of dried fruit each, is enjoyed while we hike.

I have a stash of trail mix and some nuts that we will start on once we finish everything else, and I have one very special item I've been holding on to for as long as I can.

By the time we stop for the evening, my legs feel like jelly.

Nyla hasn't spoken about what happened this morning at the ravine. She's been quiet and deep in thought all day.

When I drop my bag to mark our camp for the night, she fidgets with the strap on her duffel bag. "Maybe we should keep walking—through the night."

She's spooked.

This morning was a little too close; it was too real.

I shake my head.

"You know we need to rest. If we push ourselves through the night, we could get hurt. If we do make it until morning, then we'll be tired, and we'll need to sleep while they make good ground catching up to us." I lean over and pick up the hatchet. "I'll cut some wood for a base under our sleeping bag, to get us off the ground. You look around for anything we can eat, and we'll sort out dinner. Then I have a surprise."

She does a double take.

"Is that a euphemism?" She lifts one brow in accusation.

"What? No. Well, unless the answer is"—I raise my voice an octave, pretending to mock her tone—"*Yes, make me scream like you did last night, you beast!*"

She laughs until a snort comes out, and she covers her mouth in embarrassment. It's adorable.

"Okay. Then maybe we can talk?" she says.

"I'd like that." I smile at her, and she spins in place, scanning the ground around us before she seems to spot something she likes.

I hope this means she's decided to tell me about the microfiche.

The penalty for breaking a contract is severe. At best, no one will ever hire her again. So I've been trying to find a way to get her to help me without hurting her livelihood. So far, I've come up with nothing. Our agreements are ironclad. I hope this means she's found a loophole.

I pull my phone out like I have a couple of times before and power it up. One bar briefly registers before it is replaced with NO SERVICE, and I power it down. Hopefully we'll find that bar again in the morning.

Nyla reaches into her duffel for a plastic bag. When she pulls it out, a few of her items fall out and onto the ground. Her focus is already on a plant growing at the base of some trees.

I turn my attention to some thick branches twenty feet away from our camp. After fifteen minutes of hacking away with my little hatchet, I decide the next item I'm going to add to my go bag—if I make it out of here—will be a chainsaw.

My shoulder aches with a sharp pinch every time I tense my neck muscles.

When I return, Nyla is on her hands and knees, picking the leaves off another plant. I drop my armful of branches, then turn my attention to the sleeping bag. I pull our tarp out from inside and use the string we have left to secure it to some trees.

This should keep us off the ground, and we should be able to share our body heat to stay warm, so we won't need to risk a fire. We'll probably wake up cold in the morning, but it will ensure we don't sleep in.

Look at me, thinking like a survivalist.

My thought gives me pause. It's only been a few days, and I'm an entirely different person than I was.

Nyla brings out something different inside of me.

I guess time will tell if it's good or bad.

Whatever it is, Cole will shit a brick when I tell him everything.

I chuckle as my eyes drift to Nyla's fallen items. I stuff an extra plastic bag back into her duffel, then reach for a round trinket. I turn it over; it's a compass, and I pack it away in her duffel as well.

Then I see her phone.

The one that doesn't work.

The memory of her snapping at me the last time I held it forms an empty pit in my stomach.

I lift the corner of the duffel to put it back when my thumb brushes along a ridge on the back of the case.

I didn't look at it close enough before, but now that I flip it over, I see it has a compartment that slides out.

I draw my thumb along it, curiosity whispering in my ear to *just slide it open.* After a few seconds, I shake my head, snapping myself out of it, and return it to the—

"Wait!"

I didn't hear Nyla approach, and when I look up at her, worry creeps in.

Her face is red, and tears glisten on her cheeks.

"Are you okay?" I stand, placing my hands on her arms, and look her over.

She doesn't answer my question. Instead, she starts to ramble. "I wanted to tell you. I tried to—and—I don't know how to say it."

"How to say what, Nyla?"

She sniffles, then wipes her nose with her sleeve. "Open my phone case." She points to her duffel.

I remove her phone from the duffel and stand, facing her.

"Are you sure you want me to see this?" If this is the microfiche we've been looking for, then her whole reputation is on the line.

"I should have told you four years ago, but I was scared, and I made a mistake."

I freeze. My thumb rests on the compartment as I remember the other night, when she said she made a mistake. This sounds eerily similar.

But she hasn't had the microfiche for four years.

When I don't open the case, she lifts her hands and slides the compartment open before clasping her hands to her mouth and sobbing, "I'm so sorry."

My head swims with this overload of information without context, and I lower my gaze to the case and pull out the item contained within.

It's a photograph of a little girl.

"I don't understand." I say the words to myself more than anything.

The girl in the picture looks like it could have been Nyla as a child. She looks just as troublesome and feisty.

Nyla's sniffle draws my attention back to her, and I hold the photo up against the woman standing in front of me. I shift my gaze from the photo to her, then back to the little girl in the photo.

Then I turn the picture over and read the back out loud: "Vaughn: age four."

My world shatters, then comes into focus clearer than it ever was. "My middle name is Vaughn."

Nyla nods, then whispers, "I know."

16

NYLA

*D*agen looks like I've both slapped him and kissed him at the same time as he stands in front of me, holding Vaughn's photo.

"You named her after—me?" His eyes glisten in the setting sun as he chokes on his last word. All expression is gone from his face, along with most of the color, when he meets my gaze. "We have a daughter."

It isn't a question, and it isn't lost on me that he said *we* and not *I*.

He returns his attention to the photo before I get the chance to nod.

Cradling her image in the palm of his hand, he runs his fingers over her hair before murmuring, "She's perfect."

I open my mouth, unsure of what to say, but Dagen holds up his hand, sniffling in a deep breath to steady his emotions. "Just—give me a moment, okay?"

He doesn't sound angry or hurt. It sounds like he's asking for a time-out, a moment of peace to let this new reality sink in.

I take a step back to give him space, and he holds the photo in front of him as he crosses the small clearing and walks into the trees.

He's only partially hidden by bushes.

We shouldn't be too far away from each other, not while we are still being hunted. Even though I'm sure he wants more space, he is still watching over me, so I turn my back to give him some privacy and focus on picking the best plants to eat tonight.

I think back to when I first found out I was pregnant.

I imagine I had his same response.

I remember I was scared.

I wasn't alone, but I was close to it.

The moment I laid eyes on Vaughn, I knew I would do anything for her. My world changed on a dime, and suddenly I couldn't imagine my life without her, nor did I want to.

I stay quiet, picking at some wild chamomile to add a little flavor to our salad bag. I contemplate asking Dagen for a package of nuts as well.

There isn't much to eat tonight.

It will mean one less meal later, but we can't afford to starve ourselves right now. We'll definitely need to find a lake to fish in or something more substantial tomorrow.

The plants in front of me turn fluid, then clear when I blink and watch as a tear falls on the back of my hand. I didn't realize I had started crying.

I keep my head bowed as though I'm working away.

This isn't about me.

Dagen just found out some life-altering news, and none of this is about me. He has every right to yell or stay silent, and so I give him the space he asked for while I quietly break apart all by myself.

I've just handed Dagen the one piece of me I cannot lose.

Losing Vaughn is the only thing in this world that will crush me to the point where I won't ever recover.

"Hey." Dagen crouches beside me, hooking his fingers under my chin and lifting my gaze to his.

His worried eyes search mine, and my lower lip trembles in response.

"I should have—I'm so sorry. I just didn't know how—"

He shushes me as he lowers himself to the ground, stretching his legs around mine, before tucking my head under his chin and pulling me into his chest.

Dagen rocks slowly as he combs his fingers through my hair.

I don't deserve his kindness, and the remorse in knowing that makes me sob harder still.

When I finally come up for air, I take a deep, shuddering breath against him.

He takes advantage of the break.

"Tell me about her. Please."

He returns her photo to me, and we look at her for the first time together, as her parents.

Being able to talk about her lifts a heavy weight off my heart.

I sniffle, wiping the tears away with my sleeve. "She's so fierce. She's a force, and if you let her dress herself, she will always choose a sundress. She loves candy."

Dagen laughs at this before saying, "Then I already know which uncle will be her favorite."

We sit together like this for the next ten minutes, sharing the plants I found while I tell Dagen stories about Vaughn.

I'm over the earthy taste of our dinner, and I scrunch my nose each time I take a leaf. I try to wave off the bag when Dagen offers me another bite.

He simply frowns at me, then tosses out some of the bitter-tasting plants and hands the bag to me again. He watches me carefully to make sure I chew and swallow them. Then he praises me with the hint of a pleased smile.

He will make a great dad.

When I move on to Vaughn's favorite books and shows, Dagen opens a package of nuts and pours half of them into my cupped hands.

He doesn't ask many questions. Instead, he prompts me to continue sharing everything I love about her, which happens to be a long list. He watches me with a soft smile on his lips, and it settles my nerves.

I eat the last nut in my hand, then fall quiet. I sit in silence with my thoughts before I finally change the subject.

"Are you—mad?" I think, when I imagined telling him, I expected yelling and rejection. Not of Vaughn, but of me.

I think I was holding on to my secret for fear that he would hate me, and up until this moment, I didn't realize how important it was to me that he didn't.

Dagen considers my question in silence before carefully choosing his words.

"I don't know. I'm a lot of things, but I don't know if I'm mad. I just can't move past her face right now. She looks like you." His words are candid, and his tone is easy.

I tell him my favorite feature of hers. "She has your eyes and my toothy grin." To emphasize my point, I show him my lame smile, and he chuckles.

Dagen's smile consumes his face, and he lowers his eyes to the photograph sitting on my lap between us. I imagine he's trying to see those eyes I'm talking about, but then a hint of sadness creeps onto his face.

It's later than I thought.

When I follow his gaze down, her image is hidden in the darkness.

Dagen draws a frame with his forefinger around the image on my lap.

"It's getting dark. I'll show you her picture again in the morning." I know he was hoping to get a better look at her, but we should get into the sleeping bag before it gets too cold. Judging by how numb my butt is from sitting on the ground, I'd say we should have packed it in a while ago. "We should get to sleep."

I'm careful to pack Vaughn's photo back into my case, then I store it away. There's no point in hoisting our bags off the ground anymore. We don't have much left in the way of food that will catch the attention of a wild animal.

I walk to the sleeping bag, which is set atop some freshly cut branches, then wait for Dagen to hop in first like he has the last two nights.

I step out of my hiking shoes and stand on top of them, and he closes the distance between us, his natural scent embracing my senses.

"You go in first this time. I don't want you to lose body heat."

I stare at him. My mouth hangs open for a hot minute before I snap my lips shut and crawl in first.

I liked the banter we had before all of this. Oddly enough, I think I miss it, but it's been replaced with something deeper. Something I also enjoy.

Dagen's knees meet me at eye level as he steps out of his own shoes and pulls the sleeping bag back to accommodate his size before reaching behind him and zipping it up.

The branches bow under his weight but don't break, and he slides his bag up to use as a pillow this time while offering me his bicep to cradle my head.

"Where is she now?" Dagen's breath blows through my hair.

"She's safe. She's with my cousin, Philomena. She's being spoiled rotten and probably eating too much junk food, but she is safe."

An owl hoots in the distance, and I wonder if Dagen will push for an address, but he doesn't.

He lowers his voice, and a hint of insecurity laces his words. "I need to know, Nyla. Why didn't you find me to tell me?" He lets the question linger, and when I take too long to respond he attempts to answer for me. "Or did you look for me?"

Dagen peels his body back from mine, as though he's trying to get a look at my face, but the night has settled in and there are too many clouds blocking the moonlight to make anything out.

"I did look for you. It's what I thought I found out about your family that made me stay away. I made a mistake."

It's hard to scan his features to determine his thoughts in the darkness, and maybe that is for the best.

Without assuming what the other is thinking and schooling ourselves accordingly, we have no choice but to just say what we need to say with good old-fashioned words.

"Tell me what you found out about my family. Tell me everything."

Dagen shifts his weight and adjusts my head on his arm. I have a feeling it is so he can better hear my answer.

"At first, I didn't find anything—anything *illegal*, I mean. Some of the businesses your family runs are on the spicy side." Dagen's body jerks. I imagine he's chuckling. He must know I'm referring to the sex clubs his family owns. "But everything was legal. I was about to stop looking when an associate of the club sounded familiar to me. It was a business listed on a joint venture that I remembered from a job I took when I was first starting out. I followed it, and I found out your family was using your legitimate companies as a front to hide human and drug trafficking with direct ties to one of Mexico's worst drug cartels."

Dagen's arms tighten around me. "WHAT?"

His muscles are so tense that he is shaking.

"You really didn't know?" I hear the relief in my own words.

I was taking a chance by coming clean with this, but I was sure Dagen was innocent. Especially after he spoke about taking his father down.

"I swear to you, on my life, that none of my brothers know about this. We've—" He pauses to take a deep breath, but he stays beside me. "We knew our father was up to something. We had thought he was retired, but it was all a lie. We found out he's been going behind our backs to make deals that none of us would have ever backed up. We aren't turning out to be the successors that he hoped we would be. I need to get this information to my brothers. This is worse than we thought."

He hugs me to him then and kisses the top of my head before speaking again.

"I know you can't break your contract. The microfiche you took from the archives is a birth certificate for the head of the Lucciano crime family in Portland. It probably doesn't mean anything to you"—it does—"but a lot of people are trying to find Elia Lucciano's missing heir. It is believed that whoever controls the heir controls the future of their organization, which is currently split in two. They're at war with each other. Our father is fighting to support the side we do not want to take power. From what you've just told me, I think he needs the backing of the organization's winning side to expand his trafficking plans." I'm not sure if his pause is for dramatic effect, but it works. "But I know what it means for you if you go against the job requirements you agreed to."

Then he stops talking.

He doesn't directly ask me for the microfiche or the name of who created the job in the first place. He puts the future of his family in my hands and leaves it at that.

No pressure.

The microfiche sits no more than five feet away from him, but letting him know that comes with dire consequences, for me and whoever is close to me. Dagen must know that not only would my life be forfeit if I broke contract, but if Vaughn was ever linked to me, her life would be as well.

This is why Dagen hasn't outright asked for it.

He must know the stakes just got higher.

I haven't even weighed his information against my need for revenge on Elia Lucciano.

I don't push it right now. We still have to get out of here alive to find the equipment we need to view the microfiche.

"My name isn't Nyla." Dagen's rhythmic breathing stops at my confession. "I mean—it is. Nyla is my middle name. My name is Blanche Nyla Jensen. If you're looking for me, use my first name and my last name. You'll find a death certificate from about ten years ago."

I focus on sharing the information instead of what I worry this means.

"Why are you telling me this?" Wariness lingers in his tone.

I close my eyes and try to keep my voice steady. "It's just that—if something happens and I don't—you need to find your way to Vaughn. She needs her—you."

Time stretches awkwardly between us, as Dagen doesn't respond for what feels like an hour, but I'm sure is only minutes.

"Now tell me what you really want to say."

It's a challenge.

I've only ever been strong around Dagen, and I've caught

him looking at me when I struggle to keep my cracks from breaking open.

He's telling me to bend a little, just enough to let him in.

The pressure of holding in my worst fear makes my eyes sting.

"I'm scared I won't see her again and she'll forget me."

It was the thought I had when I finally allowed myself to breathe when the plane took off in Alaska. It was the fear that sent me into the downward spiral that Dagen witnessed.

"My own mother doesn't recognize me anymore. She doesn't remember my face, my voice, my love, and I don't want to be no one to Vaughn too. If I leave now, my daughter won't know me either. I'll be—nothing."

I've never shared how hurt I am that there is no loving recognition in my mother's eyes when she looks at me. I'm angry and crushed, but I can't direct it anywhere. I can't be mad at my mom for something she has no control over.

Soft kisses on my tear-soaked face pull me back from falling apart. I swallow my pain at Dagen's touch. His fingers comb through my hair to settle near my scalp before he clenches his hand into a fist. The pull on my hair is soothing. It releases some of my anxiety, and I take a deep breath, one I wasn't able to just moments before.

"You aren't nothing, Nyla. You're—everything, and you'll see her again. I promise."

He continues to clench and release his hand in my hair at my scalp, and it feels amazing. My body relaxes and surrenders in his hold.

When I've calmed enough to speak without crying, I whisper into the dark between us, "What do we do now?"

Dagen's voice is the one I hear when the darkness whispers back:

"Tomorrow we find our way home to our little girl."

17

DAGEN

Once Nyla fell asleep, she was out for the night.

Her guilt at not telling me mixed with her fears about not seeing our daughter again drained her of any energy she had left.

I closed my eyes, but my thoughts refused to let me rest.

Nyla had asked me if I was mad. I probably would have had a right to be, but I wasn't. I was filled with regret that I have a daughter I've never met, a niece that my brothers haven't spoiled, and a granddaughter my mother would be over the moon to hold. She always wanted a daughter, we all knew it. She loved the four of us fiercely, but a daughter would have stolen her heart. I can't imagine how she'll react when she learns she has a granddaughter.

Anger wasn't a dominant emotion until Nyla told me what she found out about the secrets my father has been hiding.

That, I didn't see coming.

I would have kept my daughter far away from him as well. I *will* keep her away from it, because I will do everything in my power to destroy the tarnished legacy my father has created for our family.

As I lay there with Nyla sleeping in my arms, I finally understood how it was easy for Lennox to sacrifice himself for the three of us. I haven't met Vaughn yet, and I'm ready to kill to protect her.

Positioning the sleeping bag off the ground was a good idea. We stayed warm through the night, and I woke Nyla up as the sky turned a tenebrous shade of blue.

We dragged our tired asses out of the sleeping bag, slowly shucking our fatigue away, then packed away our things.

I didn't realize how sluggish we had become until I glanced up to find the sky alarmingly lighter than it had been.

"We need to get moving. Be ready in a few minutes." I point my thumb over my shoulder to signal my need to relieve myself before we leave.

Nyla nods in understanding, returning her attention to stuffing the last of our supplies into our sleeping bag.

A small animal skitters under a bush as I approach my spot, and I watch as the leaves rustle then still.

We need to find a break out here: a road, a farm, something, anything. We can't walk in a straight line forever and not find civilization. Eventually we will find something, or the bars on my phone will make an appearance.

I step out from the thick of the trees. Then I stop, frozen to the earth.

They're here.

Through the trees, the backs of two men face me. Nyla slowly stands in front of them.

"Where is he?" One of the guys asks, and she holds her hands out to her sides, showing them she is not a threat.

"He—I lost him a couple of days ago. I'm alone." She shrugs. Her tone is void of emotion.

My heart swells against my rib cage.

I know how scared she is.

She wants more than anything to see our daughter again, but she's chosen not to rat me out to buy herself more time.

"We know he's with you." My skin prickles at that piece of information.

How would they know for a fact I was with Nyla, unless—

My gaze lands on my go bag at the same time the thought hits me.

Nick must have placed some kind of tracking device on me.

My bag was on the plane with him while I retrieved Nyla from the hotel. But if that was the case, they would have been able to find us on the first day.

We would never have made it this far if they were always able to see where we were.

"Look, I took his stuff, and I ran when he slept."

The guys exchange a glance, then look over at my bag sitting neatly beside hers. The second guy shrugs, seemingly accepting her answer.

"This will be easy then." The first one speaks as he pulls something out of his jacket, and the other chuckles in response.

I'm quickly losing the element of surprise.

When the one who spoke takes a step toward her, I burst through the cover of the trees and tackle the other one to the ground.

The one still standing jumps back in surprise, and I level my order on Nyla.

"GO!"

Nyla takes off running through the trees before I turn my attention to the guy with me, and I roll both of us so he's seated on top of me, giving him a false sense of strength.

"Get her! I've got this. Don't kill her!" the guy shouts from on top of me, and he takes off after her.

As soon as he leaves us, I turn the tables.

Lifting my feet off the ground, I wrap my legs around his front near his face and pull him off me, sitting up as I take him down before lifting my weight onto him and crushing my knee against his chest.

But I don't have the right leverage on him, and he rolls, tossing me off before flipping over onto his hands pushing himself up.

We stand at the same time, and his hand instinctively goes to his jacket.

He's carrying.

I don't give him enough time to get his gun out of his jacket. I run at him, tackling him to the ground a second time.

He grunts on impact, coughing and gasping for air, and I reach in, wrench the gun out of his hands, and lift myself off him just enough to point the gun at the center of his chest and fire.

His eyes widen in shock before panic washes the determination off his face.

He's not dead, but he will be soon.

I didn't miss.

I stand, put the safety on, and slide the gun into my belt at my back. Then I take off in the direction Nyla ran.

Stray branches whip across my face and upper body as I tear through the forest. Wild thoughts urge me to go faster and push harder to get to her, my promise from last night making my throat close in on itself.

I told her she would see our daughter again.

I promised.

There's no mistaking the scream that cuts through the crisp morning air.

It's Nyla.

I adjust my direction only slightly and use her pained cry as a beacon, guiding me to her.

When I break out of the trees, an open field separates us. A small herd of elk grazes off to the left, about half of the way between us.

Movement from the right catches my eye.

At first, I don't see anything in the trees, but motion in my peripheral vision pulls the culprit into focus. Then I return my attention to Nyla.

She is on the ground, her arms pushing away her attacker.

He kneels over her body and pulls something small out of his pocket before stabbing it down, and she screams again.

The elk startle and take a few cautious steps away.

The animal hidden in the trees to my right stays still, watching.

"Hand it over or tell me who hired you," the man demands, and Nyla groans in pain.

"The microfiche!" I yell across the field.

The guy stops what he's doing.

Keeping one hand on Nyla, he turns his head in my direction before standing.

Nyla stays down as the man yells back to me, "This isn't your fight. But I'll tell you what. You turn around and walk away, and I'll forget your name is on the contract."

I stay quiet, hoping to give him the impression I'm considering his offer.

He tries to sweeten the deal. "I'll even point you in the direction of the nearest town."

The corner of my mouth ticks up.

He must have a way out of here.

He takes my silence for acceptance and turns around to look down at Nyla.

I yell again. "I have the microfiche. I'm willing to trade. She owes me a debt."

That gets his attention.

"I'll need to see it."

I have the gun tucked in the back of my pants, but I can't pull it out.

I don't know if this guy has a weapon of his own. If I draw now, he could shoot Nyla before I get close enough to ensure a hit.

I reach into my pocket and pull out the only thing I have: an empty bag, neatly folded into a square, that once held a snack-sized amount of trail mix. I hold it up beside my head.

I should be far enough away that he can't clearly see what it is.

By my calculations, I need him to close just under half of the distance between us.

The guy walks toward me at a slow pace, watching me for signs of betrayal as he goes. With each step he takes, my confidence in my plan falters.

My twelfth grade science teacher had better have been right about the bullshit he spouted on one of our field trips to Olympic National Park.

I start wishing I had come up with a plan B when everything clicks into place.

Without warning, a bull elk breaks out from his cover in the trees and charges toward the guy in the field.

For a split second, the guy turns to watch as a scene from *National Geographic* plays out in front of his eyes. Then he realizes he is the animal's intended target.

I stay completely still as the man, now terrified, turns to run in the opposite direction of the bull and toward the herd, causing the bull to scream at an awful high pitch that ends in a threatening roar.

The sound rattles the man, and he trips over his feet, going down just as the elk tramples over top of him. The bull rears up on his hind legs before dealing a devastating blow with his front hooves. The sickening thud makes my stomach dry heave as the guy's body spasms once then stills.

The bull steps back, looking around for his next target, but Nyla and I are both far enough away from him.

Nyla keeps her eyes on the majestic animal and half crawls, pushing herself away, clutching her hand over her shoulder. When I see the knife sticking out of her upper chest, I instinctively start running toward her.

Her eyes widen, and she holds out her good hand, blood coating her fingers, to ward me off before returning her gaze to the elk, who is now looking my way.

Seeing Nyla hurt almost erased the memory of what just happened to that bastard.

I angle myself away from the herd of elk and circle wide to get to Nyla's hunched form.

I reach for her, cradling her as I take us both to the ground, careful not to jostle the knife further. She winces, gasping for air.

Nyla's body is locked up in pain. "Is it bad?"

The knife is lodged in her upper chest, below her clavicle but closer to her shoulder.

I hold her still and ask, "Can you breathe?"

She inhales through her nose and parts her lips to exhale a shaky breath before whispering, "Yes."

There's only one more danger I'm worried about.

For the most part, the guy who stabbed her knew what he was doing. He would have needed to keep her alive for her to lead them to the microfiche, so he shouldn't have cut into anything life-threatening, but there is a main artery that runs near her wound.

The amount of blood that comes out will tell me if it's damaged.

My gut twists at the thought of what will happen if it is.

I'm not prepared to help her if she starts bleeding out, but I can't leave the knife in, or it will eventually slice through everything.

A wave of nausea courses through me.

I can't lose her.

"I need to pull the knife out. Stay with me, okay?" I brush her hair out of her face.

Nyla's hand rests, trembling, on her stomach. She's most likely jacked up on adrenaline. Regardless, this is going to hurt like a bitch.

"Okay." Her wide eyes stare me down. Tremors in her chin betray the bravado she's trying to maintain as a tear rolls out of her eye and back into her hair.

Judging by the size of the hilt protruding from her chest, it's a pocketknife with a blade between two and three inches long.

"Will you count to three for me? Then I'll pull it out."

I hold her head to my chest with my hand loosely bracing the knife, waiting.

Her eyes flit from mine then down toward her chest. She can't see the knife, and I don't allow her to move enough so she can. Her gaze returns to mine.

"One—"

I tighten my hand and pull it out in a straight line, firmly pressing my palm over the wound to control the bleeding.

Nyla sucks in an agonizing breath, arching her back off my lap and opening her mouth wide in a silent scream before gritting her teeth and hissing.

Thankfully, the blade was only two inches long.

Once Nyla settles and her breathing evens out, I slide her off my thigh and twist to help her lie flat in the field.

I glance up to see if the lingering threat is still close, but the herd has moved away, taking that beast of a bull elk with them.

I clench my jaw, anxiety flowing through my arms. Dragging my sleeve across my forehead, I attempt to wipe away both the sweat and the apprehension settling into my mind.

I don't want to look.

"You need to check it." Nyla answers me as if reading my thoughts in the expression I've failed to hide from her.

Slowly releasing pressure, then lifting my palm away from her chest, relief floods me when blood doesn't spurt out of her.

The artery wasn't severed.

I'm failing to mask my emotions, and Nyla picks up on my reaction, dropping her head to the ground and sighing.

She eases into survival mode and attempts to sit up. "We need to get out of here before animals pick up on the scent of blood and come to investigate."

I allow her to stand, but I keep her from walking away.

The elk have already cleared out, no doubt distancing themselves from the dead body. I take advantage and run over to where the guy lies dead in the field. His cheekbone has been crushed in, and I avert my gaze to his body to keep myself from dry heaving.

I go for his pockets first. It looks like the knife was his only weapon. There is nothing else on him except for an empty package of gum, a phone, and a wallet with no ID. His phone powers up to a sign-in screen. It's a new phone, and I don't need to look at him again to know that facial recognition will no longer work, so I leave everything behind with him.

Returning to Nyla, I tell her what I know.

"This guy mentioned pointing me in the direction of the nearest town. One of them has a map or something. I noticed the other guy dropped a backpack. It's back at our camp. We need to go through it and pack one bag of our most important things. You can't carry anything heavy."

Nyla recoils inwardly. I sense she's getting ready to argue, so I hold up a hand and continue, "What do you need from me right now?"

"I'm good."

Clutching her arm to her front, she attempts to take another step.

It's clear in the way she takes control of the situation that she isn't used to being taken care of, and we don't have time to argue, so I go for a different approach.

"You're no good to me bleeding out all over the place, *Blanche*." She growls, baring her teeth at my use of her first name. Good. I need the fighting attitude, but I need her to drop the independence for a bit. "If you don't tell me how I can help you, I'm just going to start guessing, and it'll start with me tossing you over my shoulder and carrying you back to camp like a caveman."

I raise my eyebrows at her, daring her to try me.

She huffs in resignation. "Fine. Maybe a sling to hold my arm to my chest until we can get to the bandages."

She's referring to the first aid kit we found in the wreckage of the plane.

I smile, satisfied with her answer. Then I unbuckle my belt and slip it out of the loops. I round her, then stand at her back and wrap it around her upper body and her arm before fastening it and stepping back to examine my handiwork.

"You know, belts have many purposes." I smirk at her, running my finger along the leather before I lean in and lower my voice. "I've been dying to show you one of my favorite uses for it, so keep up the sass, lass."

Her face flushes the deepest shade of red yet.

Interesting.

"Come on. We'll talk more when we start hiking. I think we're on our own for a while now. I'm pretty sure I know how they were tracking us."

18

NYLA

When we return to our camp, Dagen stops and tilts his head to me with a hesitant look. I lean to the side and take in the aftermath.

Dagen was able to thin those guys out by tackling one to the ground, and I remember hearing a gunshot as I ran. My heart seized in my chest, and tears threatened to breach my eyes at the thought that it might be Dagen who was hurt.

A chill runs down my spine at the bleak memory.

The lifeless body lies at an odd angle. His dead eyes are open and staring up at the sky above. The blood that trickled out of his mouth is already darkened and drying on his face.

Dagen steps in front of me, blocking the grotesque sight and drawing my attention to him. "I'll search the body. You go through his pack."

His eyes lower to my chest, and I understand the unspoken concern written on his face.

"I'm okay. My shoulder is throbbing, and I have a headache"—most likely brought on when the guy tackled me in the field; I went down hard, unable to brace myself against the fall—"but I got this." I angle my head to the guy's backpack.

Without skipping a beat, Dagen turns and kneels beside the guy's prone form.

With my good hand, I lift the bag, set it upright on the ground, and lean over it. I hold it taut with my bound hand and unzip it with my free one.

A zing of pride shoots through me.

Dagen knows how to read a room, and I'm grateful he's giving me the chance to stand on my own right now. At the same time, I did need his help out there in the field.

He seems to know when to push me and when to allow me the space to do my thing.

Excitement bursts through me at the jackpot I find in the stranger's backpack. I start pulling items out and listing them as I go, loud enough so Dagen can hear me.

"There's a thin jacket in here." It looks like a lightweight, expensive fabric that will keep us warm. "And a sweater." I look up to see Dagen removing the guy's belt. Considering I'm using his as a sling, these are proving useful. I'm about to tell Dagen we finally have some bug spray, but a quick shake of the can tells me it's empty. I toss it aside and reach in for the next item. "A water jug." It's sturdier than ours, and a pang of sorrow hits me when I realize I'll be leaving ours behind in favor of this one. It's funny how we become attached to such simple things when everything else has been taken away from us. Then I hold up a little black GPS tracker. "I found it."

Dagen abandons his task, crawls over to close the distance between us, and crouches at my side as I turn it on.

"Huh." I grin as it powers up. "It's the first thing I've seen turned on in days."

Dagen levels me with a serious expression. "I'm offended."

It takes a few seconds for the double entendre to sink in, and I snort-laugh to hide my embarrassment.

My cheeks flush with heat again, remembering our time in the cabin, and Dagen smirks, knowing full well the effect he has on me.

I have a feeling that once we get to know each other, I won't be able to hide much from him, and that both thrills and worries me.

I hand him the tracker as the terrain displays, and Dagen moves the screen around, occasionally looking up and over his shoulder in different directions.

Finally, he turns it off and points into the distance. "We're about forty miles north of Hazelton. There isn't a lot there, but it's more than what we've got, and we should be able to get to a landline and maybe a vehicle." He turns to size me up before continuing, "We'll walk for a lot of today until we reach this river." He points to a curvy line on the screen. "We'll camp overnight, and I'll catch some fish. Then, in the morning, we'll follow it until we get into town."

Dagen moves the GPS around, tagging a city west of us, and I assume he's doing it to throw anyone off our trail. Then he turns it off and tosses it aside. We won't be taking it with us. Since it's their equipment, whoever these guys are working for may be tracking them as well.

"There's some food in here." I reach my good hand into the bag, pulling out a new stash of bars and three apples before reaching for Dagen's bag to transfer everything into.

His hand settles on mine.

"We're leaving my bag." My questions must be written on my face, because Dagen answers my thoughts. "There was a period of time when my bag was on the plane with fake Nick. I don't want to chance that he might have tagged it, and I won't know for sure, so I'm leaving it behind." Then he mutters to himself, "Speaking of which..."

He pulls his phone out of his pocket, uses his multi-tool keychain to open the side, then removes the sim card and snaps it in half.

He doesn't wait for me to ask.

"It's too much of a coincidence that the first guy found us the morning after we settled into the cabin. Now these two found us the morning after we made camp. I did one thing both times."

He leaves the riddle with me, and I answer instantly, "You powered your phone up to check for bars."

He nods, a hint of pride in his smile.

If his phone is being monitored, we'll be sitting ducks every time he turns it on.

I watch over his shoulder as he resets it to its factory settings before powering it off.

I look around at all of our supplies. "So we're taking the sleeping bag and my duffel and everything we can fit inside."

"Yes. Right after I clean your wound."

I groan.

I knew it was coming, but it's going to suck, because now I've snapped out of my adrenaline-induced haze, where the pain was numbed by the onslaught of fear and self-preservation.

Dagen points to the backpack in my hand.

"Put that down, take your shirt off, and get comfortable, Nyla. We need to hurry this up." He unfastens the belt holding my arm up, and I do as he says while he pulls the small first aid kit out and opens it, fingering through the items inside.

Dagen grabs our old water bottle, the one we'll be leaving behind, opens it, and uses it to clean my wound. It's painful but manageable, and it could be worse.

Then he reaches into the kit and pulls worse out.

He offers me an apologetic look as he rips open an alcohol cleansing wipe.

"Fuck me." I scowl at him, and he chuckles.

"Believe me, if it would help, I'd already be doing that."

I laugh at his joke then hiss like I'm some kind of cornered, feral animal when he wipes at my wound.

Dagen leans me forward, examining my back before muttering that it didn't go all of the way through.

I relax when he drops the wipe in his hand and reaches for a tissue. While he works, I try to distract myself by thinking about our morning.

"Did you know that would happen? Um, with the elk— back there?" I clarify.

Bull elk are the most dangerous animals out here during rutting season, which we are going into, but we hadn't come up close to any yet, so I didn't think to mention it.

The corners of his lips tick up into that smile I've come to enjoy. It's a cocky, confident smirk, and it hits me in the feels.

"I was on a field trip in high school. I didn't retain much from my senior year—I was more interested in girls than grades." He waggles his eyebrows at me, and I roll my eyes. "But I remember hearing about how aggressive the bulls get around the elk during mating season. We even got to see two fighting each other. Their antlers were locked. It was impressive. Anyway, I remember our guide telling us that bull elk will consider anything that comes in between them and the female elk a threat and will charge just the same." Then Dagen looks directly into my eyes, entirely serious and possessive when he says, "There was something so visceral and primal about an animal that would fight to kill anything that got in between him and his mate."

I don't blush at that. I shiver and swallow—hard.

That last part was definitely meant for me, and I sit beside him, compliant, wrapped up in his unspoken vow to keep me safe.

"Anyway, that's a lesson that stays with you." His smile returns, and he lowers his eyes to my wound as he sticks a large bandage over it. He stands, removing his undershirt and offering it to me. "Yours is bloody; we're leaving it behind. I'll take the sweater." He points at the stranger's backpack.

I stand, gingerly pulling his shirt over my head and taking a deep breath when his smell hits me. When it's on, he helps me into my jacket, telling me I'll wear it to stay warm while we walk. Once I'm dressed, Dagen wraps both belts around me at different angles, and my arm sits more secure against my body, allowing me to relax the muscles in my shoulder.

Then we look over the supplies around us and take turns listing the most important items. The flashlight and matches stay in my bag, and Dagen brings everything else out to look at.

The first aid kit, food and water, and fishing gear are the first items added back in the bag, followed by the knives and the gun. We're now wearing most of the extra clothing, and he packs the lightweight jacket.

"I almost forgot this." Dagen unzips an inside pocket in his bag and pulls out a—

"Is that...a chocolate bar?" My eyes strain, then bug out of my head.

Dagen snickers. "Well, I was going to surprise you with it last night, but your surprise kind of took the cake. We'll have it tonight, as a reward for hiking thirty miles." He steps to my duffel and tosses it in.

I look around at the remaining items.

A ripped tarp is better than no tarp, and I point at it, asking Dagen to stuff it in the sleeping bag. Then we take a last look around and head out in the direction Dagen pointed in earlier.

Dagen steps to my side, handing me an apple. "We'll walk for most of the day, and I'll start fishing as soon as we find the lake. We have enough food now to get us to tonight. I don't think anyone else is out here searching, and we should be able to get a nice fire going when we stop. We shouldn't be targets again until we surface in town."

He takes a bite of his own apple, and the juice dribbles down his chin. I've never wanted to eat an apple as badly as I do right now. Dagen bends down, lifting the sleeping bag, and I hold out my good hand that's clutching the apple, asking him to hang it over my arm. He sizes me up before deciding to let me have it, but I get the impression he won't let me carry it the whole way.

I take my first bite of the apple, and it tastes divine. I was never a fan of apples, but this one tastes so sweet and juicy.

Maybe that's what happens when you eat plants for a few days.

It feels good to step out knowing we have a final destination in mind.

I only hope we can get all the way back home before they find us again.

19

DAGEN

I've either sealed the deal with Nyla or she'll never want to see me again after all of this is over.

If I had a watch or a phone that worked I'd know for sure, but by my estimate, we walked for close to ten hours today, maybe a little more.

That is a hell of a lot of time to get to know someone.

If Nyla wasn't injured, we might have been close to signs of life by now, but I won't share that thought. I don't want her to push herself beyond what she is capable of. Her health takes priority.

I've quickly learned how fast things can go sideways out here.

The truth is, I didn't think we'd get this far today.

I'm continually impressed by how Nyla pushes the boundaries of what I start out thinking she's capable of.

I spent most of our hiking time telling Nyla about my brothers and my mom. I even told her about some of the contract jobs I took in the past. Of course, names and places were changed to protect the not-so-innocent—and my life.

I told her about the inevitable love story between Ryder and Amara and how she fought for her life in the back of a car as we tried to catch up to her. Nyla told me if I wasn't careful, she'd steal Amara away to be a member of her team. I chuckled at that, but sobered quickly. If Amara was going to be on anyone's team, it would be mine. I should have thought of that sooner, although I'm sure Ryder would finally try to kick my ass if I ever put that idea in her head.

I told her how Cole met Harlow and how their ships very literally passed in the night, how he went from her pursuer to her protector while they tried to solve her sister's murder. I also mentioned the way to his heart is through candy, which made her laugh.

I told her about Sloane and Henry and about the secret we're all keeping. Then I told her about Grayson and how we think he might be the missing heir based on his birth date, and if that is the case, neither of them are safe.

Then we talked about Lennox.

I began to ramble once I got to him.

He is the source of my guilt and regret.

When Lennox finally hit his breaking point, he had no choice but to bring us in on what was happening. I'm glad he did, but he should have come to us a long time ago. He didn't because I decided to go out on my own, leaving him to carry the responsibility for our younger brothers on his shoulders alone, and I can't stop thinking about that.

If I'd stayed, there wouldn't have been a break in our chain. I caused a gap between Lennox and my two younger brothers, and Lennox went into full-on protector mode.

Lennox told Cole the reason he was attacked was because they couldn't find me.

I had taken a massive contract that required months of work and a false identity. Knowing my own father tried to kill me off for twelve percent of our family business, and because he was pissed that I wasn't demented enough to do his bidding, is one thing. But knowing Cole was attacked because I wasn't there for him is what keeps me up at night.

I bared my heart while we walked, and that ate up the time.

Through it all, Nyla listened.

A few times, when I looked over at her, she would quickly flash me a smile, but it never met her somber eyes.

I know she hasn't heard from her brothers in a long time, and she has her own demons. I get the impression she doesn't share herself with many people, and I wonder if maybe she's become used to not talking about herself.

I've shared everything with Ryder and Cole. I talk a lot with Lennox, but there has been a divide between us for the longest time, so I understand the uneasy feeling when you change what you have become used to. Now, when Lennox and I talk, it feels like we're learning how to be brothers again.

From what Nyla has told me, she hasn't spoken to her brothers in over ten years. They would have grown in that time. They'd be strangers now, and Nyla doesn't strike me as someone who shares her feelings.

Her thoughts? Yes.

Her ideas? Absolutely.

The stuff that hurts her heart? Her worries? Her fears? No.

When I think back on last night, when she told me I had a daughter, I realized that she had been working herself up all day to say something—maybe longer.

It was a challenge for her to tell me she was afraid she wouldn't see our daughter again.

When she finally opened up, she sobbed against my chest, and I don't think it was all because of her fear of losing Vaughn. It might have been because it was painful for her to open those floodgates.

So I've been upping my game. I've been paying attention to Nyla like she's some kind of science experiment. I've been learning how to read her cues.

Like right now.

We found the river we were looking for, and we've been walking along it for close to an hour. I've been checking in with Nyla, who keeps telling me she's good to push on, but for the last ten minutes, the distance between us has marginally grown. She stiffens when I look back in an attempt to hide the toll the hike has taken on her.

It's time to make camp.

"There." I stop, giving her time to catch up. "We'll set up there and fish."

Nyla glances to where I'm pointing. It's a good spot, level ground and an open area near the river.

We can easily create a fire.

Her eyes move to mine, then back to the site, then return to me again, her lips pinched tight, as if holding in her words. I can tell she wants to push on, but we both know she can't...and it is a good spot (and this is coming from someone who thinks camping is a four-letter word).

A few curt nods in agreement are all I get.

I get Nyla settled on a rock near the bank and drop the bag and rod between us.

We took breaks during our walk, to stretch her arm, keep her muscle memory strong, and help her heal. I unbuckle the belts from her upper body, and she winces as her hand settles in her lap, loosening the atrophy that has set in since we last stopped.

I leave her with the stretching exercises we made up while I gather twigs and branches around us.

I pause once I clear the area and step into the cover of the trees. From here I can eavesdrop on her to see how she's really doing.

Nyla takes a deep breath and exhales with a groan.

I knew she had passed her threshold for pain, and her deep sigh confirms it.

I don't try to be quiet as I step farther into the bushes, searching for dry wood. I want her to know that I know she's in pain.

I want her to know she can't hide from me.

I won't allow it.

I return and leave a few times more before we have a wood pile high enough to get a fire going, then I use the matches we've been saving.

If all goes well, tomorrow we'll get to Hazelton, and our need to ration our supplies will end.

Nyla has finished her stretching, and an assortment of fishing gear sits on her lap. She holds the little metal hooks in her bad hand and works with her good one to fasten everything together.

"Why don't you go by your first name?"

Nyla's hands stop for a moment as her eyes flit up from furrowed brows to meet mine. I'm used to this look from her by now. She's sizing me up. She's trying to figure out if my question is sincere, or if I'm about to try to get under her skin.

I'm being sincere.

"My mother and father made a deal for the first and middle names of my brothers and me. If they had a boy, my father picked the first name, my mother the second, and vice versa. My mother wanted to name me after my great-grandmother. She was a feminist in her own right back in the day, pushing for equal rights and fighting for the right for women to enter the workforce." She pauses to look at the hook in her hand and smiles to herself before continuing, "All amazing things to be proud of, however"—she levels her gaze on me—"her name was Blanche." She shrugs. "But I honored it. That's what they called me my whole life, until I decided to do what I do now. Then I changed my name."

"Fair enough."

The name is rather vintage. I don't know any Blanches these days...well, one now.

"Hey, can we—maybe—have that chocolate bar?" Nyla's hopeful eyes drop to the duffel bag, where she knows I've stashed it away.

I walk over to where she's sitting and hold out my hand, waiting for her to pass me the hook for the rod. When she does, I crouch down to her eye level.

"If we eat it now, I'll never be able to get the fish down." She pinches her face in mock chastisement, but I know she agrees with me. "I'll tell you what." I lean forward, kneeling on one knee to get close to her ear, and lower my voice. "You be a good girl for me, and we'll have it for dessert."

Nyla pinches her lips in a tight line, urging her body to settle, but the blush in her cheeks gives her away. Even though she's hurt, my little trooper reacts to me.

I peel myself away from the curious vibes she's giving off to fish for our dinner. As I walk to the shore, I try to remember everything she taught me about fishing.

I press the button, swing the rod back, and cast like a pro.

When I look back at Nyla, she quickly averts her gaze to some branches lying at her feet. She picks one of them up and holds it steady with her bad hand. She opens the pocketknife, the same one that was used to stab her this morning, and begins whittling away at the tip, making a spear.

It doesn't take long until I catch the first fish. This one is smaller than the ones at the lake, and it was easy to get it out of the river when the line seized up. I was able to reel the other three in with minimal problems.

It turns out fish are slippery fuckers, and Nyla struggled to hold them with her wounded arm and get them ready to be cooked, so we worked together. I made faces while I held them down, and Nyla tried really hard not to crack a joke about my lack of outdoor skills while she fileted them.

"I'm not going to lie, I will most likely never go fishing or camping again once this is all over. I'm not sure if you could even convince me to leave any city limits ever again," I joke as she half-assedly shows me how to spear the fish onto the branch she was chipping away at earlier.

"Hmm. I might have to work harder to show you how fun it could be out here."

I do a double take at her comment.

Is she...flirting with me?

Judging by the way she attempts to hold our stare, only to back down with a sheepish smile when I deepen the connection, I would say that is a yes, and I am here for it.

"Also, camping happens to be one of Vaughn's favorite things. Granted, when I took her camping, we had basic amenities."

I set the speared fish near the fire, then return to our conversation.

"So you're going to use our daughter against me then. That's hardcore, Blanche. I can respect that."

Nyla's expression glitches briefly, and I wonder if it was my use of her first name. But then she simply says, "*Our* daughter."

It's going to take some getting used to.

"She is mine," I say matter-of-factly, and I see Nyla's defenses building behind those fiery eyes as the expression on her face slips.

"She's mine too." I don't know how she makes her hesitant whisper sound like a challenge, but here we are.

She is fiercely protective of Vaughn, and watching her in fight mode makes me ache to toss her down and fuck her until she accepts the place I want in her life.

I flash my teeth in a wicked smile.

"That's not what I meant. I'm staking my claim—on both of you. She's *our* daughter." Primal predatory need seethes through me, and I welcome it. If Nyla thought we would simply share custody after all of this was over and otherwise go on our merry way, she is about to be corrected. "But you—you are mine, and it's time we talked about that."

20

NYLA

My stomach dropped when Dagen staked his claim, not only as a father to Vaughn, but also as a partner to me.

I had hoped for something like this when I first looked him up, after I learned I was pregnant.

Our first connection, the one built on me deceiving him, felt different.

It was the only time I had remorse about a job I completed, and that was because it felt like there was something between us to lose.

As soon as Dagen told me we needed to talk, he shifted the conversation, setting me on edge. He finished his thought with, "But first, we'll eat this fish. Then I'll clean your wound, and we'll talk over dessert." His voice cracked on the last word.

Dagen knows how to shut me up. He knows exactly what to say when he wants to lead the conversation, and I nod like a sheep.

This earns me a satisfied grin.

We ate in subdued silence, talking half-heartedly about

tomorrow: what we need to avoid, what our priorities are, and where we'll go from Hazelton. We decide we'll carry all our supplies until we reach the town limits, then we'll ditch things like the tarp, fishing rod, and sleeping bag so we can move faster and more inconspicuously.

Although he gave me space to get used to our new reality, every time I tried to help, or moved to pick up something and handle it on my own, I was met with his disapproving glare.

With the promise of dessert hanging over us, dinner didn't seem as appetizing, since it consisted of scrawny fish without seasoning. We ate quickly and without much commentary.

Then Dagen had me stand while he unzipped the sleeping bag, doubling its size so we could get comfortable while he played doctor.

Having Dagen hold me down and use the alcohol wipes to clean my wound was less fun than dinner.

I tried my best to focus on tasting that chocolate while Dagen took my bandage off and sanitized the area. A deep ache had settled into my stiff shoulder joint, and the exercises were more of a challenge than they were earlier.

Dagen muttered more than once that finding painkillers for me was one of our priorities.

Having him take charge of my care is new for me.

Instinctively, I want to jump up and say I can do it myself, but there's a growing part of me that wants to indulge, as though his simple act of kindness is a guilty pleasure.

Now that everything is out of the way, it's time for our reward.

Removing the hunting knife from its sheath, Dagen joins me on the sleeping bag near the fire, setting the chocolate between us and using the hard exterior of the first aid kit as a cutting board.

He chops the bar in half, and my deprived nose smells cocoa in the air immediately.

Spit floods my dry mouth. I lick my lips when Dagen pulls it apart, exposing the inside, and a long string of caramel thins between the two pieces.

"It's got nougat and nuts!" Damn, I sound desperate.

He chuckles as he cuts the pieces in half again, to make quarters. Then cuts each one once more, making eight pieces in total.

"I still can't believe you had a chocolate bar in your go bag. That's like bringing a gun to a knife fight."

"I think the term is 'bringing a knife to a gunfight.'" Dagen hands me my first piece.

"No, I'm pretty sure it is a gun to a knife fight, because I'm going to enjoy the hell outta this."

"You do know you keep getting your idioms wrong, right?" The look on his face says it all. He thinks I'm slow, and he isn't sure how to respond.

"I have no idea what you're talking about."

I totally do.

I've been messing with him.

It's fun.

I pop my piece of chocolate in my mouth before my smile gives me away, but all humor slips from my expression as soon as the burst of flavor hits my tongue. I drag it over every single taste bud.

Dagen hands me another piece, his eyes shifting between my own and my lips as he tosses his piece into his mouth, sucking a string of caramel off his lower lip.

Without thinking, I match his moves, sucking my lower lip between my teeth as though I can taste his mouth from here.

"You look like you're ready to devour me."

Busted.

"What? No. I was just—" I don't bother finishing whatever fib I was about to tell him.

The look on Dagen's face is clear: he knows the truth, and he is ready to challenge me if I say anything less.

I reach for my third piece, but he shoos my hand away before he takes the piece in his hand and leans into my space, holding it in front of me. My eyes jump from the piece of chocolate to his face, and my heart thuds into my chest.

I don't want to be presumptuous, so I reach for the chocolate again, only to have him pull his hand away and slowly turn his head from side to side.

The tension sends waves of nervous energy through my stomach, then lower, and I shift to ease the building sensation.

I drop my good hand into my lap, and his stern expression softens as he brings the chocolate forward once more.

I don't understand the need simmering inside of me.

If this were anyone else, I'd tell them to pound sand.

Dagen isn't doing this because he thinks I can't do it for myself. He's doing this because he knows I can, but he wants to take charge of doing it for me.

Leaning forward, I open my mouth, then snap it shut and retreat before trying again. All the while, he sits still, patiently waiting for me to come to him.

I'm so wrapped up in the anticipation swirling around in my head that I no longer want the chocolate. The expression falls from his face as I lean forward. By the time my lips wrap around his fingers and I take the morsel from him, I want him. His eyes lower to my mouth as his lips part just a fraction.

Then, because I'm one smooth woman, I lean back into my own space and chew the chocolatey nougat in silence, unsure of what to do next.

"The things I would do to you if you weren't wounded right now."

"It's—um, I'm not dying." That came out sounding way more desperate than I wanted it to. "I mean, I'm okay. It doesn't hurt." I attempt to shrug to show him I'm fine, but a sharp jab of pain has me biting back a yelp.

Dagen smirks, then lowers his gaze, taking his last piece of chocolate and leaving one for me.

"Is that an invitation?" he asks, sucking melted chocolate off of his finger.

I don't understand why it's difficult to be forward with Dagen.

Directness was never a problem for me, but as soon as he challenges me, my traitorous heart rolls over for him and hopes he calls me a *good girl* for doing so.

I bounce my head in a shy nod, and he lifts the last piece, holding it out between us.

The suspense building between us has distracted me, and I've missed the part where he's moved closer to my side. Now, when I look from the chocolate to him, his face is only a foot away.

Licking my lips, I lean in for my last bite, and he stays in my space. It's difficult to chew and swallow it down while he watches me intently. As soon as I clear my throat and open my mouth, he pounces.

Wrapping his hand around the back of my head and tangling his fingers into my hair, he guides me to him, meeting me halfway as he smashes his lips onto mine. His tongue immediately pushes through, demanding I open for him, and I do with an indecent moan.

When he pulls himself away from me, his breathing is heavy, hungry. "Still, you are injured."

My heart drops at his rejection, and I try to straighten myself and pull back before I make a fool of myself.

His hand tightens at the back of my head. "Where do you

think you're going?" Apparently his question is rhetorical, because when I try to answer, he just keeps talking. "I'm not done with you. You're injured, and I won't risk hurting you, but I am going to fuck you. Unless you tell me you don't want this." His free hand rubs along the seam of my pants, and I spread my legs for him.

He lowers his head, and his breath tickles along the shell of my ear when he says, "Yeah, you're not going anywhere, are you?"

He's taunting me, and I whimper, shaking my head as best as I can in his hold.

A deep shudder runs through me when he licks my ear, then continues down my neck, shifting his body to wrap his leg around me and pull me closer to him.

"I need to see you. Stand up." He helps me half of the way, careful not to touch my injured arm as he turns me to face him.

The day is almost done, but the area is still lit by the fire.

Dagen unfastens my pants and pulls them down, taking my boots off with them and tossing everything to the side. Having his full attention on me is both exciting and torturous, and I attempt to lower myself to his level when he stops me.

Strong hands grip my hips, and he moves me to stand in front of him with my back to the fire. His eyes hold my own. His pensive expression gives nothing away as he lifts his hand to my panties and rubs along my pussy through the thin fabric.

My hips jerk under his touch. His lip twitching up at the corner is the only sign that he is pleased.

Releasing my hip, he hooks a finger under my panties, moving them to the side, and my body bows as he slides his fingers into me. I groan at how easily he moves through my wetness, and he breaks our stare to focus on what he's doing.

"Fuck, sit down." He takes my good hand, then turns me to face the fire in front of us and helps me to lower myself between his legs before draping my legs over each of his. When he opens his legs, he spreads mine apart with him, then he leans me back against his chest.

As I rest with his chin on my shoulder, he wraps his arms around me, careful to avoid my stab wound, and returns to my panties, hooking one finger under the seam and pulling it over to expose me.

His free hand goes to my good one, and he moves my fingers to my clit. "Feel how wet you are."

I go straight for my most sensitive area, rubbing gently along one side in small circles, moving easily through my slick when Dagen joins me, sliding his fingers inside of me before curling them, and I arch my back, lifting my chest as I roll my hips, absorbing every touch.

"There's my good girl." His whisper slithers into me as he grinds his hips up, his hard cock pushing into my lower back. "Let's make this pussy come, yeah?"

My soft circles evolve into rough rubbing, and Dagen opens his legs wider, spreading me out and giving Mother Nature a perfect view. My panties are now fisted in his palm, and he's pulled them far to the side as he continues to fuck me with his fingers and I hump my hips, desperate to find the right spot.

His soft kisses on my head are a contrast to the rough fucking of his hand, and I moan when he starts talking to me. Whispers about how good I am swirl into how wet my pussy is, and when he says, "Make no mistake, Nyla. You are mine," I break apart in his arms, screaming his name and my release to the stars above.

Brushing his fingers through my hair, he cradles me against his body as my orgasm washes through me.

I take a deep cleansing breath to right myself when Dagen moves behind me. His erection still obvious, he says something about getting some sleep when he stands.

Before he is able to walk away, I grab his hand, returning his attention to me. His free hand brushes my hair out of my face, and his half smile is filled with affection—for me.

I shake my head at him, and he tilts his head, curiously taking me in.

"You're mine too, and I'm not done with you."

21

DAGEN

Nyla was attacked and stabbed less than twenty-four hours earlier, and it has been a grueling day of walking with her wounded shoulder.

I had every intention of claiming Nyla and making my position very clear to her, then settling in for the night so she could rest.

I want her to know, without a doubt, that I have every intention of being more than the guy who knocked her up.

I wasn't there to protect my own brothers, and I won't make that mistake again. Vaughn is my daughter, and God help anyone who tries to hurt her.

But Nyla is different.

She is strong in her own right.

I don't need to protect her, but I want to, and dammit, I want to fucking own her. Her fiery independence is like a challenge that my soul can't help but rise up to.

I want Nyla to wake up in the morning understanding our place with each other. I don't want her tiptoeing around, wondering what all of this flirting means. I don't want her to second-guess my attention and affection.

Her slender fingers snake their way into my hand, intertwining with my own, and she tugs, drawing my attention to her wide eyes looking up at me.

"You're mine too, and I'm not done with you."

"Is that so?" I straddle my feet on either side of her knees and crouch down to her level, searching her eyes for signs of exhaustion.

Fire and determination stare back at me.

"This isn't just a fuck, Nyla. Don't step up if you're only horny and this is about scratching an itch." I hover close to her face, lowering my voice. "I will take all of you this time, and I won't give you back." I tickle my fingers up the inside of her bare thigh, earning a sinful tremble from her.

"I—I'm not done—with you."

She has no idea what her brave words and her inability to look me in the eye are doing to me.

Placing the two fingers I just fucked her with under her chin, I tilt her head, demanding eye contact. "Unless you say otherwise, right now, you belong to me. Is this how it's going to be?"

She nods, and I shake my head. "Say it."

"This is how it's going to be." With my fingers under her chin, I gently turn her head from side to side, telling her to try her answer again, and she does. Clearing her throat, she says, "I belong to you."

"It's about time you accepted that, Jensen."

When I kiss her again, I taste a hint of chocolate on her lips. The kiss is slow and consuming, and her chest rises and falls with her deepened arousal.

I stand up and step away from her as I remove my clothes. If she wasn't hurt, I would make her undress me.

At first, she struggles to remove the shirt I gave her this morning with only one hand. I won't offer to help because I want to make sure she is up for this. Her eyebrows furrow, in frustration more than anything, and I imagine it is because she is relearning her simple tasks without the full use of both arms.

Her injury limits most of the positions I'm currently fantasizing about, but there is one I haven't been able to stop thinking about since the first night we met.

"You'll ride me." This isn't up for debate. "I want to watch your ass while you fuck yourself on my cock."

Understanding dawns in her round eyes immediately. She knows I want a do-over of the reverse cowgirl she hit me with five years ago.

This way, she is in control of the pace.

I sit on the sleeping bag beside her, not bothering to hide my erection, and clear the air of one final thing.

"I'm going to say this once. If you are hurting at any time, you will say so, and we'll stop. I'm not fucking around about this. If you're hurt and you don't tell me, you will not like the consequences. Do you understand me?"

I wasn't planning on taking it this far tonight, not with her stab wound, but if she is pushing for this to happen, I won't deny either of us.

"I understand." She tucks her legs under her and shimmies her hips so she is kneeling, and it takes too long for my brain to catch up to what is happening.

Her cool fingers wrap around the base of my shaft as she leans over me, her good arm resting on the ground. I fist her hair as she takes me in her mouth and sucks me in, and I hiss a few choice profanities under my breath.

Popping her mouth off of me, she licks my length from the base up, then kisses and sucks my tip before running her tongue underneath my shaft.

Her good hand fumbles between jerking me off and playing with my balls, but it makes no difference to me. I have all the sensation I need partnered with the view of her kneeling over me to send me home.

I lift my hand, which is still wrapped in her hair. She takes the hint and releases me before she lifts herself over me, pulls her panties to the side, and straddles my cock before she sinks herself all of the way down.

Desperate to feel her body move while she fucks me, I place my hands on her hips, feeling the way her body rolls as she lifts herself off of me only to impale herself again. I follow her movements, kneading her ass as she rides me.

Pulling her cheeks apart, I press my thumb against the tight muscle of her ass. "Is this still mine?"

She knows what I'm asking.

I told her I wanted to fuck her ass the first night we had sex, and she said it was something she hadn't tried.

Sadly, we never got around to it.

"It's still yours," she rasps over her shoulder, and I lose my shit.

"Fuck yes, it is." I spank her ass hard, watching it jiggle as her pace picks up, and she sits to her full height on me, bouncing on my cock. "You like that? You want me to spank you until you come all over me? Touch yourself. Let's make this pussy come again."

She answers me with a keening groan as she arches her back. Her ass is slapping against my pelvis, and I lose some of my controlled composure.

Sitting up just enough to tangle my fist into her hair, I pull her body tight, so she is forced to look up to the sky. I growl when she keeps fucking me through it all as I spank her ass with my free hand.

"That's it. Show me how much of a dirty girl you are,

because filthy girls get fucked in the ass, and I am dying to put you in your place."

My vulgar words spur her on, and she moans as she rubs herself while she grinds down on me.

This is a side of Nyla I haven't been able to explore yet, but something tells me I'm going to enjoy myself when I do.

I slap her ass a few more times before leaning up further, keeping my hand in her hair and taking control of her pleasure as I slide my fingers under hers and rub her clit.

"Come on, baby. Make that pussy come all over my cock."

She uses her good hand to steady herself on my thigh, and she doesn't relent. Her hips buck and hump as she rides herself before trying to stop the storm that is approaching.

I smack her ass hard, then grip her hip and slam her back down. "This is how it is, Nyla. Now come for—"

Tremors wrack Nyla's body as she tightens up around me and cries my name in waves of incoherent euphoria. I follow her quickly, holding her tight against my front while I spill myself inside of her and growl against her back, now covered in a sheen of sweat.

We sit together for a couple of minutes before she lifts herself off me and turns, sheepishly looking for a classy way to make an exit.

"Join me." I stand, reaching out my hand to her, and she takes it without considering her options, which is a step in the right direction.

We pad to the bank of the river, and I pick up my undershirt on the way, dropping it before we get to the water. "Care for a swim?" Nyla glances at her bandage, and I clarify, "You won't get it wet. We'll only go waist deep. I've got you."

She tugs her panties off with one hand but leaves her bra on. I help her lift her wounded arm around my neck, checking to make sure she's comfortable, then I walk us both into the water. We quickly sink to our waists, and I lift Nyla, wrapping her legs around me and bracing her against my chest.

The water is cool against my flushed skin.

I press my lips against her forehead. "It's selfish, but I want you again."

Nyla tightens her grip, adjusting herself around my waist. I know she's trying to give me what I'm asking for.

I comb my fingers into her hair at her temple, meeting her gaze. "It wasn't a request. Just an observation. We need to rest."

As I say the words, the extent of my exhaustion hits me. If we were attacked right now, neither of us would have the wits or awareness to protect ourselves or each other.

The image pushes me out of the water.

Once we're safely on solid ground, Nyla loosens her legs from my waist, and I set her down. I pick my shirt up and walk her to the fire, drying her off with it as we go.

I pull the opened sleeping bag closer and add two logs to the fire before I dry my body off, gather our clothes, and join her on the soft inside.

Nyla reaches for her clothes and pulls them closer to her, and I place my hand over hers. "Let me dress you."

Her independence sparks like fire in her eyes, the words sitting on the tip of her tongue. She isn't used to this at all, and her first reaction is to brush it off.

I try a different angle. "I've never dressed a woman before. It'll be sexy."

The roll in her eyes doesn't come. Instead, she keeps tugging on her clothes until they are in my lap. Then she stands up next to me, her bare pussy at eye level as she looks down on me, biting her lip.

I haven't even started dressing her, and this is already one of my favorite things.

The silence between us is heavy and hot as she watches me

fumble with her panties: the ones she pulled to the side while we fucked. I tap each ankle, and she steps into them. Then I pull them up, hiding her away from me.

By the time I'm done with everything, the fire is dying again, and this time Nyla turns to add a log while I dress myself and zip up our sleeping bag. It's a clear night with a gentle breeze from the south, so I set us up on the south side of the fire and crawl in. Then I assist Nyla with getting settled, half on my body so she isn't lying on her hurt arm.

I leave the top of the bag open while she gets comfortable. It's the first time I've taken my eyes off Nyla and our surroundings, and the stars in the sky look like something from another world.

I must have voiced my awed appreciation because Nyla turns her head, staring up with me.

Neither of us say a thing for a few minutes. Instead, we huddle together, afraid to disrupt the moment, as though words would just ruin the heavens above us.

"That's Cassiopeia." Nyla wedges her arm between us, pointing to the northern sky. "It looks like a W." I follow her finger, then look around before seeing it tilted a little sideways.

The only constellation I recognize is the Dipper, and I'm not sure if it's the little or the big one. Everything up there looks bigger than life.

"Do you know any others?"

She yawns, then rests her head against my chest, scanning the sky. "There's the Little Dipper." Ah, so it's the little one. "And I think that bright star right there is actually a planet. I'm not sure which one."

I don't ask anything else, and five minutes later Nyla's breathing has evened out. Her body molds into mine like it is meant to be here.

It is.

I gawk at the expanse above us for a few minutes longer before pulling the sleeping bag over us, zipping it up, and cocooning us in for the night.

Tomorrow, we will find our way back to civilization. Then the real fun will begin.

NYLA

True to the GPS we left behind when we were attacked, the first building comes into view after an hour of hiking south from our riverside campsite the next morning.

Granted, it's a bit broken down, and missing a third of its roof, but sounds around the side caught our interest, and we circled the barn until we saw two horses grazing in a field.

Beyond that, and farther away from us, a farmer worked on a tractor. It was the first sign of life that hasn't tried to kill us in days.

I glanced at Dagen, who was focused on the same sight I was. He tore his gaze away from the farmer long enough to look at me and shake his head.

We had already decided we would try to make it all the way into the town before we searched for a phone. If we approach the wrong person out here, they may panic and alert the local authorities.

We shared the last apple by the river this morning, and we

ditched all our unnecessary supplies just before we crossed the river over a bridge about five miles back.

By the time we finally reached Hazelton, we were eating the last of the granola bars, and Dagen had my duffel hanging over his shoulder.

We earn a few curious glances and hushed whispers from the first people we see, and I suddenly feel like I've been lost in a time warp. I try to do the math in my head, but I'm not sure how many days we've been missing.

Dagen and I have been in survival mode for all of that time, and stepping back into life like this is jarring. A little piece of me wants to turn around and run away. A much larger piece needs a hot shower and a massive cup of coffee.

If the town were bigger, we could have blended in easily.

From what I've seen, Hazelton is only a few streets wide and long. It's the type of place where gossip is spread like it's a game of Telephone.

Our presence will be announced long before we enter any of these places.

I miss the part where Dagen stopped walking to look at a sign, and I run into his back before grabbing my sore arm and backing up a step.

He turns. His eyes land on my hand that is clutching my shoulder before traveling up to examine my face.

"Let's go this way." He points in the same direction the sign behind him indicating INFORMATION is pointing.

We walk for another five minutes before Dagen stops and turns to me.

"Can we get your arm in the sleeve?" He points at the belt we took off of the dead man, still fastened around my upper body.

I nod, and he goes for the buckle, releasing my hand from in front of me and guiding it through the jacket. Then he zips it up, concealing my wound, before tossing the old belt into a nearby trash can.

We're already drawing too much attention just by being strangers in a small town. If I showed signs that I was wounded, then we'd most definitely run into a problem.

Dagen takes a deep breath and smiles down at me before stepping up the small walkway and into the little building on the corner: the Hazelton municipal office.

An older lady looks up from the pile of paperwork in front of her. She does a double take when she sees Dagen, her eyes popping out of her head.

I know the feeling, lady. Even after a few days in the bush, he comes out looking like a god, while I look like someone who got into it with a feral cat and lost.

"Can I help you?"

It sounds more like she's asking herself the question rather than us, but Dagen rolls right over her confusion, smiling at her and laying on the charm.

"Our car broke down about twenty miles up the road"—the woman stands, removing her glasses as Dagen weaves his lie—"and my girlfriend and I were wondering if we could use your phone—to make a collect call. My brother is expecting us, and I want to let him know we're okay."

I heard everything after "girlfriend" at a lower volume, and when Dagen turns to look back at me, his smirk says it all.

He said I was his girlfriend.

I'm standing here with a tight-lipped grin on my face like I'm twelve.

"Goodness. Of course, just one moment." She leaves her desk to circle the kiosk at the front, where she lifts an old rotary dial telephone. When she places it on the counter, its ringer clatters against itself on contact.

I watch with restrained amusement as Dagen lifts the

receiver, putting it to his ear as though he doesn't believe it actually works. Sticking his finger into the rotary dial, he drags the thing all of the way around when he dials zero.

I close the distance between us when he starts telling the operator he wants to make a collect call.

The woman gives me a sympathetic smile, then steps back to her desk to give us some privacy when Dagen starts rattling off a number followed by his first name.

The rest of his conversation is broken and one-sided.

"Yeah, man. Barely. No—I don't know. Hazelton. That's it." There's a longer silence between Dagen's answers when he glances over his shoulder to meet my gaze, and I get the feeling the conversation has shifted to me. "I can't talk about that right now. Yeah—I can't. Wait a second."

Dagen covers the receiver with his hand and raises his voice, addressing the woman at the desk. "Excuse me, where is the closest place to get a room?"

"There's a motel over on Main Street." She turns to face the shelf of binders behind her and grabs a handful of papers before returning to the kiosk and shuffling through each one. "Here it is." She drops a pamphlet on the counter and taps it twice before returning to her spot.

Dagen pinches it between his thumb and forefinger and lifts it, examining it in the same way he would regard garbage before reading the address off the front. Then he lowers his voice and finishes with, "Yes. Under my first name, mom's maiden name. I have ID. I'll need some money—same name. Leave a message at the motel with the information. I'll call you later. Thanks. You too."

When he hangs up the phone, the woman sidles toward us.

"Everything settled?" She gathers her pamphlet back and glances between us.

I smile and shrug, waiting for Dagen to field that question.

"Yes. Thank you for the phone. How far is it to the motel from here?"

She scrunches her face at that and clucks her tongue. "It's almost ten kilometers up the road." Then she looks around the room, as if making an executive decision. "I tell you what. It's not too busy here today." Dagen and I exchange curious glances with each other. Is this woman for real? We're the only ones in here. "Why don't I just drive you two over."

I try to tell her she doesn't have to at the same time Dagen graciously accepts the ride, and she beams, grabbing her purse and hustling us out, telling us to wait by the white Camry parked across the street.

Dagen drops his hand to my lower back and crosses the road with me, speaking quickly.

"We are done walking for today. You need to rest. My brother is getting us a room." As soon as he's done, he flashes his smile at the woman as she approaches, and she looks like she's going to melt into a puddle when he begs her to forgive his poor manners and introduces us as Doug and Blanche.

When I shoot him my death glare, he bites the inside of his cheek to stop himself from laughing our charade away.

The woman gushes something about us being the cutest couple and tells us her name is Agatha. Apparently first names are all that is needed in this little town to establish trust, because with that, she opens our doors and welcomes us into her car.

Dagen opens the front passenger door and turns to me, helping me in so I don't hurt my arm, which only makes Agatha's smile widen.

The drive is short, and I take stock of any stores on the way where we can grab things like clothes, food, and supplies. I practically jump out of my seat when we pass by a hospital. Its size is deceiving. In a regular city, it would look more like a walk-in clinic.

When I turn to the back seat, Dagen nods once and returns his attention to the businesses outside.

Dagen thanks Agatha from the back seat and tells her his brother is driving up from Vancouver. He covers all of our bases when he says we are going to stay one night and we'll be gone by morning. He doesn't skip a beat when she asks if we have dinner plans. He says we should really get some rest, because I am very tired and pregnant, and it's been a long day.

Agatha falls all over herself promising we won't be interrupted and wishing us a safe journey home.

It's impressive how fast Dagen can think on his feet and answer as though he, himself, believes the words coming out of his mouth.

The thought is unsettling.

It plants a seed of doubt.

Is Dagen saying all of the things I want to hear?

I push the thought away.

When we get out of the car, Agatha rounds the car and pulls me into a hug, and I smash my teeth together in a forced grin when she squeezes tight and a sharp pain starts in my shoulder and tears through me.

Dagen wraps his arm around me, pulling me into his side possessively, and tells her she is an absolute angel, which makes her flush a deep shade of red. Then she sends us "two little love birds" on our way.

Before we step into the office, I tug on Dagen's arm. "What did you say to your brother?"

Something unreadable flashes across his face when he answers, "Just that we're alive and I'll be in touch."

I don't like the answer, but I'm not ready to push it.

My self-preservation instincts rear up, and my stomach flutters with nerves.

When we were *out there*, we had no choice but to work together. Neither of us would be alive right now if we were on our own, and we knew it. We shared our information and pooled our resources, and here we are—alive.

But now, here we are.

Dagen has his brothers, whom he trusts, and shortly he'll have access to unlimited resources.

He doesn't need to rely on me any longer.

And I told him about Vaughn. My stomach rolls at the thought.

Tucking my arm around him, Dagen opens the door and leads me into the motel lobby.

I hang back by the front window while Dagen talks to the guy behind the counter.

I've told him about Vaughn, but if anything happened to me, he would still need to put pieces together. I could run and make contact, then have her moved once more until I can get to her.

I've also been through a mountain of shit: I've been stabbed, I've barely slept, and we've walked for days. Not to mention I haven't had a shower or a full meal in—what?—almost a week.

My head and heart are not on the same side, and until I figure this out, I'll have to guard them both.

Our room is the last one on the second floor, and it is the farthest from the road. Backing up against a forest of trees, it's the best choice possible if we need to grab our things and run, since neither of us has a car.

"Can you manage a shower on your own?" Dagen steps up behind me, helping me out of the large jacket.

Disappointment sinks into my gut when he doesn't offer to join me.

"Yeah. I'm good." I turn to leave, but he stops me.

"I want to make sure it isn't infected." His expression is all business.

The flirty comments and sly winks are gone as he helps me out of my shirt.

There's no heat in his eyes as he peels back the bandage. He's detached, methodical, as he presses the area around the wound before he unbuttons my pants for me. Then he pinches his lips and sends me into the bathroom.

I want to question it, but it goes on the back burner as soon as I see the little bottles of shampoo and bodywash in the shower.

The water pressure isn't the best, but it is better than nothing, and I kick off my shoes and wiggle out of my pants, not bothering to check out my wound in the mirror.

I let the water cascade down my back and front, but I try to keep it away from my wound. I'll have to double-check it in the mirror when I get out. From this close angle, it looks like it's healing well.

Washing my hair with one good hand is a challenge, but I manage, and by the time I step out of the shower, I feel closer to my old self.

The woman staring back at me in the mirror looks a little worse for wear. I don't remember how I got the subtle bruise along my jawline, but my hair covers it. Thankfully, the guy who ran after me didn't have enough time to do anything more than stab me.

The dull ache in my shoulder brings the memory back to me, and I stare at my reflection in amazement.

How the hell am I still alive?

Dagen.

The answer fills me with conflicting feelings.

I dry off and walk into the room.

My stomach drops.

Vaughn's photo is on the bed beside my phone. My duffel is missing, and Dagen is gone.

23

DAGEN

As soon as Nyla turned the water on, I was on my feet with a plan for the day.

We passed a handful of stores on our way to the one-star no-tell motel we ended up in, and I had a long list of items we needed.

But there was one thing I wanted to do first.

Opening Nyla's duffel bag, I went straight for her broken phone, found the compartment at the back, and pulled out Vaughn's photo.

Our daughter.

Her smile lights up the whole picture, and I wonder what her voice sounds like, or her laugh. This little girl will have all of my brothers wrapped around her pinkie finger.

I set her photo aside and made another call to Lennox while the shower was still running. He's the only one out of all my brothers who still has a landline, so he can accept collect calls.

He picked up on the first ring.

It was another short call.

Lennox had the same questions as earlier, but I had to get some things done before I brought him up to speed, and I didn't want to be gone too long.

It wasn't until I promised my big brother I would call him as soon as I was done that he gave me the bank name and address I needed to access the wire transfer he sent.

Stealing and sneaking around will only get us so far before we're caught. If we can blend in, we'll be able to make our way to the US border a lot easier, and money talks.

That's another idiom I imagine Nyla would get wrong. She'd probably say something like, *Money doesn't talk, that's ridiculous!* Then she'd prop her hands on her hips and roll her eyes at me, and I'd want to bend her over and fuck her.

Man, she's dug herself deep under my skin.

After writing a note for Nyla, I gathered my things and set out. If I waited until she was out of the shower, she'd just want to come along, and she needs to rest so she can heal.

I was able to charm my way through collecting the three thousand dollars Lennox sent to the closest bank.

He wanted to send twenty. I talked him down.

I'm pretty sure there are forms to fill out if it goes higher than a certain amount, and I was able to reuse the lie I told about my car breaking down and needing the money for a tow and repairs.

From there, I went straight to the hospital, or, rather, the little pharmacy attached to the side of it. When we first drove by, I had planned to sneak in and steal what we needed for Nyla's wound, but I have more than enough to buy most of it now, and her wound is already healing nicely.

On my way back to the motel, I found a grocery store that, oddly enough, had a clothing section. Charming.

If Cole could see me now, I would never live it down.

Something on a rack catches my attention. I know what I'd like to see Nyla in, but somehow I think returning with a neon pink lace teddy that I bought for—I check the tag—$2.99 won't fly, so I keep walking until I reach the activewear section, which consists of one rack of yoga pants and some stretchy long sleeve tops, before grabbing a couple of things for myself.

I round out our wardrobe with basic socks and underwear for the both of us, then take ten steps to my left and peruse the produce.

Oddly enough, if we weren't being hunted, I might find some kind of demented amusement in playing tourist in this little town.

I still can't get over using a rotary telephone today.

I stuff the clothes and food into Nyla's duffel bag and take off for my next stop. Then I return to the motel with two cups of coffee and a bag filled with burgers, salad, and fries.

When I pass a pay phone across the street from our motel, I decide to stop to call Lennox back. Nyla will probably be out of the shower by now, and there are a couple of things I want to tell him in private.

I have a direct view of our door, and I balance the coffee on top of the pay phone.

"I'm coming to get you" are the first words Lennox says.

I have to stop myself from audibly chuckling because Lennox won't have any of it if he thinks I'm taking this lightly.

"Not here. We're leaving in the morning. I need a few things from you."

Lennox listens while I tell him I need two passports good enough to get us across the US border when the time comes. Until this hit is removed, I can't show up anywhere under my real name. Then I give Lennox Nyla's full name and tell him to get in touch with Nigel and have him dig up everything he has on her, including a recent photo to use in the passport.

"Does she have what we need?"

Hearing Lennox say "we" is a good feeling. I hate that he went out on his own for so long. Even now, when I talk to my older brother, I hear him struggle to step away from the fatherly role he took on.

Our father failed us in every sense, but it was never Lennox's burden to bear alone, and I want my brother back.

"I'm not sure yet, but there are some things I need to tell you. Just not over the phone like this."

I went back and forth about telling Lennox about Vaughn. I want him to be the first to know, but I want to see him face to face when I tell him. Lennox has been the single greatest fatherly influence in my life, and saying it like this and hanging up just feels impersonal.

He's silent for a minute.

"Something isn't right here." Lennox's hesitation makes me think he was weighing whether or not he should share this information with me.

"Is everyone safe?" I ask.

Ryder, Cole, and I have been working closely with Lennox to learn more about what our father is doing, but we haven't brought any of the women in our lives into it yet.

We all know we're going to hell for keeping this from them —hell being the moment they find out and hand our balls to us on a platter—but Amara and Sloane cannot know our father is involved until we have a way out for everyone.

"They're safe. I just haven't been able to get a location on Dad for a few days now. I went by the house today to visit Mom, and their housekeeper said they went on vacation."

Despite the warm afternoon, a chill runs across my skin.

They haven't gone anywhere since she's been diagnosed

with Alzheimer's. Not that it should hold her back, but a trip away like this would have been planned out and mentioned to us.

"Ryder and Cole?" I ask.

"He didn't tell anyone. I have my guys looking into it, but I feel like I need to get you back here."

"That reminds me." I reach up to take a sip from one of the coffee cups before continuing, "Nyla said she found out some things about Dad's business. According to her, the companies we run are some kind of sex and drug trafficking front. I mean, we knew it was going to be bad. She said there are connections with a Mexican cartel. Maybe you can verify that as well."

If it wasn't for his occasional sighs, I'd think the line was dead.

"Thanks. Leave it with me. I am coming to get you. Where are you heading?"

I'm not even going to fight Lennox on this. I need all of the help I can get.

"We're going to make our way down to Vancouver. I'm not sure how yet, but we'll head for Prince George tomorrow." As I finish talking, movement at our motel catches my attention, and it takes me a minute before I recognize the figure walking toward the office is Nyla.

"Fine. I'm couriering you a burner phone. You'll have it by the time you wake up. Keep it on you. My contact information will be programmed in it, along with Ryder's and Cole's. Until we know where Mom and Dad are, we handle our business over those lines. I'll get in touch with the boys. I'm leaving shortly, and I'm heading your way. Now that I don't have a plane, it's going to take a little longer."

I pause, trying to read the proverbial room.

If Ryder or Cole had said that to me, it would be a joke, but it has been a long time since Lennox made light of anything around us.

I decide to chuckle. He can kick my ass for the plane later if he wants.

"I'm glad you're okay."

"Fuck, have I got some stories for you."

The front door to the motel lobby opens again, and Nyla walks out, taking two steps toward the street before pausing and turning back. Then she recovers those steps and takes a few more toward our room.

Then she stops again.

"I'll call you tomorrow. I need to get back." I hang up and step behind the pay phone, obscuring her view of me, and I watch as she wages an internal war with herself.

Is she thinking about running?

I outright reject the thought at first, but it's still there.

She did leave me handcuffed to a tree in the desert, after all.

Her head swivels from the door to our room to the street and back again, and I wonder what's holding her back.

Is it me?

Or is it the fact that I have everything but the picture of our daughter in the duffel bag slung over my shoulder?

In the end, she turns away from me and takes a few steps toward our room, then she looks up and takes in the scenery. I haven't had a moment to appreciate the view out here. A large mountain dominates the landscape to the south of us.

I take advantage of the distraction. I cross the road with our food and coffee in hand and walk up behind her. "I thought I told you to rest."

She screams and figuratively jumps out of her skin, clutching her hand over her heart and almost knocking the coffee out of my hand when she spins around to face me.

"Don't do that," she huffs, inhaling deeply.

"What are you doing out here?"

"I just wanted some fresh air and to—um, look around." She points at the mountain then asks a question of her own to change the subject. "Where did you go?"

She isn't outright lying, but she isn't telling me everything, and I pack that little piece of information away.

"I have some medical supplies to properly dress your wound. I also have some painkillers, fruit and vegetables, clothing, and"—I hold up the brown paper bag and cups—"I've got lunch and coffee."

Her face lights up at that, and she reaches out, offering to help. I give her the food and drinks and tell her to get started while I check in with the front to tell them I'm expecting a delivery.

Once she's inside our room and the door is closed, I head to the office and up to the front desk, looking around in confusion. "The woman I'm traveling with, did she come in here earlier? We seem to have missed each other, and I'm trying to catch up with her."

The guy looks up from his screen. "Oh, yeah. She used our business center." He points to a computer sitting on a desk with one leg secured with duct tape. Above it sits a scanner and fax machine on a shelf that looks like it's going to come crashing down any minute now.

Classy.

I should up my internal star rating to two stars just for that.

Forcing a smile, I nod my thanks and walk over to the computer, jiggling the mouse until the screen comes to life. When I search the history on the web browser, it's been scrubbed; there's nothing there.

I check the connection to make sure she would have been able to get internet access, and it connects quickly.

She covered her tracks.

This is fine.

We're back to playing games.

I like games...especially the ones where the odds are stacked in my favor, and this time, I'm going to win.

24

NYLA

I wake with a startle, and it takes me half a minute of pure panic to remember where I am.

The room is completely dark except for a sliver of light that pours in from the cracked bathroom door.

Even once my memories catch up to me, there's still a gap of time I'm missing.

The last thing I have any memory of was during the daytime.

I don't remember getting ready to sleep. I don't recall the sun going down or any conversations after Dagen re-dressed my wound with the supplies he picked up earlier in the day.

I remember I had the start of a stomachache when Dagen returned to the room from the front office. I knew in my head I should have taken my time and allowed myself to get used to full meals again, but the pangs in my gut overrode my graceful decorum, and I pigged out.

When I asked Dagen what was being delivered, he simply answered that it was a burner phone. Then he shut the conversation down when he took a bite out of his own burger.

I felt Dagen's eyes on me while he ate, and again when he insisted on changing my bandage and re-dressing my wound properly.

I should have told him I reached out to my team, but right now it's one-sided. I won't know until they respond if they made it out okay.

Now Dagen sleeps soundly beside me in the queen bed. We had to make a choice when we checked in. We could have a room with two double beds, but we'd be close to the front of the motel, or we could be back here, where there was more privacy, but we'd be sharing a bed.

I stretch out, lying on my back and staring up at a brown spot on the ceiling. I'm suddenly wide awake, and my limbs buzz with restless energy.

When I turn my head to watch Dagen sleep, the whites of his eyes shine in the light from the bathroom. He's watching me from his spot beside me. "Can't sleep?" he murmurs.

"I don't remember falling asleep."

"You were tired. I gave you some painkillers and bandaged your shoulder, then you laid down. You were asleep before I was done with my coffee."

I answer with a simple "Oh" then return to the captivating stain on the ceiling.

He must watch me struggle to close my eyes for the next few minutes before he speaks again.

"Come here." Dagen slides his arm out toward me and lifts the covers between us, urging me into him. I slide closer until my warm skin touches his. He doesn't have a shirt on, and neither do I.

I remember taking off my shirt so he could remove my bandage. I must not have given him time to get it back on, yet I am still wearing my bra.

The contact startles me, and he laughs under his breath.

"Go to sleep, Jensen." He pulls me the rest of the way into him, partially wedging his body under mine.

Internally, I want to struggle for all of five seconds, then a wave of calm hits me.

The last few nights have created a habit in me. Sleeping on the other side of the bed from Dagen feels too far after being swaddled into one sleeping bag together.

I've slept like this before. It was the night of the storm, when he was worried about my body temperature dropping.

Dagen wraps his arms around me, hugging me into him, and I can't help but sigh against his body. This has quickly become a comfort for me, and I breathe him in. The smell of his skin reminds me of the small bottle of bodywash I used in the shower earlier.

"Close your eyes." With one arm hugging me into him, I rest my head on the bicep of his other arm, and he bends his elbow so he can play with my hair.

My eyes roll at his soothing touch before I close them once again.

The next time I open my eyes, the room is bright. The flimsy curtains do nothing to keep the sun out.

When I groan my displeasure at waking up, Dagen stirs.

He rolls me onto my back, pinning me to the mattress with half of his body draped over mine. "How is your shoulder?"

I pause to assess myself. When I feel nothing, I lift my arm off the mattress. As soon as I move, I feel the spot where I was stabbed, but it is nothing more than a dull reminder.

"It's much better."

My answer makes him smile.

"Good, because I'm about to defile you in this shithole.

Then I'm taking you for breakfast before we catch the bus."

Somehow, it doesn't seem like the best time to ask where the bus is going when Dagen fists his fingers into my hair and angles my face to kiss me, groaning against my mouth.

Sliding the strap of my bra off my shoulder, he pauses to examine my face for signs of pain before he continues tugging it down and away from my chest. He cups my breast in the palm of his hand and pinches my nipple between his thumb and forefinger. As he squeezes, he watches my face, keeping his expression impassive until my lips tremble and I hiss. At the first sign of pain, something wicked flashes in his eyes, then he lowers his head, licking the sensitive spot as he releases me.

His hand glides farther down my body, settling between my legs. I hadn't noticed that my pants were gone, but I do still have the modesty of my underwear, although I'm not sure how long that'll last.

Dagen dips his fingers under the elastic at my waist and wastes no time covering my mound with his hand and sliding his fingers into my folds.

His mouth returns to mine as I groan.

"You enjoy a little pain. Don't bother denying it. You're soaked." To drive his point home, he easily pushes two fingers deep inside of me while he tightens his hold on my hair.

"I don't deny it," I pant into his mouth.

I didn't know I had a penchant for rough sex until I met Dagen. When I left him, I couldn't put my time with him behind me. He stirred something inside of me, and I haven't been able to find someone who could duplicate it since.

At my answer, the muscles in his lips curl up at the corners against my mouth. Breaking away, he stands, moves to the side of the bed, and gives me a front row view to his ridged abs and his lean thighs.

Then my jaw drops when he bends over, takes his boxer

briefs to the ground, and returns to his full height with a thick erection pointing right at me.

He turns my body at a ninety-degree angle and slides my head to the edge of the bed, in line with his cock. Then he rips the blankets off the bed, slides his hands under my upper body, and releases my bra, exposing me to him.

Any propriety I held on to evaporates the moment he braces his body above mine and pulls my panties down and off before pushing my legs open wide for him.

Need replaces self-control, and I reach my hands above my head, cupping his balls and drawing my fingers along his sensitive skin.

"So good" is followed by a few other words I don't make out when he leans over, bracing one hand under my ass and sliding his other along my folds before spreading my lips open and licking the length of my pussy, then sucking my clit into his mouth.

I open my mouth to moan, then wrap my hands around him and feed his length into my mouth. Dagen's hips surge forward, and I struggle to take all of him in. Pulling back, he eases himself in once again, and this time I accommodate him easier, and I drop my hands away, holding on to his upper thighs and allowing him to lead.

His tongue hits every sensitive spot as he keeps his mouth firmly on me, only lifting to spank my breasts with one hand while he fingers me with another as he fucks my face.

Pleasure builds at an insane pace, and I buck against his mouth as his tongue alternates between sucking my clit and pushing inside of me.

"Are you going to come like this, baby? Getting eaten out in a seedy motel while I fuck your head into this cum-stained mattress?" He spanks my breast again before pinching then twisting my nipple, and my pussy clenches around his fingers.

Those words and the image they create send me into another world, and I spread my legs wide, allowing my knees to fall open when he mutters, "Fuck, yes," and lowers his mouth to me again, eating me like he's starving.

His hips thrust into me, pushing his cock to the back of my throat before he adjusts his position and drives further, my throat opening for him.

It's the farthest I've ever taken anyone, and it takes me a moment to adjust to him.

His finger presses against my back entrance, testing the tight muscle. "Atta girl, open for me."

I obey his words as though they are a command. I let my body go, giving myself to him, and he takes everything. He pushes his thick finger into my pussy, then he trails it to my back hole. His finger swirls around the outside of my tight muscle, then he applies pressure, easing his digit in. "I'm going to enjoy fucking your ass."

My orgasm possesses me with the depraved promise in his words, and I hump and buck in his hold, my mouth wide open as he continues to thrust down my throat, pushing all of my screams back down.

His legs shake, then his hips jerk a moment before he spills himself down my throat, reaching under both of us to fist my hair at the base of my skull, holding my head to him as he growls my name.

Easing off of me, he braces my shoulders, helping me back to the pillow before kneeling on the floor beside the bed. His eyes are level with mine as he brushes his fingers through my hair.

This time when he kisses me, it's gentle, almost loving, and my head swirls at the deep intimacy behind it.

"I wish we had—time." His tone is soft, filled with regret.

We haven't stopped moving since Alaska. I haven't been

able to scrape enough of a moment together to reflect.

Our damn plane went down, we've been attacked, I've been stabbed, and I don't have time to process any of it. The decisions I've been making haven't been carefully thought through because I don't have the benefit of time for that.

So, without time to talk ourselves out of anything, we've been following our strongest instincts, and they've led us to each other.

I just hope we're not wrong.

Dagen looks around the room at all of our things before returning his attention to me.

"We need to pack up. The bus leaves around noon, and there isn't another one for a few days. Do you have an alternate ID?"

"I have an alias. It might be hot." I have no idea if the people looking for us are aware of the only other identity I have with me.

Dagen considers the risk for a minute. "We have to try it. Let's get going."

We can't afford to stay here for much longer.

I sit up, sliding my feet off the bed and onto the floor. I stand on shaky legs, and Dagen manages to help me steady myself before I fall over. It's taking more than I thought to recover from what he just did to my body.

"We shouldn't be on our own for much longer. My brother is making his way to us, and my team is working on a way across the border."

I excuse myself and gather my new underwear, pants, and a top on the way to the washroom.

Knowing his brother is on his way to us is bittersweet.

There is strength in numbers, and it will be nice to have someone else on our side, but at the same time, I have a bad feeling this will bring new threats to our front door.

2 5

DAGEN

The burner phone was waiting for me at the front desk when I went to check on the status of my package. As soon as I turned it on, there were check-in messages from Cole and Ryder, and I responded to both, telling them we were alive.

Then Cole started a group chat to ask me if I was able to get my money back in kind, and I threatened to block him.

It turns out, all of my joking around about Harlow and Amara is about to bite me in the ass.

After we checked out, Nyla and I stopped at the coffee shop on the corner, then walked a couple of miles to catch our ride.

There was nothing memorable about the bus depot.

If it wasn't for a placard five times too small hanging over the door, we would have walked right past it.

Once inside, we walked up to a booth, asked for our tickets, and showed our fake IDs. Nyla visibly settled when the attendant behind the counter barely looked her way to confirm if she was the person in her photo.

We waited until ten minutes before the bus was scheduled to depart before buying the tickets just in case Nyla's alias is being monitored.

Given the way the kid behind the counter wrote everything down instead of typing it on a computer, it was clear that it was only a formality, and we'd be getting out of here with nothing more than a paper trail.

And now we have nine and a half minutes to kill before boarding.

Nyla and I exchange a conspiratorial glance when I turn to hand her her ticket, and we make our way through the doors into another room.

The pungent smell of diesel fills the waiting room at the back of the building. I guide Nyla past all of the seats and through the doors leading to the open area outside. The last thing I want is for either of us to get sick from the fumes.

Judging by the amount of people inside and out here with us on the platform, the bus is going to be only about half full. I lead Nyla to a bench to wait until boarding is called.

A few people glance our way, but most of their attention is on Nyla.

I don't blame them.

Nyla has a way about her that makes you want to be near her. It's like the air smells clean, and she makes me feel pure and whole. Her smile—her real smile—makes me feel like I can fly, and when she looks at me, nothing else matters.

"Is everything okay?" Mistaking my admiration for judgment, she lifts her hand to her face, then huffs when her fresh sling holds her back.

After I changed her bandage this morning, I set her arm properly in a sling I bought at the pharmacy. She most likely won't need to wear the thing for long, as her wound is already healing, but I want her to be careful and remember to take it easy.

"Everything is fine." I shove my hands in my pockets and glance around the area.

Twenty feet away, a mother with two little kids looks around, notices us, then lowers her eyes to Nyla's arm before one of her children tries to make a run for it and she takes off to wrangle him in.

Three newspaper dispensers sit side by side to the left of our seats, and I open the first, looking for reading material during the ride to Prince George. The first box holds a magazine for new parents, and I myself just happen to be a new parent...to a four-year-old.

Jesus. My reality hits me. I have no idea what the hell to do. The only kid I know is Henry, Sloane's son, and I don't get to see him often. When I do see him, I'm the fun pseudo uncle. I don't know the first thing about being a father.

I grab the magazine, then quickly open the dispenser beside it and add a home rental guide for the area to my pile. I'm confident I will never be coming back here, but I need something to hide my new dad's guide under, so it'll do.

The last dispenser carries a local newspaper, and I grab a copy to round out my collection.

When I turn back to Nyla, movement out of the corner of my eye catches my attention. The bus doors are open, and the line is moving.

I sling the duffel over my shoulder, twist my reading material into a roll, then guide Nyla to the bus. An older gentleman waves as I approach, asking if we want to store our bag under the bus, and I shake my head, sending him to the elderly couple behind us.

Most seats near the front are taken. I walk past everyone,

heading straight for a couple of empty seats near the back and a couple of rows away from everyone else.

I stuff the duffel under the seat and step into the aisle, offering Nyla the window seat. When she sits down, she points at my hand.

"Mind if I read one of those?"

I'm second-guessing picking up the parenting magazine now. I unroll my stack and give her the local news from the top of my pile.

A woman stands at the front of the bus, going through announcements before we leave. Nyla flattens the paper on her lap and starts to read a story on the first page about a summer harvest festival.

I half listen to the woman ramble on about not smoking on the bus, which includes the bathroom at the back, and I pick at the corner to the parenting magazine that is hidden under the home rentals.

Curiosity gets the better of me, and I lift the corner and open the magazine to a random page. A What Kind of Mother Are You? quiz is the first article on the page, and I sneak a peek at Nyla out of the corner of my eye. She's onto the next page of local news, and I return to find out what type of mother I am when the bus jerks, then rolls away from the station.

The first question seems easy enough—until it comes time to answer it, then I begin to doubt myself. I decide to pick my top two answers for the first question, then narrow it down with a game of Eeny, Meeny, Miny, Moe.

When I move on to the second question, none of the answers fit what I would do. I lean into the aisle and glance toward the front of the bus, as if the answer is hidden up there somewhere.

My confidence really wavers by the time I'm on to the fifth

question, and once I answer the last one, I've all but convinced myself that I am not cut out for this.

"This isn't good." Nyla hiss-whispers beside me, and I have to agree with her.

"You're telling me," I huff in response.

It turns out I'm a "helicopter mom," and I need to ease up on my kid and let her learn some things on her own. I haven't met Vaughn yet, and I'm already smothering her.

"What are you talking about?" Nyla glares at me before swiveling her head around the bus, and I match her movements.

"What? Nothing. What are *you* talking about?" I close the magazine and hold it shut with my hand, as though it'll open up and start telling everyone on the bus that I'm *that* mom.

When Nyla is done scanning the bus, she sinks into her seat and huddles near me, bringing the paper between us and opening it.

I stare long and hard in confusion at the picture of myself before I look back to Nyla. Her warm brown irises swim in the whites of her eyes as they bug out with panic.

The story of our downed plane takes up a small section on the page. The pilot's body was found near the crash area, and my picture is shown because it's suspected that I was on board, but it hasn't been confirmed by family.

It adds that I may have been traveling with an unknown woman.

The grainy black and white image of me is almost four years old. It was taken at a charity function, so I was dressed to the nines. My hair was close to a buzz cut, which doesn't match the way I look right now. This photo was given to the authorities by one of my brothers. It's their way of being helpful —to a point.

"That reminds me." I reach into my pocket, pull out the

burner phone, and hold it up to Nyla. "I need a photo of you to send to my brothers. If Lennox sees you first, I want him to recognize you."

She weighs my request for a second before nodding in agreement, and she leans back toward the window. She purses her lips together in a strained smile. I consider asking her to try again, but the chances are good that this is what she'll look like until we're safe, so it's perfect, and I send it off.

"And what about this?" She tilts her head to the paper, returning my attention to the problem at hand.

I consider what this means.

"I'm not concerned." I place my hand over hers, closing the newspaper.

Now, if there were a photo of Nyla with me, that would be a different story. Her identity is still hidden to everyone except those who are trying to find us. I'm positive none of my brothers would have told the authorities that I might have been on board, so either someone saw me at the airport, or whoever is chasing us is trying to flush us out, and they don't have a photo of Nyla.

I watched the evening news last night as Nyla slept, and there was nothing about the crash or any efforts to find survivors, so I'm assuming my family is being tight-lipped about any information leading to me.

There is no record of me leaving the country under my real name, so once I'm stateside, I will miraculously appear and be accounted for.

When Nyla doesn't relax, I open the paper to the small snippet at the bottom of page four and point to it. "It's not front-page news, and that photo looks nothing like me now."

She looks at it again, then shrugs, seemingly pacified for the moment.

She mutters something to herself before closing the paper

and staring out the window. Her fingers switch between tapping nervously on her lap and clenching into a fist.

I glance down at my lap, then try to make it sound like I'm casually changing the subject. "So, what kind of mom would you say you are?"

That was poorly executed.

Nyla stops fidgeting, and she turns her gaze back to me. "What?"

At least she doesn't look anxious anymore.

"So let's say there is a bake sale at Vaughn's school. What would you bring to it?" I ask the first question I remember from the quiz hiding on my lap.

Nyla's forehead creases. "She's not in school yet."

I try a different approach. "Say she was. What would you bring?"

She crosses her arms, giving me a look that says, *Okay, I'll play.*

"I would bake something with her. She had fun making my mom's cookie recipe last year, even though she wore most of the ingredients and ate half the chocolate chips." She smiles at the memory.

I steal a glance at the answers.

It's not there, so I'll just choose "make something simple."

Then I ask the next question.

"Your kid is having a playdate. What types of snacks do you have on hand? I mean"—I change my tone, trying to pile on some disinterest—"let's say Vaughn has a friend over. What do you give them for a snack?"

Nyla tilts her head, and her gaze drops to my lap. "What are you—"

She wedges her finger under my rental guide and lifts just enough to see the cover. Then she pulls it out, reading the words on the front before turning it to face me.

"You're not, by chance, asking me the questions in this quiz, are you?" Her arrogant smirk tells me she already knows the answer.

"Pfft! Whatever. No. I already know what kind of mother you are." I snatch the magazine back, and she crosses her arms.

"And what kind is that?" The feisty snark is evident in her tone.

"The nosy kind." I mutter to myself, and she tosses her head back and laughs, causing the person nearest to us to glance over.

She ends her chuckle with a sigh, then nudges her shoulder against mine. "Come on. Let me see it."

I'm half tempted to deny her request, but this whole thing has distracted her from the shitstorm that seems to be following us, so I act like she's won this big battle and open the magazine to the page for the quiz.

Nyla reads over the first question before huffing her disdain. She turns the page for the next question, then skips to the results at the end.

Shaking her head, she sets the magazine on my lap before looking at me. "You took the quiz, didn't you?"

"Maybe."

"And let's see." She leans into me, skimming the final page. "Are you the 'perfectionist'?" She sizes me up before she answers her own question. "No. What about the 'hot mess'?"

I don't let her list all of them. I speak quickly and under my breath: "Imthehelicoptermom."

"Really? Hmm. I can see that." I must look wounded by her answer because she backpedals. "I'm kidding. Look." She points to each of the options. "Do any of these look like labels that any mom would strive to achieve? I used to take these quizzes all of the time when I first found out I was pregnant."

"You did?"

Nyla is already nodding. "Hell yes. Second-guessing your choices when it comes to your child means you care. Worrying that you aren't doing enough means that you probably are. The answers to the questions you have aren't in these magazines. The answer to if you are a great parent can only be found in your child's heart. Only Vaughn will be able to answer that question for you."

I kiss her out of nowhere, and she squeaks in surprise when my lips crash around hers. I take advantage of her initial shock to lean into her space, deepening my connection, and I'm about twenty seconds away from finding a way to fuck Nyla in the bathroom of this bus when my phone rings in my pocket, drawing attention from the person closest to us once again.

I swear under my breath and dig my burner out.

There are only three people who have this number.

"What is it?" The happy expression has already slipped from Nyla's face.

Lennox: I'm seven hours out on 97. You can't stay in PG. Start heading south.

We won't arrive in Prince George for another two hours. Lennox wouldn't tell us to stay moving if he didn't think there was an incoming threat.

"Not sure, but it doesn't look good."

NYLA

The rest of the trip is filled with patches of tense silence followed by the occasional brainstorming session of how we're going to continue moving south toward his brother.

Between Dagen and I, we have over twenty-five hundred dollars in cash, which is more than enough for another bus ticket if the times are right.

As the bus pulls into the depot in Prince George, I open the newspaper to the page with Dagen's image, tear it out, fold it, and tuck it in my jacket pocket.

I test my arm in the sling, first rubbing the area where I was stabbed, then lifting and stretching my arm.

The ache is barely noticeable now, and I slip the sling off my shoulder and leave it on the seat as we leave.

Any little thing could draw the wrong kind of attention my way, and I don't want to be noticed at all.

Dagen grabs our bag and hangs the strap over his shoulder. Once we're off the bus, he walks to a screen listing all of the departures. We missed the last bus heading to Vancouver today by an hour.

"Let's get out of here." Palming my hand in his, he lowers his head toward the ground and leads me outside and around the side of the building. He's about to cross the street when someone parking their car catches my attention.

I stop and tug on his hand, and he hangs back. "What's up?"

"Give me a minute." I watch as the guy gets out of the beat-up old car and takes a suitcase out of the trunk.

Instinctively, I release Dagen's hand and tell him to hang back and wait, then I cross the parking lot toward the guy.

"Hey. Is that your car?"

The guy stops mid-step and turns to look me over. "What's it to you?"

I take the last few steps to him and look around at the buildings bordering the parking lot.

There are no cameras.

I'm pretty good at reading people. It was how I could bribe the bartender so easily when I first met Dagen. I have a feeling I'm going to get what I want from this one.

"I need to get out of town, and I want your car. I'll make it worth your while."

When his eyes roam down my front, stopping at my breasts, I correct his fantasy. "How about a thousand dollars cash?"

His eyes light up. It seems I was right about him.

"You want to buy my car?" He looks over my shoulder, and I turn to see Dagen has taken a couple of steps toward us, his expression uneasy. I hold my hand out, telling him to stay back, then I return my gaze to the guy.

"No. I want to steal it." I hook my fingers in air quotes around the word "steal," and he looks confused, so I lay it out. "You look like you're leaving town for a bit. How about you give me the keys to your car and take your trip with a thousand dollars extra spending cash. You can report it stolen when you get back and claim any insurance."

His expression is suspended in disbelief. His eyes flit between me and Dagen when he asks me why I don't just steal it.

"If I steal it, I run the risk of it being reported too early. We need to head north"—I lie—"and we can't risk being stopped before we get to where we're going. So you take a thousand dollars for your troubles and report it stolen later."

He takes a minute too long to answer, and I'm close to walking away to look for another way out of here when Dagen steps forward. "Fifteen hundred—cash. Which we both know is more than this car is worth."

"Deal!" The guy extends his arm, stepping past me to shake Dagen's hand, as if to seal the bro code or some bullshit. Dagen pulls the wad of cash out, removes a few bills from it, and slaps it in the guy's palm, then holds out his own hand for the keys.

Dagen doesn't wait for the guy to leave us. He opens the driver's door and hops in, starting the car up and waiting for me to take my place in the passenger's seat. I fasten my seat belt and glance over when he doesn't immediately drive away.

He checks his phone for messages, then tells me we're going to drive until we find the next town then stop for dinner. As he says the words, my stomach growls its displeasure at the delay, but I agree.

If something has spooked his brother, then we need to keep moving.

Neither of us knows where the hell we are, so it doesn't surprise me when Dagen pulls into the first gas station we see. He tops the tank off, then tells me to lock the doors and keep my head down while he goes inside to pay.

When he returns, he hands me a bag of chips and a bottle

of water, then opens a map, folding it back down to a manageable size.

"We're here." He points to a spot. "And this is the road south to Vancouver." He drags his forefinger across the map.

It doesn't look too difficult to navigate. "Got it." I look at the street, then back to the map before pointing back over my shoulder. "We should go back that way."

He starts the car up, and we drive back the way we came. When we pass the bus depot, I tell him to take a right at the next light.

It continues like this until we are on the road out of town, and I set the map in the back seat before opening my bag of chips.

I eat in silence until the city gives way to another stunning countryside. The speed limit increases, and a distance sign lists four cities, with Vancouver being the farthest away.

"The guy at the gas station told me we have around an hour to the next town. Why don't you use that time to tell me what you were looking up online in the hotel lobby yesterday."

I'm slow to react, and by the time I understand what Dagen is asking of me, my silence is doing me no favors.

"It's not what you think."

"Tell me, Nyla, what do I think it is?"

I walked into that one.

Dagen keeps his eyes on the road, but the muscles along his jawline flex as he grinds his teeth.

He's disappointed, and I don't like the way this is making me feel.

This man is a master at waiting for the perfect time to handle his business. He's methodical and patient. He's a planner, and he planned to wait until he got me here, in a controlled space, just like he did our first night, when we were wrapped up in the sleeping bag.

I don't know what is more confusing to me: that he was able to easily lull me into complacency, or that I like the way he handles me.

"It's nothing bad."

He chuckles sardonically. "Try again."

I huff and cross my arms, leaning away from him and toward the passenger door, using my defiance as a shield.

This draws his attention, and he breaks his gaze away from the road for half a second to witness my disobedience. My stomach drops when he raises an eyebrow, clearly unimpressed by my spite before he looks forward without a word.

On the outside, I hold firm. I don't know why I'm pushing back. I didn't do anything wrong. My answer would have easily pacified him, but I'm poking the bear like I want to be eaten alive.

Maybe I do.

My heart thuds into my chest when the *ticka ticka ticka* of the turn signal echoes in the quiet car, and he says, "Have it your way then."

The little rest stop comes into view, and my brave front crumbles away when the only other car here pulls onto the highway and drives away.

"What are you doing? We need to keep driving." My questions are met with a soft chuckle.

Dagen finds this funny.

A row of bushes separates the rest stop from the highway, and he pulls behind the densest section.

He turns off the car and pockets the keys before twisting his upper body and squaring himself on me, waiting for me to push him again.

My fire has fizzled quite a bit, and I don't know if I'm brave enough to back up my actions, so I give him the answer I probably should have to begin with.

"There was nothing to say. I contacted my team, but I won't know if any of them received it until they respond, so there's nothing to report."

His gaze lowers, taking in my body as he considers my words. Unlike my reaction to the guy in the parking lot earlier, energy zaps at my nerve endings when Dagen looks me over.

"How do you contact your team in a situation like this?"

I'm not sure if he really wants to know or if he's testing me, but I answer anyway. "We communicate through the back end of an untraceable web address. We use files within the cPanel to leave messages. I left one, and now I wait for a response."

Headlights flicker through the trees as a car drives by, unaware of us parked only twenty feet away. I hadn't realized how fast the day slipped into the evening.

"And what message did you leave?"

"I said I was alive and making my way to the Peace Arch at the border. I would contact them again once I was across."

I open my mouth to say something else, then stop myself.

I also sent an image file to my team. I scanned the microfiche and attached it, asking if they could work their magic and extract the information Dagen would need from it. It's a long shot. As far as I understand, it can only be viewed by an archaic machine built specifically for microfiles. Telling Dagen this is admitting that I have the file, and I'm not ready to yet.

Dagen catches my gaze and glares at me in warning.

I'm no match for him when he has the scent of something, so I skip my thought and tell him the last thing I did before I powered off the computer. "I told them to pass your information on to my cousin. If I don't contact them again, she will find you."

Judging by the look on his face, I don't need to explain what it means if I don't get in touch. If something happens to me, my cousin will make sure Vaughn knows her father.

His face softens briefly before his dominance returns.

"You have a strong independent streak, and you're a fighter, Nyla, but you need to understand that I only appreciate those qualities when you accept that you are mine, and you act accordingly. This means you are to tell me everything, even if you deem it insignificant."

This triggers my attitude. "And what about you?"

Dagen cocks his head to the side. "What about me?"

"I heard you. On the phone to your brother—when you said, 'I can't talk about that right now.' I know you were talking about me, and I didn't appreciate being left out."

When Dagen smiles this time, I know my trouble just got worse.

"My brother asked if I retrieved the microfiche that—by the way—I haven't pushed with you. Then he asked me what was holding me back from getting it. I don't want to tell him about us or that I'm a father over the phone. Lennox has missed out on a lot because of our father, and when I tell him about something this important, I'll do it to his face."

I'm in the wrong, and I feel like a sack of garbage. No wonder I've caught him looking at me like he wants to throw down. I shouldn't have assumed the worst.

"Dagen, I'm s—"

His burner dings with a notification, and he pulls it out and reads a message before typing a response and pocketing it once again.

"Save it. We'll be late if I discipline you the way I want to."

My breath gets stuck in my throat.

Discipline me. The thought turns me on. My nipples are sensitive and tight in my bra at the fantasy.

Dagen retrieves the keys from his pocket and starts the car up, pulling onto the highway to continue south.

"So, you aren't going to discipline me?"

I don't know what I want his answer to be.

"I don't have to." He smirks. "You're going to do it for me."

27

DAGEN

Nyla made me crave tension: the sinful moment between one action and the inevitability of its consequence is now my favorite kink.

It electrifies my blood and courses through me as though it is possessing my very essence, making my fingers tingle, aching to touch, punish, and claim.

I'd been living with five years of pent-up anticipation, as it built at an excruciatingly slow pace from the moment she double-crossed me and left me in the desert until I found her again.

Now, as she sits quietly contemplating my words, the tension builds again.

If I had time to discipline her as I wanted, she'd be bent over the hood of the car with her pants around her ankles while I spanked and edged her until she begged me to fuck her ass so she could finally come.

My cock strains in my pants at the mental image.

She was saved by the literal bell when I got Lennox's

message that he would be meeting us in a town up the road about an hour and a half from here.

Every second she sits in silence is going to make what's coming that much worse for her.

While she doesn't make a sound, I sense she's deep in thought.

Nothing about any of our times together has been gentle. She knows I'm rough, and she gets off on it in spades every single time. While I haven't had the opportunity to sit her down and spell out what I like and ask the same of her, she has been receptive to the directions I nudge her in, and this punishment is just another push.

I keep my eyes on the road in front of me.

"Pull down your pants." I steal a glance from my peripheral vision, and even though she doesn't question me, I can tell by the way she sits that she's about to treat this like she has an option. "I won't ask again."

And I don't have to.

My face heats when she obeys quickly. She shuffles beside me, lifting her ass off the seat and pulling her pants down around her ankles. I allow her to leave her panties on.

Those damn yoga pants I picked up for her have been taunting me since she pulled them up over her firm ass this morning.

"Open your knees, pull your panties to the side, and show me what's mine."

Nyla peeks out the back window before slouching in her seat and spreading her legs.

I take a quick glance over.

Her pussy must have been shaved bare when she was in Alaska, as her hair is still in the stubble stage. She attempts to cover herself with her hand, and I lean over and smack it away with my own.

I return my attention to the highway in front of me, but not before I notice a glimmer of wetness at her center.

"It's important you tell me everything. So if you want to cover yourself from me, you'll have to use your words to ask. Am I making myself clear?"

"Yes," she answers, but she doesn't ask to hide herself.

"Good. Now turn your body so I can see you, and use your fingers to spread those lips open nice and wide for me."

A large semi is driving toward us in the opposite lane, and I keep my eyes on the road until it passes. When I glance over at Nyla, she's done what I asked.

I examine her face. She stares back at me in humbled silence. Her eyebrows are drawn together in contrition.

As I return my attention to the road, I catch movement out of the corner of my eye.

She's let go of her underwear.

"Did I say you could cover your pussy?" I chastise her.

"No."

"Did you ask to cover yourself?"

"N-no. Um." She curses at herself under a hissed breath, and I bite the inside of my cheek to stop myself from chuckling. "Can I cover myself?"

"You can, but keep your legs open." I allow it, but only because the sight of her is intoxicating, and I'm going to drive this piece of shit car off the road if she keeps showing me the one thing I can't have right now.

This punishment is meant to make her feel exposed and on display because she hid herself away from me when she failed to communicate properly.

"The next time you decide to hold information back from me, you will be doing this completely naked"—I grip the steering wheel as I say my next words; the visual in my mind is testing my restraint—"and you'll be wearing a butt plug and nipple clamps."

I am on a fucking roll tonight.

I leave her with the thought and drive in silence, forcing myself to keep my eyes on the road. She remains still beside me, suffering the consequences of her actions. The silence draws on for another fifteen minutes as I drive toward our destination.

Not once does she move or speak.

Eventually, she slips into a comfortable position and startles when I give my next command.

"Spank yourself."

I keep my attention on the road, but I sense her shifting beside me.

"What?" Nyla twists her weight to one side and lifts her hips, as though she's going to attempt to smack her own ass.

"No. Your pussy. You can do it over your underwear"—I level her with a side-eyed glare—"this time."

She places her hand over the cotton fabric, making one-syllable sounds as she fumbles around while staring down at herself with a mixture of shame and confusion.

"Why don't you lower the seat and lie back, get comfortable." When her gaze shoots up to meet mine, I soften my features to comfort her. "It's just us, Nyla. You're safe with me—in all ways. If you'd like to stop and discuss thi—"

"No!" She cuts me off. "I want to—I mean—I don't want to stop."

She turns away from me, searching around the side of the seat for the release before reclining the seat halfway.

The sight of her pants twisting over her boots is doing some strange shit to my control.

She reclines, slipping back from my peripheral vision. I sense this is very new for her, and having the buffer of me not being able to look her directly in the eyes while she disciplines herself might make this easier on her. This is a mercy I will allow her this time because she is keen to continue.

When she stills in the seat, I lean over. Keeping my eyes on the road, I trail my fingers up her inner thigh, reveling in the sensitive little tremors caused by my touch. I feel along the thin fabric covering her and zero in on the warm, wet spot I was hoping to find to further push her shame to the surface.

"Wider," I command, and she pulls her knees farther apart.

Her hips push up to meet my touch, and I remove my hand before slapping it against her clit.

Her lusty gasp tells me Nyla is exactly who I need, and I groan in response.

"That's how you'll do it."

Removing my hand, I return it to grip the wheel. I'm surprised I haven't ripped the steering column out of this car with all of my pent-up energy, but the night is still young.

I steady my breathing when a slap from Nyla catches me off guard, and my heart hammers into my chest at the little grunting sound she makes in response.

"Again."

I watch as she raises her hand and spanks herself a second time, and the sight is mesmerizing.

Quickly, I tear my gaze back to the road.

I can't continue to watch as I'd like, so I listen to each slap. Every groan, every heady breath, is music to my ears, but I don't look again.

"Do it again," I command, and she obeys. The sound of her panting is more prominent.

I tell her to spank herself a few more times before giving her a new command.

"Harder."

She increases without hesitation or question.

A highway sign catches my attention. Our destination should only be about five more minutes up the road.

"Again. Why are you punishing yourself, Nyla?"

She smacks her pussy before answering me.

This time, her voice is throaty. "Because I didn't communicate."

I tell her to ease off as I place my hand over hers just as the gas station comes into view. I take the turn into the station a little faster than I would have liked, and I park the car in the first free space I see, still well away from anyone else, and turn off the engine.

My hand remains cupped on top of hers over her mound when I lean over and unbuckle her seat belt.

"We're in this together. Tell me you understand."

Her shiny eyes stare up at me as her lips tremble, then she sniffles. "I didn't. But I do now. I'm sorry."

Then I kiss her, because I feel like I'm going to suffocate if I don't taste her pretty mouth again, and she hooks her arms under my jacket and around my midsection, pulling me into her.

I scan the area around the gas station, then lean closer to her and feel alongside the passenger's seat for the lever to drop the seat all of the way down.

"Tell me how it felt to spank your pussy. Was it dirty?" I whisper close to her ear, and she shudders underneath me. "It was, wasn't it? You liked it. Whipping yourself for me. Tell me, are you sensitive? Do you think I could make you come by punishing you like that?"

She nods, staring up at me with big round eyes.

"Let's try, shall we?" I lower my head, sucking in her lower lip before nibbling it, and she whimpers.

Now that the seat is all the way back, Nyla can't see out of the windows.

Pushing her hand aside, I tuck my fingers under the elastic of her panties and slide through her slick folds, and she groans.

My little hellion growls in frustration when I remove my hand and push her legs open wide, then I land my first smack.

Her sounds are telling. She was spanking herself in discipline; I know how to spank in pleasure, and she grinds her hips, arching her back in response.

I look out the window. "Hmm. There's my brother." Then I return my attention to her. "Are you going to come for me before he gets to the car, baby?"

"What?" Mortification laces her voice, and she tries to sit up.

I brace my arm across her chest, pinning her down.

"Ah, ah, ah." I spank her again, and her desire wages war with her pride. "If you're going to come for me, you better be quick, or he's going to see you lying here like my dirty little whore."

The threat of being caught does it. Nyla's eyes become unfocused, and she moans into my mouth as I smack her again.

"Yes." The word is drawn out and supplicating as she grinds against my touch. When I smack her again, her hands clench into fists around my shirt.

"He's almost here, baby."

I smack her again, then rub my discipline into her clit.

"I'm going to come. Please just once more?"

The movement in her legs is frenzied, and I lift my palm off her one last time. When the last strike lands, Nyla seizes underneath me, her foot bracing the rest of her body against the dashboard, her orgasm keening out of her, and I take everything in.

Her face, contorted and stretched in pleasure as her body heaves and bucks around me, makes me want to sink my cock deep inside of her right here, but I can't. Not yet.

As soon as her senses return to her, she tries to hurry up, reaching for the waist of her pants.

"We have to hurry. Your brother—"

"Isn't here yet." Bringing my fingers to my mouth, I coat the product of her orgasm on my lower lip as I finish her sentence for her.

Propping herself up on her elbows, she looks over the vacant lot before chuckling to herself. Then a vehicle pulls in, passing us and heading to the front of the gas station.

We watch in silence as the driver steps out of the vehicle first, followed by—

"That's Lennox. We need to get going."

Now I let her pull up her pants and fix herself until she is comfortable enough to tell me to approach them. I try to use the time to settle my raging erection, but the sight of Nyla and the smell of her sex isn't helping matters.

When I start the car, both men stop their approach to the building. They turn to watch us pull out from the last spot then drive toward them, their hands ready to grab the weapons they're hiding.

I turn off the lights and park five car lengths away, and Lennox visibly relaxes when we make eye contact.

Turning my attention to Nyla, I tell her to gather everything that is hers because she won't be getting back in this vehicle again. Then, adjusting myself as best as I can, I open my door.

Lennox waves his guy off when I get out of the car. He walks toward us, and I meet him halfway.

My brother looks like he's aged ten years since I last saw him, which was only about ten days ago.

I was going to introduce him to Nyla, but something feels very off.

"What don't I know?"

Lowering his gaze to the ground, Lennox drags his palm over the scruff of his neck.

"We can't find Dad, and I just heard from Cole: Elia is in palliative care. He has a few days left." Then his eyes drift over to Nyla standing five feet behind me. "All hell has broken loose, and they're coming—for her."

28

NYLA

The way Lennox looks at me as he tells Dagen people are coming for me sends chills down my spine. He doesn't know me at all, and he sizes me up like I'm a commodity.

The exchange affects Dagen too, and he steps in between us, cutting me off from his brother's stare.

"Nyla is mine."

The way Dagen challenges his brother makes the little hairs all over my body stand on end. They both look like they are not to be messed with, but Lennox is downright terrifying.

This claim goes deeper than possession, and Lennox takes a half step back and tilts his head, looking around Dagen's body at me with a different expression on his face.

The meaning is understood.

"Noted." Lennox takes a confident step toward me as Dagen wraps his arm around my shoulder and pulls me into his side.

The mood between the brothers feels strained but not dangerous.

"Do we know who put the hit on Nyla in place?"

"We have a lot to discuss, but we need to get somewhere safe first."

For the first time, Lennox looks troubled. Dagen notices it too.

"I just want the name. Is it Ratchet's group? Please just give me that. We can discuss it later. I need to—"

"It was Dad."

Dagen recoils like he's been slapped in the face, and my blood runs cold. We both know that I'm not the only one on that hit—Dagen is too, and that means his own father is trying to have him killed.

The answer knocks him back, and Lennox takes advantage and turns on me.

He gets right to the point. "Do you have it?"

While Dagen has spoken up for me, Lennox and I don't share the same understanding of what breaking my contract means.

I'm close to breaking it anyway, but there is no point in painting an even bigger target on any of us right now. Not until we can do anything with the file I'm carrying.

"Leave this with me." Dagen resumes his protective stance, stepping between us enough to stop the interrogation.

Lennox mutters something about *wasting time* before he turns to the man standing behind him and jerks his head to the side, telling him to approach.

"This is Leon. He's going to handle the car." Lennox points at the beater we drove here in, then he points at the gas station. "If you need anything, make it quick. We leave in five minutes."

Dagen reaches into his pocket and tosses the keys to Leon, who steps to the car without any further instructions.

"Give us a moment." Dagen drops his hand to my lower back, leading me toward the building.

When we are far enough away, he turns to face me. A world of pain is written all over his face. I can't imagine being betrayed on this level by my own family member, and it crushes my soul to see him like this.

"Dagen, are you o—"

He holds his hand up between us, silently asking me to avoid the question.

I don't think he's prepared to answer it.

He changes the subject when he pulls me into him, cupping my head to his chest. His chin moves against the top of my head as he speaks. "My brother won't hurt you. He's protective, and he can be an ornery asshole sometimes, but I trust him with my life, and you are a part of it now."

Dagen and Lennox are pillars of strength, and all three of these men are on high alert. Something tells me that surviving the wilderness was the easy part.

The severity of our situation and my uncertainty finally spill over. I use the comfort of Dagen's embrace to let myself feel, and I cry.

Dagen kisses my head and shushes me to comfort my anxiety. It feels good to have him in my corner.

"Let's get you some water and something to eat. Do you need to use the washroom before we go?"

I tell him I do, and he takes my hand, leading me into the gas station. "Washroom?" He addresses the attendant, and the kid behind the counter points to a hall at the back.

I try to pull my hand away and go on my own, but Dagen holds firm, walking in front of me all of the way to the door. He opens it and looks inside first before stepping into the hall and allowing me to enter. Then he tells me he'll grab some food.

I do my business at record speed and check myself out in the mirror. My eyes are puffy. I don't normally wear a lot of makeup, but I would pay good money for some concealer right about now.

I brace the palm of my hand against my stab wound and lift my arm. The pain is deep and dull; it's barely noticeable now.

When I rejoin Dagen, he is carrying a full plastic bag and a couple of water bottles. He tilts his head toward the snack section filled with sandwiches, salad, bananas, and other items. "I wasn't sure what you'd like, so I grabbed one of everything." He lifts the bag with a grin, then adds, "Except the granola bars. I've kind of had enough of them."

I chuckle when he sticks his tongue out in mock hurl as though the mere thought of it is making him queasy. I have to agree with him. It'll be a long time before I want a granola bar again.

Lennox and Leon are deep in conversation by the car we bought-stole, and I follow behind Dagen as we approach. Dagen's brother breaks away from their talk to look down at the large bag of food in his hand, then his gaze travels up to the both of us before he dismisses Leon and walks to their SUV.

Dagen offers me the front seat, but I decline, instead pointing at the back, and he opens the door before joining his brother up front.

We drive in an uncomfortable silence for a few minutes, and I dig through the bag, picking out a turkey sandwich, a banana, and some chips before handing the rest to Dagen.

He reaches behind the driver's seat and sets the bag on the floor, then opens his water, and I stare at him in surprise. We haven't eaten all day. He should be hungry.

"It's good to... I'm glad you're okay. I should have been there." It's clear Lennox isn't used to sharing his feelings. To an extent, this is something we have in common.

For someone so overwhelming and domineering, Lennox sure doesn't get along with words, and I stuff the sandwich in my face to ease the awkward moment and give me something else to focus on.

"I'm glad you weren't," Dagen answers matter-of-factly. "Did you find Nick?"

"Local authorities found his body in Fairbanks last week. It looks like he was killed right after he landed." Then Lennox turns his head toward both of us while keeping his eyes on the road, and he includes me in the conversation. "We have a couple of rooms about an hour up the road. I'll bring you both up to speed there. Ryder and Cole have been busy trying to find Dad and any of his closest associates. We've been locking down our businesses because we don't know what he has planned. There's no word from Mom. She hasn't texted Ryder in over a week."

Behind us, headlights flash between regular and high beams, and Lennox signals, pulling over to the side of the road before turning off his vehicle and looking between both of us. It isn't lost on me how much he is trying to include me. "We're going to ditch the car here. Give us a second."

Dagen looks like he wants to join them, and I nod at him, telling him I'll be fine in the car by myself. They leave me, locking the doors behind them, then cross the street as Leon turns the car around to face the opposite direction.

It's a smart move. It'll make it look like we were headed north when we abandoned the vehicle.

I watch them from the back seat while I peel my banana. The three of them gather around, pointing into the ditch on the far side of the road, then gesturing at a few more things before Lennox and Dagen step back and let Leon do his thing.

As they watch him start the car up, Lennox takes a side step closer to Dagen. He puts his arm around his brother, then taps him on the back before tugging him into him, and Dagen returns the little bit of brotherly affection.

The moment is overshadowed when Leon guns the engine, then gets out and steps away to pick up a thick branch from the ground. Leaning into the vehicle, he does something that makes the car rev louder, and I glance up the empty highway. It's getting late, and only one vehicle has passed by since we've pulled over.

I look back in time to see the back end of the car as it drives itself off the shoulder and into the ditch. Then all three men turn to walk toward me without watching where it ends up.

Dagen joins me in the back seat. As soon as he's buckled in, I reach into the bag and get him a sandwich. He holds his hand up to tell me no, and when he meets my stare I glare at him.

I know things are bad, but he needs to eat, and he must realize I'm not going to back down when he deflates in his seat, fastens his seat belt, and takes the sandwich.

I tap Lennox—who is now in the passenger's seat—on the shoulder and he startles. His wide eyes meet mine before they lower to the plastic bag in my hand, and he clears his throat to say thank you as he takes the bag.

He opens a sandwich and hands it to Leon, who has taken over the job of driving. Leon accepts it and eats, and Lennox doesn't take anything for himself.

Like brother like brother, I think to myself.

For as gruff as Lennox is on the outside, he takes care of the people around him. If I didn't know he was Dagen's brother, I would have first assumed he was Dagen's father. They are too close in age for that, but there is a paternal quality to the way he protects his inner circle.

Lennox and Dagen talk for a while about their mother. Dagen mentioned she is in the beginning stages of Alzheimer's when we were in the woods, and they are both concerned for her health since they don't know where their father has taken her.

I follow Leon's lead and keep my mouth shut.

Dagen shares snippets of our time together after the plane went down, and Lennox turns to look directly at his brother in surprise a couple of times as he recalls some of our more harrowing moments. A couple of Dagen's stories even earn me an impressed glance from his older brother.

The sky is pitch-black by the time Leon pulls into the motel parking lot. We are in the middle of another small town, and no businesses are open this late.

Dagen's low groan is the only indication I get that he can't wait to find more suitable accommodations.

I, however, just want a hot shower. Then I want to hop in bed and replay what Dagen made me do to myself in the car earlier before I fall asleep.

Lennox's voice cuts into the opening scene of my fantasy.

"We have the two at the end. We'll talk in my room." Lennox gets out of the SUV as soon as Leon turns it off. He steps to my door, opening it before Dagen can get to me first. Holding out his hand, he forces a smile. "I apologize, Nyla. I'm Lennox. That is Leon. Please forgive my—"

"Not necessary." I throw myself out of the vehicle, a little too excited to start over. "It's nice to meet you—both. Thank you for, um, coming for Dagen."

The pretense of his smile turns genuine by the time Dagen gets around to my side of the SUV, and Lennox turns to lead us toward the rooms.

Exhaustion hits me in a sudden wave.

I fall back and tug on Dagen's arm, and he stops just before entering the room behind the other two.

"Would you mind if maybe I could just take a shower and go to sleep?"

Dagen doesn't answer me. Instead, he ushers me into the room and gets Lennox's attention.

"Listen, Nyla's had a long day, and we need to talk privately—about a lot of things." The heavy way Dagen speaks makes me think he's planning to tell Lennox about our daughter. "Can Leon sit with Nyla in the other room while we catch up?" Lennox and Leon exchange a glance, and Leon shrugs as Dagen continues, "Just until we're done, then we'll switch places. I want someone with her at all times."

Lennox waves his hand to the door and tells me we'll talk in the morning, then Leon leads me out.

Just before I leave the room, Dagen hooks his fingers around my arm, turning me to face him, and, in front of everyone, he kisses me like he owns me. I'm panting to catch my breath when he breaks away. He reaches into my pocket, pulls out my phone, slides the back case open, and retrieves Vaughn's photo before returning the phone to me. Then he smirks and sends me out the door.

I follow Leon to a second room on wobbly legs with a dopey grin on my face.

I'm sure my cheeks are a bright shade of red under the harsh lights hanging over the door when Leon turns and speaks directly to me for the first time in his baritone voice: "Damn girl, that Saint has it bad for you."

29

DAGEN

As soon as the door shuts and I'm alone in the room with Lennox, I struggle to find the words. We have so much to talk about, and I don't know where I want to start.

Sensing my unease, Lennox walks to the sink and runs the water before taking off his jacket and hanging it in the closet.

He splashes some water on his face, then leaves the tap running while he braces his hands on either side of the sink and stares at his reflection. Finally, he hangs his head, turns off the tap, and reaches for a towel.

He opens the little fridge on his way back to me, pulling out a bottle of bourbon, then grabs two cups wrapped in paper. He joins me at the table, taking a chair across from me.

While he pours, I mentally list all of the things I want to say, then I just decide to suck it up and start with what is most important to me.

"I'm a dad, Lennox. I have a daughter."

Lennox stills. His hand holding his drink is halfway between the table and his lips. His eyes turn glassy.

"Nyla—Nyla and I have a daughter. It's—I found out a few days ago. You're the first person I've told."

Lennox's lips move, and he blinks rapidly before he speaks. "That's—I have a niece. Dagen, congratulations."

I slide Vaughn's photo across the table, and Lennox sets his drink down to pick it up. His eyes flash between taking me in and her smiling face.

"What's her name?" Lennox looks up from the photo with glossy eyes.

I clear my throat. "Vaughn."

"Vaughn," he repeats. "Wow, that's—"

"Fucked-up." I answer for him, and he shakes his head.

"No, you dumb shit. That's your middle name." I haven't seen Lennox genuinely smile for a long time. "Did she know?"

"Yeah," I answer with a smug pride I feel in my chest. "She gave her my name."

"And Ryder and Cole don't know?" Lennox glances at me warily.

I tell my younger brothers everything, but this is different.

Out of all of my brothers, I am the closest to Lennox. We're the two oldest, and we spent the most time together growing up. It's part of the reason why I carry so much guilt about not noticing he was in trouble. I was close to his age; I should have recognized the signs when he pulled away. I shouldn't have been so quick to assume we were just "becoming men."

This is also why I wanted Lennox to be the first to know about Vaughn. Because of the choices he's made, he has been pushed out of all of our lives.

Ryder and Sloane's engagement is a sham, and Henry isn't his. Ryder and Amara have since been married, and Lennox knows none of this.

Cole and Harlow might as well be married, and, while he knows about them, we still haven't had the luxury of getting together over drinks so he can meet the women in my brothers' lives.

I couldn't deny him being left out of another secret.

I know all of these things will come to light eventually.

My brothers desperately want to come clean with Lennox and let him in, but our situation is too volatile to add this type of fuel to a fire that is already burning out of control.

Lennox stands and takes two steps around the table, lifting me up by my arms and pulling me into him.

"I am so happy for you." He doesn't break the embrace until I hug him back. "How do you feel about it? I mean, yeah, how are you?"

We sit back down, and Lennox lifts his glass, this time to clink with mine.

"I'm—I haven't met her yet, but I can't imagine not being her dad. At the same time, I'm terrified of what kind of dad I'll be. I'm more worried about failing her than I am of getting out of this country alive. How fucked-up is that?"

For the first time in a long time, Lennox laughs. "It's not fucked-up. I know the feeling. I used to worry about Cole and Ryder all of the time."

I smile at the camaraderie in his answer before his words sink in.

Lennox shouldn't have had to be worried like that for any of us. He is our brother, not our father, but he gave up the experience that comes along with being our older brother in order to be the parent we should have had.

"I shouldn't have gone out on my own." I speak my thoughts out loud, and Lennox's smile slips. "You never should have had to do what you did on your own. I should have—"

Lennox cuts me off. "Here's what we're not going to do: we are not going to regret the choices we made"—he holds up

Vaughn's photo—"because if life hadn't happened exactly the way it did, my beautiful niece wouldn't be here."

Lennox drains his glass, then pours himself a little more and adds to mine. I take my first sip; the burn in my throat is welcome after the week we've had.

"You didn't abandon us, Dagen. You lived your life. This shit is all on Dad. Our father fractured us. He made us compete against each other, to weaken us, but that's in the past. We are together; we will overcome this together. I'm taking my fucking brothers back. Then I'm going to kill that son of a bitch, because I'm done being his *son*." He chokes on the last word, and I feel it in my heart.

Lennox clears his throat with a cough before taking a sip and standing to put the bottle away. That's his way of telling me this particular conversation is over. He hasn't shared what our father has done that made him decide to step up and protect the three of us by setting the boundaries he did. I know he will, but now isn't the time. Now, we have to get out of Canada, find our father, and bring our mother back.

"So Dad wants me dead then?" I raise my glass in cheers to the air with that nugget of information.

I can't say I'm surprised. He tried to have Cole murdered when he couldn't find me the first time.

"He wants all of us dead." Lennox's acerbic tone sours my stomach. "Ryder and Cole have the house on lockdown. We have our own lawyers and accountants going through everything. Dad's ship is sinking, and we're working around the clock to cut ourselves free before we get dragged down with him. Cole spoke to Creed earlier today. They're up to their eyeballs with their turf war. He didn't mention anything about the hit on Nyla or you, and we've decided not to share that information until we can get you across the border and figure everything out."

"Who did Dad send? As far as I know, he didn't have a lot of men when he 'retired.' He just kept the bare minimum, to keep him and Mom guarded."

"I found out he's been working with Ratchet's group for a few years at least. They were doing his dirty work for him. It's not Ratchet who is planning a takeover of Elia's organization —it's Dad. He wants to absorb Lucciano under the Saint name, and he's promised Ratchet the second-in-command position."

"If Creed finds out about this and we don't have solid evidence showing our loyalty to him, he'll think we've betrayed him. That's how I would see it."

Lennox points at me and nods.

This is why they haven't mentioned that I'm out here after Nyla and the microfiche.

It's bad enough that Dad sent Ratchet's men after us. If Creed came after us with all of his firepower as well, we would be dead in the water.

I was going to ask Lennox to reach out to Creed and ask if he knows anything about Nyla's brothers, but I can't tip him off about any of this until we can bring him what he needs.

"Where do we go from here?" I ask, draining my drink. My arms feel warm from the alcohol.

"Tomorrow, we head for Vancouver. I'm going to take a better picture of Nyla and send it off, and we'll have passports for both of you waiting by the time we get there. Ryder and Cole are adamant about being there to escort you both across the border. They actually wanted to be here now, but they saw reason."

"And by 'reason,' you mean..."

"I told them no, and they're both pissy about it."

The image Lennox weaves of our brothers throwing a fit because they didn't get their way makes me chuckle, even though I would feel the same frustration if either Ryder or Cole were in trouble.

"And the girl—" Lennox stops himself and backtracks. "And Nyla. How did this happen?"

I'm reminded again about how little I've spoken to Lennox over recent years.

"Do you remember me telling you about a woman who handcuffed me to a tree during one of my jobs?"

He smiles as familiarity dawns in his eyes. "Oh yeah. That was—what?—five years ago?" Then he sits up straight. "Shit! Is that her?"

When I nod, he looks at the closed door of his room with a new sense of fascination in my little vixen. I had told Lennox I was hunting someone from my past, but I didn't go into great detail at the time. When I set out to find Nyla, I had told myself it was to settle a debt and recover the microfiche. I didn't want my brothers asking too many questions because I didn't want to answer them.

"I'm bagged. Thanks for this." I stand, tapping my empty glass, and Lennox rises too. "And thank you for coming up here. This"—I wave around the room to indicate, well, everything— "was getting hard."

"There isn't anything I wouldn't do for you." There's something in the way Lennox says it that makes me believe he's already sold his soul to the devil for us, and he'd do it again without blinking.

At the same time, the guy is still carrying around the sins of our father, and I hope to hell that one day he'll let us all shoulder them with him.

Instead of telling him that, I say good night and excuse myself. The liquor and the long day have finally taken their toll, and I step into the cool air outside. Leon stands from his place on a bench outside our door, and I join him.

He points to the door beside their room. "This is yours." He hands me a key. "She took a shower, then crawled into bed. Out like a light."

"Thanks, man." I don't stick around to talk.

I slide the key into the lock and let myself in.

The room is dark, but there is enough light from the bathroom that I can make my way across the room without running into anything.

I kick off my shoes and strip down, then slide under the covers until I'm pressed against the warmth of Nyla's freshly showered body. She's turned away from me, but as soon as I touch her, she rolls over, shimmying across the mattress and curling herself into my arms without waking.

I've become used to having her near me when I close my eyes. Her washed hair smells like strawberries, and I kiss the top of her head while combing my fingers through her damp strands.

Something happened between Fairbanks and here that has altered my path. We had to rely on each other, we saved each other, and we worked together. She taught me how to fish and how to forage. She carved her presence into my soul, and I can no longer be without it.

I went into the wild a very different man. I came out better. I came out *more*, and Nyla once told me she stayed with me the first night we met because she wanted more. I hope I'm now the more she is looking for, because I won't let her go.

Being this close to Nyla settles my demons.

When I know she's safe, I'm calm.

Lennox laid out our next steps as though they were a walk in the park, but I have a feeling getting across that border is going to be one of the hardest things any of us has ever done.

NYLA

When I fell asleep last night, I was alone. Waking up, I'm alone again, but I know Dagen was here at some point.

His side of the bed is messy, and I'm hugging a pillow. I've never woken up with my arms around a pillow before, and I wonder if I was curled around him and he used the pillow as a surrogate, to comfort me and help me sleep longer.

When I bury my face into the pillowcase, it smells like him.

"Dagen?"

No answer.

I toss back the covers and jump out of bed, opening the curtains to a bright, sunny morning.

Leon's unmistakable large frame sits on a bench just outside of the room, and I open the door to catch his attention.

"Good morning." He points down and across the street. "They went for breakfast. Get dressed and packed, and I'll walk over with you." He takes a sip from a mug that looks exactly like the ones near the single-serve coffee maker in our room. Then he grimaces, and I decide to wait to grab a coffee until we get to the restaurant.

"Why are you drinking that if it tastes bad?" I ask with a hint of humor in my tone, and Leon smiles.

"I'm fitting in." He gestures to the empty parking lot with his cup. "I'm just a guy traveling through, drinking a cup of coffee to start his day. If I had carried out your *boyfriend's*"—he winks at me when he uses the term—"instructions to the letter, I would have been standing in front of your door with my arms crossed, silently threatening anyone who looked this way. Now, I don't know if you've noticed, but I'm a big, scary motherfucker, and shit like that draws attention."

We stare at each other in amused silence for a while before I decide I like Leon, and I take a few steps and join him on the bench, yawning and stretching.

Leon is built like a linebacker.

On the bench, our side-by-side size difference is obvious.

"How did you come to work for Lennox?"

Leon looks down the street toward the diner in contemplation before he answers. "The Saints own a group of —clubs. I wanted a fresh start, and I was new to town. I was... looking for someone. Anyway, lots of stuff happened, and Lennox helped me find her and get her out of the situation she was in."

"When you say, 'lots of stuff happened,' is that your way of saying it's none of my business?"

He grins at that. "You're a perceptive little pet, aren't you?" Leon smirks, and I blush before crossing my arms, leaning back, and changing the subject.

"So this is a debt you're repaying?"

"No. To call it a debt insinuates that Lennox asked for something in return for being a decent human being. I work for Lennox because finding honorable men these days feels like navigating a minefield. You work for a bad man, and it's just a matter of time before you find their knife in your back."

His gaze travels just over my shoulder, and he smiles, lifting his cup in greeting like a good neighbor. When I follow his line of sight, a young woman a few doors down smiles back as she straightens her maid's uniform and goes back to her business, pulling towels out of a cart.

I sit quietly beside Leon for a few minutes more. Then he tells me to get ready and we'll get some greasy food in us before we leave town.

I tell him I'll only be about five minutes, and he holds the mug up before taking another sip. It's followed by that same scowl, and I chuckle as the door closes behind me.

I cross the room to our duffel. I peel off the yoga pants Dagen bought me and exchange them for a matching pair. Either Dagen must like yoga pants, or the store had an extremely limited selection, because I ended up with two of the same thing. I exchange the top for a cleaner version of itself as well.

I decide to leave my old clothes behind on the bed. This isn't a vacation. I want to be practical, and these clothes will only be deadweight.

It looks as though Dagen has packed everything he wants to take in the duffel already. I'm surprised he was able to do that this morning without waking me.

I scan the items he chose to leave behind. The bag of sandwiches has been left out for too long, so they won't be good to eat. I check the bathroom one last time and end up taking the small package of mouthwash and an unopened bar of soap.

We've been on our own and in survival mode for too long, and these feel like luxuries I don't want to leave behind.

I grab my phone out of the duffel and check the empty compartment before slipping it into my pocket. I want to ask

Dagen if I can have Vaughn's photo back. It's more of a comfort than anything; it's all I have until I see her again.

I also want to hand the microfiche over once I know we're all safe.

I've been tempted to give the microfiche to Dagen for days now, and each time I try a wave of dread hits me and I decide not to. At first, I thought that I subconsciously didn't believe he was telling the truth, or that I shouldn't trust him. I've come to realize that I knew he was, and I knew we had unfinished business between us. I felt our connection, and I know how much of a bargaining chip this microfiche is now.

More than anything, I want to see Vaughn again, but Dagen is quickly becoming just as much a part of my family, and I think he feels the same.

That being said, I haven't told him I have the microfiche on me because I'm afraid he'd give it up to protect me. I know I would do the same for him.

I know these men are coming after me.

Dagen isn't their priority, and as long as they believe this, they won't use him to get the microfiche from me. No one knows about Vaughn's existence except Dagen, and I know neither of us would ever divulge this secret because we both know what is at stake.

I lift the straps of the duffel and hook it over my shoulder. I take two steps before I realize I'm carrying it on the same side where I was stabbed. The pain is gone now, and I'm able to carry the weight without problems.

I walk once around the room, opening drawers and closets and looking under the bed for anything I may have missed. Then I join Leon outside at the back of the SUV.

"I thought you had more than this." He slips the duffel off my shoulder and slides it between two cases in the back.

"It was just this and the big bag of food Dagen bought last night."

"Right." Leon responds over his shoulder as he organizes a few items. He pulls a barrel bag to the top and unzips it before muttering to himself, "Dammit."

"Everything okay?" I ask.

Leon glances at his closed door before looking at me. "I left my travel kit in the room. I'll just be a minute." He searches his pocket for the key, then turns to level me with a "stay here" glare before jogging to his door.

I lower the trunk but don't close it, since Leon will need to pack his kit into his bag when he returns.

The sun is hot on my back today, and I turn around to soak it up. Closing my eyes and tilting my head in the direction of the warmth, I take a deep breath.

I should talk to Dagen about checking in with my team to see if they've uploaded their own message. I'm sure two teams working together is better than one, and I can probably speed up the passport process for me since we have a list of unused identities all ready to go. I also want to get a message to my cousin to let her know I'm okay. I know her better than most, and if she doesn't hear from me soon, she'll search out Dagen herself in order to find me.

When I lower my head and open my eyes, I have to blink rapidly, as it takes a few seconds for my surroundings to come back into focus.

We're on the main road through town, and there isn't a lot of traffic right now. Lennox's SUV looks out of place among the more rugged trucks parked around us. The only other car that looks as out of place just pulled up and parked across the street from us.

Three men, dressed almost entirely in black, get out of the vehicle. I freeze, unable to move as the hairs on my body stand on end. Their backs are turned, and they're all staring at the closest building to them across the road.

I take a slow step to the side, sure they'll turn around and see me. When they don't, I take another, telling myself I just need to make it into one of our rooms.

It isn't until one of them turns around that my world tilts on its axis.

As our eyes meet, memories and familiarity pull me forward. On impulse, I take one step forward, my arms falling limp at my sides.

The man I think I recognize says something to the men he's with, and they all look over at me, but no one moves.

A hurtful pang slices at my heart, and I take another step.

This can't be.

He's a lifetime older than I remember him, and I wonder how I must look to him.

Then it hits me.

He thinks I'm dead.

With my father's blessing, I quietly had the documents created for my passing and subsequent cremation. There was no funeral. I had no close friends that would have torn apart the world looking for me, and my cousin is the only other family member who knew, understood, and kept my secret.

He circles the car and looks both ways before crossing the road toward the motel, and I walk across the parking lot in a daze to meet him with the sting of tears in my eyes.

I've imagined this moment for so many years. I used to cry myself to sleep wondering where he was and if he was alive. I wondered if he thought about me or if he missed me.

When I'm two steps away, I stop.

He looks over his shoulder, lifting his hand toward the men he is with, and they get back in their car.

Then he looks at me once again.

His smile isn't the same as I remember, but it could be the shock of seeing me alive.

The fleeting thought that I must be dreaming hits me, and I blink, causing a tear to roll over my cheeks.

There's only one way to know for sure.

"I don't believe it. Carson, is that you?"

DAGEN

I want to say this is the best cup of coffee I've ever had, but I think going a week with little to no coffee at all might be swaying my judgment.

The waitress, an older woman wearing a stained apron, fills our mugs for the second time as Lennox thanks her with a curt smile. She's glanced over at us a few times in the last ten minutes. No doubt, we stick out in this little town like sore thumbs.

"How are Sloane and Henry doing?"

I'm worried about the little guy in all of this. Ryder has limited his connection with our father since we found out what was happening, and he's told me Sloane has been asking him why.

We made the decision not to share what we know about our father killing Grayson until we had enough leverage to stop him.

Sloane loved Grayson, and there is no way she'd have survived these last months knowing what our dad had done. Still, keeping this from her has been hard on all of us.

Lennox tenses across from me, so I give him a moment to answer. I use the pause to look outside and across the street at our motel. Leon is still sitting on the bench. Just before I look back at my brother, the door to our room opens, and Nyla pops her head out.

Seeing her makes me smile.

"They're fine." His answer is clipped.

He never hovers on Sloane.

We all know bits of what happened between them, but Lennox is a private person, and he holds his feelings close to his heart. I still don't know why he sent Sloane away when she chose him, but it isn't my business. That, and Sloane has asked all of us to respectfully stay out of it.

I know it hurts her more than she shows.

They've both moved on since then, and Sloane tries to keep the peace for our and Henry's sake.

When I look back across the street, both Leon and Nyla are gone. The waitress comes back to ask if we're ready to order for the fourth time. Lennox is ready to wave her off, but I stack the menus and order four of their early riser specials. When she cocks her head at me, I tell her we are expecting company and ask for two additional cups of coffee.

I have no idea how fast the cook is, and I know Lennox is agitated and ready to get on the road.

"Still nothing on Dad?" I take another sip of my coffee, and Lennox's shoulders relax a fraction.

He won't admit it, but I can tell he's happy to move on from talking about Sloane.

"No. I spoke to Cole this morning. He has his tech guy looking into a few things. I have people looking for his inner circle now."

Lennox glances out the window, and I look again. Leon and

Nyla are at the trunk, packing up. They'll be on their way over here any minute.

"You care for her." Lennox doesn't mean it as a question, but I nod anyway.

"I think I always did." I look over at Nyla while I talk. Her eyes are closed, and her face is tilted up toward the sun. She looks peaceful and happy, and I want her to always feel that way. "There's just something about her that—fits. I mean, we have a way to go before we really know each other, but she makes me want to fight for it—for her, for us. I can't describe it."

"I know what you mean." Lennox's words catch me off guard, and when I meet his gaze, there is a lot of unspoken regret written all over his face.

I'm tempted—so tempted—to ask him why he let Sloane go way back when.

We all see the way he looks at her, even now. Don't get me wrong, Grayson was like a brother to me, probably to all of us, but witnessing Lennox in his self-imposed exile from Sloane over the years has been torturously hard to watch.

The question is in my chest, dangerously close to surging up my throat and out of my mouth, when Nyla catches my attention from her spot in the parking lot.

She's looking across the street, almost right at us, and her face has lost the carefree ease it held just a moment earlier.

A world of emotions I don't recognize have replaced her smile, and I squint at her, trying to make out if she's crying. Her expression is pained as she takes a few steps across the motel parking lot and toward the street.

Then I pull my attention away from her long enough to see a man has crossed the street and is walking toward her. I only see the back of his head, and I grunt in confusion, drawing Lennox's attention out the window.

A flash of recognition crosses her face, and she smiles at

whoever's approaching. I wonder for a second where Leon is—then everything tilts sideways and goes off the rails.

Leon yells at Nyla, and I hear it from inside the diner.

The expression on Leon's face spurs me into motion, and I'm up and at the door to the diner in a flash.

I all but fall onto the pavement behind a parked car as a gunshot echoes through this little town, and screams erupt from all around us.

I look for Nyla, and my gaze settles on Leon as he stumbles back, dropping his gun and falling to the ground.

Lennox is already beside me.

Nyla is playing tug of war with her own arm, and she slips out of the guy's grasp and runs back to Leon. She doesn't try to save herself; she's trying to help him. She leans over Leon, but I can't see what she's doing.

Tires peel from a block away, and Lennox draws his gun. The guy in the street also has a gun drawn, and he quickly closes the distance and pulls her off of Leon, who remains down and unable to help her.

"CARSON!" Nyla screams when he fists a handful of her hair to try to control her.

A wave of nausea hits me when she yells her brother's name, and I try to get a look at the man with her.

I finally see his face when he spins them both around, holding her back to his front and using her as a shield while he tries to locate us.

"Ratchet," Lennox hisses. "I'm going to kill—"

"Don't."

I won't chance him hitting Nyla.

I try to stand up.

I already know offering myself in her place is a bad decision. There's no way he'll take me when they must know she's the one who has access to the microfiche.

When he sees me, he doesn't try to negotiate. Tightening his hold on her hair, he yanks Nyla into him and aims his gun at us.

She lifts his arm high, and the shot comes nowhere near me, but it's given Lennox time to get to me and pull me down behind a car.

Lennox braces himself on the hood of the parked car and aims his gun once more, telling me he isn't going to fire unless he has a shot, but a car pulls between us, blocking our view.

Seconds later, it squeals out, heading south.

Nyla is gone, and I'm off and running across the road with Lennox toward Leon.

He coughs and groans as we approach, muttering how sorry he is followed by a string of profanities. Lennox covers his wound with his hands and pats Leon down. He finds what he's looking for when he pulls Leon's phone out of his front pocket.

"I've been shot." Lennox pretends to be Leon when the emergency operator answers. He rattles off our location, then hangs up before turning his attention to Leon and slipping his phone back into his pocket where he found it. He examines the wound. "Hang on. They'll be here—"

We exchange glances. We're in the middle of fucking nowhere. If we were in the city, then it might only be ten minutes until help arrives. I don't even know how far we are from a city.

Leon lifts his bloody hand, holding the keys between us. "You need to go," he says to Lennox, then looks at me. "Take my gun."

I look over at the weapon lying a few feet away.

"Leon—" Lennox is shaken.

My brother is a good man.

He is loyal to the people who are loyal to him.

"No. Here." Leon shoves a phone into my hand before saying, "She gave me this just now. Go—help her."

It's a good sign that Leon is still able to speak with little effort.

"And you?" Lennox asks.

"What do you mean?" Leon groans in pain. "I'm just a guy on vacation, trying to enjoy Mother Nature and all that shit." His cough ends with a humorless chuckle.

It's his way of saying he'll cover for us.

"I'll be in touch." Lennox clasps his hands around Leon's, then meets my gaze. "Let's go."

I reach over, grab the gun, and run to the SUV, slamming the trunk shut. Lennox already has the car started, and it's rolling back as I jump in the passenger's side.

Tires screech as he speeds out of the lot and heads south.

"How did he know where to find her?" I watch the road in front of us, hoping to see the ass end of their car. They know we'll be coming, so they'll be driving just as fast as we are.

"I think it was just luck. We still have a couple of guys who are close to him. Ratchet isn't pulling any punches this time. He put most of his men on this. Now that they have her, he'll probably call them back to the front lines in Portland to deal with Creed."

I grip her phone in my lap, sliding the compartment on the back open and closed. This was where she hid Vaughn's photo—the photo I still have. She doesn't have it with her, and that thought makes me furious before another moment of clarity hits me.

"She yelled her brother's name."

"What?" Lennox shoots me a look before returning his eyes to the road.

Our speed increases.

"Carson. Nyla yelled that name before Ratchet took her.

She was yelling it at him." The voice in my head begins to repeat the word "no" over and over again. "That's her brother's name. Nyla told me that she's estranged from her brothers because they had gotten into something their father didn't approve of." The car is silent for a few horrible minutes as we continue to speed down the highway. Eventually I put my fear into words: "I think Ratchet is her brother."

"Shit." At first I think it was me who said that out loud, but then Lennox keeps talking. "If Ratchet is her brother, then—"

"Just a minute. I'm thinking. I didn't know Ratchet had a brother in Elia's organization. We need to find him before—"

Lennox returns the favor, cutting me off just as fast. "You already know him." He swears under his breath.

Lennox swerves to the side of the road, and I'm ready to yell at him to keep going when he squares himself on me. "It's Creed."

My ears ring.

So this is what an epiphany feels like. I'm physically sick as a wave of tremors blindsides me, and my life as I know it drains out of me.

"What? How do you—"

"I met Creed when he first started with Elia a long time ago, before any of you were introduced to the family business. When I met him, he went by J-something."

"Jonah."

Lennox nods, then continues, "A little later, he started going by his middle name, Credence. Anyway, I guess there was an incident, and Creed stepped up, saving Elia's life. Elia took to Creed fast after that. He groomed him and trained him to be his next in line after his second was gunned down almost fifteen years ago now. I knew they were brothers, but it's a piece of information that has been left out over the years, especially now that they're trying to kill each other. Blood means nothing when all you want to do is spill it."

I lean into the passenger side door as though this information just physically assaulted me.

Ratchet and Creed are related, and worse—way worse—is that Nyla is their sister.

Then everything settles on me like the very epic shitstorm it is, and I grip her phone to my chest.

I'm fucking Creed's sister, and I'm the father of his niece, and he is going to deadass murder me if we make it out of this alive.

NYLA

I remember three things after Leon was shot.

I remember running to him to make sure he was okay. Leon put himself in danger to warn me, and he was shot because of me. I had to tell him how sorry I was. Carson isn't the brother I remember, and I needed to get the microfiche off of my person, but I didn't have time or privacy to tell him it was in my phone case.

Then next thing I remember was the look on Dagen's face when Carson fisted my hair and pulled me around to try to locate him. There is a point when fear becomes tangible, when it creates its own gravity, tearing everything you wish you'd said and moments you'll never have away from you.

The anguish on Dagen's face will be etched into my brain for whatever time I have left to live.

The last thing I remember was being shoved into the back of a car. My initial shock and the localized pain at the back of my scalp made me easy to maneuver.

My memories garbled when a sharp prick in my shoulder sent adrenaline through my body. Two sets of arms held me down while I struggled against them until my body grew weak. Then I lay across Carson's lap like a sack of potatoes, unable to fight back and staring at the back of the passenger's seat until I blacked out.

My brother didn't say one word to me the whole time.

"She awake yet?"

The unfamiliar male voice is followed by a kick to my back, and I groan from my place on the floor.

"Give her a few," comes the impassive reply from a second man in the room, and I listen to the thud of footsteps retreating along the floorboards when the same man says, "You can sit up, but don't try anything."

I realize his threat is pointless when I try to push myself into a seated position only to find my hands tied behind my back. My fingers are cold.

The back of my eyeballs hurt, and my head feels like it weighs ten pounds more than it should.

Folding my legs, I roll my weight onto my hip and peel my upper body off the spot on the floor.

The sun shining through the window is bright, so I can't have been out for long. I haven't peed myself, so it isn't the next day.

"Where are we?"

My question goes unanswered, so I look around the room for clues.

Family portraits sit on every shelf and across the top of a piano against a wall, and two knit blankets cover an old couch. The room smells like nutmeg, and a cross-stitch project has been abandoned on a chair.

We were hours from Vancouver, and this isn't a hotel.

My stomach twists.

Carson wouldn't own a piece of property all the way out here in the middle of nowhere.

Where are the people who live here?

My stomach growls. "Can I have some water?" There's no point in asking for food, but maybe I can get away with asking for the bare necessities.

Nope.

Not getting an answer to that question either.

I cross my legs and use the silence to try to listen for any hint of where I am or what's going on. There is nothing but a gentle breeze blowing through an open window, causing the curtains to flap.

After a couple of minutes, the sound of footsteps approaching makes the man in the room with me stand up and straighten his jacket.

When the door opens this time, it's my brother who enters.

"Cars—"

"Leave us." Carson addresses the man with us but holds his gaze on me.

The guy leaves without a word as Carson walks to a small desk in the corner, lifts a chair, and sets it in front of me before sitting on it. He makes no move to help me up.

"Carson—"

"Isn't my name. Not anymore. You can call me Ratchet." He threads his fingers together, clasping his hands and bracing himself against his elbows on his lap.

I guess the nickname makes sense. Carson was always working on an old car he bought himself with money he saved from his first job.

"Whose place is this? Are they—okay?"

He levels me with a scowl. "You don't want that answer. They are in the barn."

I feel sick.

My stomach rolls, and I'm close to dry heaving.

"Where's Jonah?"

His mood sours when I say our brother's name.

Growing up, I was closest with my oldest brother, and Carson always seemed to be distant from our family. He used to tell me to get lost when his friends were around, so I stopped searching him out after a while.

He ignores my question with one of his own: "Where's the microfiche, *BJ?*"

My expression turns to match his at the name he used to call me when no one else was around. At first, I liked it. I thought he used the initials of my first and last name because he cared and that was our thing. Then one of my friends overheard him call me that and told me what a BJ was. After that, I felt stupid.

"It was destroyed, per my contract. Why do you want it anyway?" I play dumb, hoping it will keep me alive until I can figure out how to get out of here and back to Dagen.

"That's none of your business." He leans forward, dragging his hands over his face. "Who hired you?"

"That's none of *your* business." I throw his words back at him.

I'm not fast enough to avoid his backhand. The impact ricochets through my temple and into my skull as my body timbers to the side. I'm unable to brace myself with my hands bound behind my back.

I suck in a deep breath to replace the air that was just knocked out of me.

He sighs in frustration, leans over, and lifts me without care into the position I just fell over from, as though he's lining me up to do it again.

This is not my brother, not anymore.

"I don't know who hired me. Our channels are encrypted. It protects everyone for this exact reason." I run my tongue along the inside of my cheek to soothe the tender spot I bit when he hit me.

I don't bother telling him I originally took the job because I wanted to stick it to Elia Lucciano, or that I was looking for him. The mere concept that I wasted my time wondering if he was okay is ridiculous to me now.

"You're going to give us access to your freelance account. We're going to hack it to find out who hired you."

"I won't."

He looks at me as though I've challenged him. Then he leans forward, hovering in my space, and I hate that I flinch.

"You will, but you're in luck. There's no internet out here, and we don't have the equipment we need, so we're heading out at dusk and driving overnight to Vancouver. You have until tomorrow morning to decide if you're going to help us gain access. If you don't, you'll never see Mom or Dad again."

Or Vaughn or Dagen. My eyes well with tears, but I keep my secret to myself. It's best for them if Ratchet thinks I'm crying over our parents.

There's no hesitation, no uncertainty in his threat.

He means what he says.

If I don't help them when we reach Vancouver, he'll kill me.

"You should have stayed dead, *Nyla,*" he says. It's the same tone he'd use if he were saying *I told you so.*

He's never called me by my middle name before. He's telling me he heard about my death, and he's telling me he didn't care and I should have stayed gone.

I'm no one to him.

I often wondered if hearing that I had died bothered my brothers. If they ever took a moment to mourn me, or remember happier times. I wondered if losing their little sister mattered.

Now I know.

"I'll send in something for you to eat." He stands, moving the chair away from me.

My brother's apathy hurts more than the actual slap in the face I took. He won't even sit in the same room as me for what little time I have left.

He stops before he reaches the door and returns his attention to me.

"You asked me about Jonah." He says his name as though it makes him sick. "He goes by Creed now. He's hunting you too. You always saw things the way you wanted to see them, not the way they are. We are not the brothers you think you know. You will do well to remember that. It will make what's coming easier to accept."

Credence was Jonah's middle name.

Hearing that he is hunting me too is a harder pill to swallow.

Jonah always looked out for me.

He called me Lady Bug. He said I was a lady, and no boy would ever be good enough for me, and he said I was a bug because I always bugged him. Then we'd laugh. I knew he wasn't being the same type of mean that Carson was when he called me BJ.

My friends used to tell me how hunky Jonah was. He'd go out of his way to lavish me with attention whenever they were around, and he'd leave them in jealous, googly-eyed fits. I thought about trying to find him over the years, but Dad said it would only lead to my broken heart.

He was right.

I was never close to Carson, but I thought family meant something.

I'm so lost in my thoughts that I didn't notice the changing of the guard.

Ratchet is gone without a goodbye, and in his place stands

his chatty friend, carrying a tray. When he sets it on the coffee table in front of the couch, my stomach growls at the sight of the bread and jam.

Returning to stand behind me at my spot on the floor, he wraps his hands around my upper arms and lifts me to my feet, not bothering to wait to see if I can stand on my own. I'm threatened with the unknown when he says, "Don't try to get away, or else," as he tugs on my binds.

I can tell by the way it chafes against my wrists as he works the knots loose that I'm tied with coarse rope. As soon as my hands are released, I hold them in front of me, rubbing along the raw, red lines the strands have burned into my skin.

No wonder my hands felt cold. My fingers are a ghostly shade of white due to lack of circulation, and they tingle when I press them against each other.

He points to the food on the tray with a one-word command: "Eat."

It's the last thing I want to do.

I take a seat and reach for a sealed bottle of water. My tongue is dry and fuzzy, and I can't deny myself the hydration that my body needs, but somehow the food is different.

Ratchet said the people who live here are in the barn, and I'll be surprised if they aren't dead.

I can't eat their food.

None of us should be welcome to use their home and enjoy their food.

These people are most likely dead because of me.

Then I think about Leon.

His gunshot didn't look life-threatening, but it incapacitated him, and he looked like he needed urgent medical attention to make it through.

I hope he's okay.

I can't build my strength on water alone though, and in the end, I eat the bread but leave the jam.

The strawberry jelly looks like it was homemade and preserved with care. I don't think I'll be able to keep the sweet taste of something so pure and natural down knowing the person who made it might be lying dead in the barn.

Ratchet is right about one thing, and it's that I should have stayed dead.

I should have seen my brothers for who they really were, not for who my stupid kid brain built them up to be, and I should have buried them when I buried Blanche. I should have listened to my father, and I never should have martyred them in my memories to the point where I took that job as soon as I saw Elia's name on the docket.

But Ratchet is also very wrong about one thing.

I have no intention of helping him once we reach Vancouver.

I'm suffering no schoolgirl delusions this time around.

If I get the chance, I'm either running, or I'm going to kill him.

33

DAGEN

nger slices through me every time my brain tries to accept that Nyla has been taken. I can't manage the despair and hopelessness that comes with it.

My brothers and I are used to having, at the very least, a modicum of power and control over the situations around us.

But this is different. Nyla has become my power, and she's been taken from me. The control I used to feel on my own has been replaced with a new dominance, and I've come to prefer it over the way things used to be.

Lennox pulls over to the side of the road a second time, and I lose my shit.

"We have to find her. WHAT THE FUCK ARE YOU DOING?" Spit flies out of my mouth, landing between us.

I'm a lost man.

I've never spoken to any of my brothers with so much rage.

Lennox looks over at me as though he's seeing someone he doesn't recognize. Then his features soften for a moment in what looks like sympathy before he throws the SUV into reverse and backs up, kicking rocks into the air around us.

When he stops, he points at an airfield sign on the side of the road and says, "I'm calling in a favor." Then he pulls out his phone.

I listen over the next five minutes as he calls Cole. Lennox says a name and tells him to get him on the phone now. A minute later, it sounds like Cole has the guy on the other line, and Lennox tells Cole to relay that he's cashing in on a debt and wants to know where Ratchet is going. I sit, holding my breath, while they go back and forth. Whoever Lennox's guy is, he is too scared to give up the information.

The most we get is that Ratchet has called everyone back to their places, so he's sending everyone home. Then Lennox tells Cole to text him his informant's number, and he hangs up.

His stony expression lowers the temperature in the vehicle as he dials the number.

There are no pleasantries when he speaks.

"You know what you owe me. You'll tell me where they're heading, or you're done." He points to the glove compartment and makes a writing motion with his free hand.

Opening the little compartment at my knees, I hand him a pen and a notepad, then resume my position.

Lennox's reputation is scarier than he is.

He is a fair man, and he usually doesn't overstep his boundaries. But when he wants something, he comes in with his best offer, and that's it. He doesn't know how to negotiate. He doesn't need to know.

I've seen men piss themselves around him.

The person on the other end of the line must understand this about my brother, because Lennox hangs up half a minute later with the answer.

"They're heading to Vancouver. They are expected tomorrow morning." He tosses the notepad with an address on my lap, then points to the sign with a single plane on it again. "We'll be there later today."

Rocks spray behind us as Lennox merges onto the highway, then the tires squeal their displeasure as he makes a sharp turn onto the dirt road heading toward the airfield.

"Thank you."

My brothers and I hold on to the favors we collect. They are as good as currency, often better among the people we do business with.

"Not necessary." He blows off my outburst as though it were a temper tantrum. "Besides, I won't let anything happen to the mother of my niece." Then he glances at me and winks.

We both know he just gave me an out.

I lost my shit and all but declared I loved Nyla, and this is Lennox's way of letting me claw back a little of my heart until I'm willing to share it.

If it were one of my younger brothers, I wouldn't stop hearing about it, but Lennox is different. He's the one we can share our real secrets with, and we know he will take them to his grave.

"Get Cole on the phone. He and Ryder are already in Vancouver. The fuckers couldn't wait. Tell him to find a place near that one"—he points at the notepad on my lap with Ratchet's destination—"where we can meet up." Something catches Lennox's attention, and he straightens. I follow his line of sight up the road, and the first signs of an airfield are just up ahead as we pass the start of a chain-link fence. "Tell them we'll be there in a couple hours."

I dial Cole.

He picks up on the first ring. "Fuck, man, where are you? What's going on?"

"Ratchet has Nyla. They are driving your way. We're going to try to charter a plane." I rattle off the address Lennox wrote down, along with his instructions. Then I tell them to find a place we can use close by.

I tell him we'll have more once we land, then hang up.

I don't have time to go into everything, as the airfield is a lot smaller than I imagined it would be.

My excitement wavers when we drive up to the main building. This isn't a professional airfield, per se, so much as it's a place for hobbyists.

A low growl of disappointment comes from Lennox as he turns off the SUV and exits. I follow him into the main building —actually, it is pretty much the only building.

An older gentleman straightens up when we walk in, and he calls over his shoulder to someone in the back before asking if he can help us.

Lennox meets the guy on the other side of the counter. "I need a plane and a pilot, but if you don't have a pilot, that's fine. I've got my private pilot's license."

The guy winces and groans, then shakes his head. "We only have one plane here today, and her insides are all over the shop." He points at his buddy, who is covered in grease, and the guy holds up a metal gear as though we completely understand what he has in his hand. "The only thing we have here is the chopper, and I can't pilot it unless there's an emergency."

The guy shrugs like his hands are tied, and I look at Lennox for his response. His jaw ticks in annoyance as he fists his hands and leans on the counter.

My brother is like a shark when he smells blood in the water.

"How much?" Lennox asks.

"How much what?" It's clear this guy has never been propositioned before.

"How much for you to fly us to Vancouver in the helicopter right now?"

Lennox and the man are squared off in a staring contest, and I almost see the abacus in the guy's head counting dollar signs. Then he says, "Like I said, I can't fly unless there is a medical emergency. It's in the regulations."

Lennox breaks his stare to look at the second man before returning to the one he is dealing with.

"How's ten thousand dollars? And if the answer is no because you're concerned about regulations"—he cocks his head to the guy behind him—"I can make it so that there is a medical emergency on board." Both men adjust their stance at his unspoken threat, and Lennox continues, "I would prefer to just hand over the ten grand—each."

The color drains from their faces as they exchange a glance with each other.

Hell, I feel a little woozy at the threat and the hefty bribe.

The man in the back shrugs his agreement, and when the first guy turns back and asks how Lennox would get the money to them, I know we have a ride.

Lennox hands me the keys and asks me to bring our bags in while he deals with the money transfers.

When I return for the last of our luggage, the slow, high pitch of an engine revving up out back cuts through the still silence around us.

I join Lennox with the last of our things, and he takes the SUV keys from me and hands them to the guy as he tells him that some men will come by in a couple of weeks for it, and to park it wherever they need to.

A surge of panic hits me when I see the helicopter out back with its blades whipping around, slicing through the air. For a moment, I feel as though I can't physically board. I don't want to be in the air again. It occurs to me that I haven't worked through what happened when our plane went down.

But there is something I want that is greater than the fear of crashing a second time. I want my power and control back, and I will overcome anything to have Nyla safe with me.

I pick up my pace and board, taking the back seat and allowing Lennox to sit up front with the pilot.

As the pilot does his checks, I pull Vaughn's photo out of my pocket, then turn my burner on and bring up Nyla's grainy photo. Setting them side by side, my eyes jump from one to the other, losing myself in their features. They are my anchors. My world is spinning out of control. They are the only things keeping me grounded, and I'm barely holding on.

I have them and Lennox.

If it wasn't for him, I would be lost to my worst fear and driving aimlessly along the highway right now.

The whirring scream of the helicopter permeates my senses, and only Lennox's hand, waving to get my attention from the edges of my vision, snaps me away from their photos.

Lennox points to the headset beside me, then to his head, and I put it on, cutting out some of the sound.

"Are you going to be okay?" he asks.

He isn't asking if I am okay. We both know I'm not. He's asking if I'm working on it, and I am, so I nod.

Then he smiles.

It isn't brotherly or jovial.

It's the savage smile of someone who is ready to kick some ass, and it's the smile I need to see.

"Good. Let's go get your baby mommy back."

34

DAGEN

Our younger brothers are waiting for us by the time we land, and my feet barely touch the ground before Cole half tackles me with a hug.

He's become a hugger over the last year, and it's been odd to watch, as he's more of the family enforcer. I think almost losing Ryder and Amara then finding Harlow has changed him.

"How did you know we were landing here?" I ask as Ryder steps in for his usual almost-hug that's mostly a heartfelt pat on the back.

Ryder breaks away from me to help Lennox with our bags, leaving me with Cole to answer. "We connected Nigel to Dark Webb, and they've been working together on a few things for us. They're focused on finding Dad and his associates, but they've been tracking the helicopter since you took off. I've been trying to get information, but my means are a little more hands-on." He rubs his palms together, and I catch a few scrapes along his knuckles that weren't there when I last saw him and Harlow at their new cabin.

Ryder rejoins us and further clarifies, "Cole's been on a

rampage trying to find out where Mom is. Anyone still on Dad's side has gone into hiding. It's like they know what he's capable of, or maybe it's what we're capable of."

I catch Lennox over Ryder's shoulder, talking to the pilot who brought us here. He's distracted, and I use the space to ask, "Where is Sloane—and everyone?"

My cryptic question is understood.

Ryder steals a glance back before answering, "They're all under lockdown at the house. It's easier to watch them if they are together, and that way our manpower is concentrated in one location. They know we're keeping things from them though, and they want answers."

We had agreed not to tell Sloane and Amara about our father killing Grayson. They loved Grayson more than any of us. Their broken hearts would have ruled their actions, and they wouldn't have been able to be as methodical as we have been over the last few months.

They would have shown our father our hand, and we weren't ready to deal a strong enough blow to end him.

The time to come clean with everyone is quickly approaching. I think it's going to happen as soon as we're all back together in Seattle.

We're keeping things from Lennox too.

"We need to tell him." I jut my chin in Lennox's direction as he turns and walks toward us.

"We will—first thing—once we're done. You know it shouldn't come from us," Cole hisses before Lennox gets too close to suspect our conversation is about him.

Sloane asked Ryder if she could be the one to tell Lennox what they've been doing. She thinks he'll take it better if it comes from her, and at this point I'm inclined to agree. We are all still in for a world of reckoning, but he'll understand where our hearts are if she explains it.

"Are we ready?" Lennox asks as he reaches our group.

Ryder walks to the trunk of their car and stores my duffel as Cole reaches his hand to Lennox for the remaining bags.

"It's not far. The address you gave us is a warehouse near the harbor. There are a lot of places we could use close by," Cole answers before joining Ryder at the trunk, and I slide into the back seat, tempted to pull out the photos again.

Cole slides into the driver's seat, and I expect Lennox to claim the passenger's seat, but he joins me in the back, glancing over to examine me with tempered concern in his frown.

He knows I'm carrying my secret and that I'm struggling worse than our brothers realize. He's always been our protector, and he's staying near me for moral support.

I force a smile, and he matches it

As we drive to our next location, I sit quietly, listening to my brothers talk. I answer the occasional question, but my mind is on Nyla. Finally, when Ryder directs a question to me about the crash, Lennox levels him with a scowl and shakes his head, telling him to move it along. Cole and Ryder exchange a worried glance before they do, and the conversation returns to finding our father.

I spend the rest of the drive watching the city go by outside as their muted voices drift in and out.

I think about Nyla.

If they aren't due to arrive until tomorrow morning, then Ratchet must be worried about exposing himself and driving while it's light out.

He'll think we are still scouring that highway looking for him, and this will work in our favor.

I glance to the sky to try to tell the time, the way Nyla and I have so many times over the past week, before I realize I can just look at the clock on the dash.

It's dinnertime.

I hope Nyla's eaten today.

Ratchet will be leaving whatever hole he crawled into soon and making his way here with her, and they don't know we are already waiting for them.

She has to be alive. I push the thought down as far as I can as tears threaten to show. I'm not ready for any of my brothers to see me wrecked like this.

Five minutes have passed before I realize no one is talking. My younger brothers have picked up on my distress, and Lennox sits beside me, offering silent support.

We pull in front of a nondescript warehouse, and a few men from Ryder's team stand and disperse around the area. Ryder tells them to cover the perimeter and stay close, then he looks at another and tells him to grab food for everyone and prepare to settle in.

I relax a bit knowing we are staying here for the night in case Ratchet shows up sooner than we expect him to.

As soon as everyone clears, Ryder leads us through the large doors.

I drop Nyla's duffel on the ground and plunk myself into the nearest chair as my brothers stand a hesitant few feet away from me, waiting for me to lead.

I take a breath so deep it makes my stomach ache.

"There's something you need to know, so I'm just going to say it. Nyla and I have a daughter. She kept this from me because of shit she found out about Dad, and she assumed it included all of us." It's clear by the lack of all emotion on their slack-jawed faces that this is the absolute last thing they expected me to say. "There's more," I add, throwing my hands in the air, and Cole looks at me as though there can't possibly be anything I could say that would top the bombshell I just dropped on them. I drag my palms over my face before I open my mouth to prove that, oh yes, there can. "It turns out Creed and Ratchet are brothers, and I just recently found this out at the same time I realized that Nyla is their little sister."

I clasp my hands in front of me to signal that I am done spilling the tea.

No one moves a muscle.

The stunned expressions of Ryder and Cole as they blink rapidly at me are mirror reflections of each other.

There is a long pause before Cole speaks up. "I have some follow-up questions."

I release a delirious chuckle with my next breath. I can always count on my brothers to pull me back from the ledge.

I have my best chance of getting Nyla out of this when I have my brothers with me.

"What's her name?" Ryder comes at me with a more sobered expression.

"Vaughn," I answer, reaching into my pocket for her photo.

"Holy shit. That's—" Ryder's sentence is cut off.

"Fucked-up. We know." Lennox rolls his eyes, repeating the response I gave him last night.

"I was going to say it's your middle name." Ryder finishes his initial thought.

"Yeah. She named her after me." I hold out Vaughn's photo, and Ryder reaches for it.

Before he is able to grab her picture, Cole shoves him out of the way and steps in, taking the photo. Ryder recovers and punches him in the arm before they look at it together.

"Damn." Cole looks up with a genuine smile. "Your woman must be hot, because she's taken half of your ugly DNA and turned it into this adorable princess. It's like she did all of the work for you."

"Fuck off," I say through a smile that is cut short when Ryder steps into me and shakes my hand.

"Man, that's—congratulations."

I thank him and smile proudly as Cole claps me on the shoulder.

"Henry has a cousin." Lennox tries to show his excitement, but his words are noticeably forced, and it dampens the atmosphere in the room.

We all know that, while Lennox cares for Henry, it's a source of pain for him to think that Ryder is Henry's father.

The expression on Ryder's face slips, and when he doesn't immediately respond, Lennox looks down to his feet, then takes a few steps away, as if to busy himself.

Finding our way back to each other isn't going to be easy, and it kills me that I can't be the one to settle his demons.

My regret takes a back seat when Ryder speaks up.

"Henry isn't my son."

When Lennox faces us, he doesn't need to ask Ryder to repeat himself. The look on his face says it all.

Ryder tries to explain anyway. "We're past the point where you need to know, and I can't stand here and keep this going when it does nothing but hurt you. Grayson is Henry's father. We kept it quiet after he was murdered in case it made Henry a target. I promised Grayson I would take care of Sloane. He never knew he was going to be a dad."

Lennox exhales as though his whole life has just left his body, and he staggers backward a step.

Ryder opens his mouth to say something else, but Lennox holds up a hand, shutting him down. "Can you give me some time with this? I just—can't."

Ryder nods, shoving his hands into his jacket pockets and taking a step away.

I change the subject, covering for Lennox this time. "Did you know Mom and Elia have a history? Creed mentioned something about it when Cole and I met with him in Portland."

Cole's phone rings at the same time I say his name, and he glances down before signaling to tell me he'll be right back.

Placing the phone to his ear, he steps outside.

It takes Lennox a moment to compose himself, then he stands tall and straightens his jacket. "I knew about it. When I was little, just before Cole was born, he showed up demanding a paternity test for me. I heard them yelling about it through the vent upstairs." When Lennox senses our next question on the tips of our tongues, he continues, "I'm not his. Elia accused Dad of purposely knocking up Mom to make her decide between them, knowing how much of a big heart she has. Elia Lucciano's goodwill toward our father ended when he took our mother from him, but he's always been good to the four of us because we are her sons, and I think he never stopped loving her."

None of us have time to process the apparent soap opera that was my mother's love life. The door to the warehouse opens, and Cole walks in looking two shades paler.

"We have a problem." He holds up his phone. "The clock has run out. Elia is dead, and Ratchet sent a team to kill Creed. Ghost is down. He's at the hospital, and it doesn't look good. Creed heard that Ratchet is on his way here. He's coming for him, and it's going to be a bloodbath."

"Does he know his sister is with him?" Ryder asks.

I shake my head. "Creed thinks his sister died—over ten years ago."

"How is that possible?" Ryder sends the question to me.

"It's a long story, but Ratchet must have realized she was alive when our father put the hit on both of us. Creed wouldn't have access to that information because he's been trusting us to get the microfiche for him while they fight their war. Ryder, keep your main team on the women; get everyone else up here now. Ratchet and Creed have moles on each side. If Creed is coming, Ratchet will know about it. The only thing that might still be a surprise is us. Cole, you need to call Creed back and have him come here—to us. Tell him he has our full support, but I have information that he needs to know before he goes into this."

Cole gives me a you've-got-to-be-kidding-me glare, then shakes his head with a smirk. "Hey, remember when you told Harlow's brother that I was"—he looks up to the ceiling, tapping his beard in mock contemplation—"what did you call it...*schtupping* his sister?" he says with a hint of wicked mirth. "When I tell you I cannot wait to see Creed kick your ass once this is all over, I mean it, Dagen."

35

NYLA

After Ratchet left, I spent some time burying him in my mind.

My brother died a long time ago, and I'm just realizing it now.

There was an hour in the afternoon where the sun shone directly on me through the window, and I closed my eyes, letting it warm me like I did just before I was taken this morning.

I'd been so stupid.

I let my guard down, and I allowed myself to feel safer than I was.

There was no way Dagen could have saved me from what happened. I'm here because I messed up.

I spent the rest of the day sitting by myself, staring at the walls that housed the family who once lived here.

Technically, I wasn't alone.

One of Ratchet's men was always with me, but I may as well have been by myself, since my questions and requests went unanswered.

Ratchet didn't come back until later in the day, after I had another crusty bun delivered, this time thankfully without the jam.

He didn't acknowledge me, he just told the guy I've nicknamed Lackey that we were leaving in an hour.

"You didn't have to kill them," I murmur before he leaves me once again.

This makes him glance my way in annoyance before tilting his head to the door. Lackey gets the hint and takes a break, leaving us alone.

"Who are you referring to?"

His question makes me examine his features more keenly.

He really doesn't know who I'm asking about.

Hurting the people who live here hasn't fazed him at all. I'm pretty sure this is a bright red flag for some kind of sociopathic personality disorder.

"The people who live here," I answer incredulously.

He nods in recognition, but there's no remorse when he says, "You mean the people who *lived* here."

His callous tone surprises me, and my face crumples in sadness before I am able to steel my features.

This further irritates Ratchet, and he sighs apathetically, chiding me for having a heart. "They were of no use to me alive." Shrugging, he explains his choice to me like I'm stupid, like anyone in his position would have done the same thing, and I can't believe this was my brother.

When I look up at him, I catch him in what I imagine must be his resting bitch face, except it's so much worse. His lips droop at the corners in a deep scowl, as though I nauseate him by just existing, and he glares at me with pure hatred in his eyes.

There is no love lost here. I wonder if there was ever any to begin with.

Ratchet looks like he wants nothing more than to be locked in a room with me so he can beat me to death, and my blood runs cold.

Starting a conversation with him was a mistake.

When he repeats "You should have stayed dead," I don't argue.

My goal now is to make it out of this alive and see Vaughn and Dagen again.

Ratchet has no intention of letting me live. If I didn't hold what little value I have with him, I'd already be out in the barn with the owners of this house.

He turns to leave, and I release a harrowing breath in relief, but it is short-lived. With one hand on the doorknob, he spins to address me again, and a chill pulls goosebumps from all over my arms.

"I had everything until you were born. You're the reason I was sent away, and it's your fault I couldn't go back. They babied you, and they were so afraid you'd break. I was always getting in trouble because of you." This is the most emotion I've ever seen from my brother, and it is all for himself. He stops from saying more and flips an internal switch that makes his eyes grow cold once more. "Defy me once, give me one little reason, and I'll break you, then I'll finally forget you ever existed."

He leaves me with a sick pit of terror deep in my gut.

Now I wish he had his apathy back.

I would prefer it if he just sent one of his guys in to ignore me.

Before the door closes, I hear him in the hall, giving one of them a timeframe and telling him to make sure I use the washroom before we leave.

I eat all of the bread on the tray and leave the water this

time. I don't want to risk Ratchet's wrath if I need to use the bathroom on the drive.

I spend the next half an hour thinking about Dagen and where he might be. I wonder if he's found the microfiche yet, or if my phone has been discarded. I don't linger too long on my happier times with Dagen or the intense moments we had together. The urge to cry will overwhelm me, and I don't want to show any emotion. I wonder about my team and if they've received my messages yet.

Then I close my eyes and picture Vaughn's smile. I recall every little thing about the photo I carried with me. I remember the little uptick on the right side of her smile that makes it look like she knows something I don't, and I remember what her laughter sounds like.

A heavy knock on the door makes me jump in my seat. No one enters, but the one who I call Bootlicker stands and tells me it's time to "use the can."

With a tight grip around my sore arm, I'm pushed into the quaint bathroom, which smells heavily of potpourri, and I'm given a minute before he bangs on the door to tell me it's time to wrap it up.

When I step out of the washroom, my hands are tied again. At least this time they are in front of me so I can blow on my fingers to heat them up when they get cold.

I'm reminded two more times how horribly I'll die if I try anything, then I'm led out of the house and across the lawn.

I start looking for their car too late. I realize they must have stored it in the barn.

Fear grips me, my feet stop moving, and three sets of eyes glower at me. I recover quickly, sucking in a deep breath to keep myself from fainting.

I don't want to see the people who lived here.

The men surrounding me are not good men, and my mind conjures images of sweet people who suffered the last moments of their lives.

I would be pressed to pick which of these men I liked the best, but if there were a gun to my head—which there may be soon enough—I would say it is Lackey. He was the one who finally untied my hands and allowed me to sit during the day with full use of my arms. He nudges me forward, and when I turn to meet his gaze, there's a hint of a plea in his eyes. I guess he wants to see me hurt as much as I want to be hurt, and I keep walking.

When the barn doors open, it's my guess that it was probably Lackey who mercifully covered the bodies with a tarp. As we pass by the covered mass on the ground, I catch the corner of a pretty floral dress sticking out from the dirty plastic tarp, and I quickly look away.

A sharp tug on my arm tightens the rope around my raw wrists, and I hiss as I'm pulled toward the car. Ratchet opens the back door, then motions for me to be set inside behind his spot in the passenger's seat.

The only mercy is that I'm joined in the back seat by Lackey.

As we pull out of the barn, I can't help but look back at the tarp and whisper a few words under my breath. I don't pray, I just tell the people who lived here that I'm sorry.

By the time we pull onto the main highway, the sun is setting.

For the first half an hour of our trip, I perk up when I see the headlights of every vehicle on the road, hoping one of them belongs to Dagen.

Ratchet makes phone calls from the front seat when he gets cell service, and he updates his buddies in front of me. I'm sure he's sharing things he believes will be kept private because he isn't planning on keeping me alive after he has what he needs.

When it gets dark and the headlights around us become sparse, I slump into the seat, using the back as a headrest, and I close my eyes. I don't fall asleep, but I feel better blocking out the view of the men around me.

Finally, Ratchet takes a call that changes his tone.

He's no longer cold and confident.

He's agitated and harsh.

I keep my eyes closed, but I listen as he barks orders and tells the person on the other end of the line to be ready.

There's an awkward silence when he hangs up the phone. I sense Ratchet has shifted in his seat, and I wonder if he's looking at me, but I keep my eyes screwed shut.

"You always were a fucking brat. I know you're not sleeping."

Slowly, I open my eyes and meet his gaze in silence.

He's unhinged, and I'm not going to give him the fuel he's looking for.

He tries to goad me again. "It looks like we're going to have a little family reunion in the morning. It turns out Creed is coming after you too, so I guess it's going to be a game of who gets to kill you first." He sneers, holding his eyes on me for signs of emotional impact.

This time, I'm prepared, and I lower my gaze. I don't change my expression, I just listen, then I close my eyes and lay my head down as though his revelation is irrelevant.

I picture Dagen's face, and I remember what it felt like when he held me those nights in the sleeping bag. He smelled good. It wasn't cologne or any type of bodywash. It was his smell, after we'd been out in the woods for days and we went swimming. There was something so primal and comforting about his real scent, and I pushed my face into his chest and inhaled deeply on more than one occasion.

When I think enough time has passed, I crack open one eyelid to check.

Ratchet has given up on me and turned back around. I blink my eyes, and the tears I had hidden away behind my closed lids roll down my cheeks. I lift my bound hands to my face and wipe them away.

When I glance over, Lackey is watching me in silence.

A trickle of snot threatens to run out of my nose, and I lift my hands to use the cuff of my sleeve again when he places his hand over mine. He reaches into his pocket and stuffs a tissue into my palm. Then he looks out his window, allowing me to wipe my nose in private.

An hour later, I do fall asleep sitting up. It isn't comfortable, and I wake up constantly during the drive.

We make one stop in the middle of the night. It's along the side of the road, and I'm led into a field to do my business by Bootlicker. My pride completely gone, I pull down the yoga pants Dagen bought for me and crouch down to go while he watches. I'm pretty sure Lackey would have at least looked away. I think.

Once we return to the vehicle, Lackey is already in the driver's seat, and my heart sinks. I won't like sitting with either of my other options. Bootlicker joins me in the back to sleep, and Ratchet keeps his spot in the passenger side and reclines, crushing my legs with the back of his seat.

The next time I open my eyes, I overhear Lackey telling Ratchet we are an hour away. I use the tissue that I managed to hold on to to wipe the dried tears and sleep out of my eyes, then look out the window at the morning sky.

It's a powdered shade of baby blue that fades into a

stunning orange. The sun hasn't broken the horizon just yet. No one else in the car bothers to appreciate it, so I tell myself it's all mine.

It's pretty.

I wonder if Dagen has seen it yet.

DAGEN

They say it's darkest before dawn.

It's a proverb to tell people to hold on and keep going, but today's light comes with an impending and inevitable hell, and I wish I could steal Nyla away and push her back into the darkness to keep her safe.

I still don't have confirmation that Ratchet has kept her alive, and my mind has been playing tricks on me with that lack of information.

I sway between feeling her in my bones and boiling with pure rage that she might have been forced to leave Vaughn and me.

My brothers stopped asking me if I was okay a couple of hours ago.

They know better.

Every one of my brothers has reached their breaking point where they'd kill our father themselves.

I was happy to stand back and let one of them have him, until now.

His actions have put Nyla in danger, and he has threatened

the security and happiness of my daughter. It doesn't matter if he knows this or not; I will kill him with my bare hands if I get the chance.

I will hack my way through every one of these motherfuckers to keep the girls in my life safe, and I think my brothers have picked up on my downward spiral, as none of them have left me alone since we've arrived.

Tensions grew as the night went on.

Rogue sounds and shadows moved through the buildings around us. Some of those belonged to men who were with us. Most of our manpower arrived an hour ago, and Lennox has been coordinating their movements.

The air crackles with suspended awareness: we know what's coming, yet we are forced to sit and wait for it to find us.

No one is prepared. None of us have the home-field advantage, and these men are desperate for a conclusion.

This has the potential to slip into a full-on slaughter.

My brothers and I are not violent men.

Even Cole, who took to the family role as enforcer, exhausts alternate tactics before he spills blood. He's not our enforcer because he's brutal; he's our enforcer because he knows how to instill the type of fear to get us what we want before he needs to throw a punch.

Today is different.

There is no negotiating.

We don't have anything they want.

Ratchet already has Nyla.

I've been sitting outside in the shadows listening to sounds that would normally go unnoticed if you didn't know men were preparing to tear each other apart.

Nyla is about to see a side of my brothers that I never wanted to show her.

The sky is already a light shade of blue. It was so gradual

that I don't remember it being dark, and I step out of my spot and into the light as a single vehicle pulls up. Cole stands at my side.

He swears beside me when the door opens and James gets out. He's Harlow's brother, and both Cole and Creed have taken him under their wings since everything went down with Harlow and their sister. I imagine he isn't happy to see her only living family here today.

"What the fuck is he doing here?" Cole rounds the SUV, punches his finger in James's direction, and gets in Creed's face.

We're about to have a war of our own before the real one starts. James joins me in getting between the two, and we separate them when Creed says, "When Ghost went down, James said he was coming under my group or going out on his own. Better he's here and I watch him than he goes off with our soldiers, yeah?"

Creed's hesitation when he talks about Ghost says it all, and Cole backs down. Ratchet cut deep when he took down Creed's second.

Lennox opens the door, calling our attention. "Get in here. We have something." He nods in greeting to Creed and his men. I turn to Creed to talk to him, but I'm cut off when Lennox says, "NOW!"

When I turn to follow our group in, I catch Cole's gaze, and he shakes his head, muttering "Harlow is going to kill me" as we walk in together.

Once I file in behind everyone and step to the side, I see someone I don't recognize kneeling with his wrists bound behind his back in the middle of the room. Blood coats his face under his nose and soaks into his shirt.

"We found him when I was setting everyone up." Lennox

looks around at all of us before he settles his gaze on Creed. "One of yours?" he asks him.

Creed lifts his hand, waving one of his men over. The guy steps out without hesitating and walks to the bound man.

No words are spoken. He steps around, looking at his hands, then pulls the neck of his shirt down. Finally, he crouches and lifts the man's shirt up, exposing a stomach and chest full of tattoos before answering Creed, "Mexican Mafia."

"Not ours." Creed answers Lennox's question.

"He's not talking, but he doesn't have to." Lennox looks at the two men standing guard behind our captive. "Get rid of him."

He waits for them to drag the man out of the room before he steps closer to Creed and speaks loud enough for everyone left to hear. "We have reason to believe it isn't Ratchet who is leading the challenge to take over Elia's organization. It's Sebastian." Lennox calls our father by his name to give Creed the chance to clear the room of anyone who shouldn't be privy to this information.

Outside of James, I know the two men with Creed. They are almost as close to him as Ghost is, and I'm confident they will need this information.

Creed gets the hint and takes stock of who is in the room with us before returning to Lennox. "Keep going."

"Our father has promised Ratchet a spot at the top, and they're planning on using the combined resources of both our organizations to expand the trafficking empire they are trying to build. They've been building a relationship with a cartel south of the border." Lennox points to the door the guy was just dragged through. "They must have access to the Mexican Mafia, so we don't know what we're walking into today."

Creed takes a few aimless steps while he processes the

information, then turns back to us. "How do you know all of this?"

Lennox looks like he's going to try to protect me by answering, but I don't let him.

I step forward.

"I was tracking the microfiche. An—acquaintance of mine had taken it, and I found her in Alaska."

Creed squares his body on mine, tilting his head to the side. "So you *were* on the plane that went down."

I nod. "And I wasn't alone. She found out this information about Sebastian, and we think Ratchet has her with him now." Saying his name is easier than acknowledging that this monster is my father. "There's something you need to know."

"Cole mentioned that on the phone. Sun's coming up, and we're running out of time. What is it?" Creed is all business.

My brothers turn to me and wait.

As I take a breath to answer, Lennox takes one step closer to me while I gather my courage.

"The woman I found—is your sister."

Creed's face twists with furious warning. "My sister is dead."

The men with him all straighten at his response. This is definitely a sore spot for him, and it's not to be brought up.

I reach into my pocket for my burner phone. Then I close the distance between us, turning it on to the photo I took of her and handing it to him.

Creed's ferocious sneer drops into shock as he looks at Nyla's image. It's the one I took of her days ago, on the bus.

"Lady Bug?" he whispers at the screen.

When he meets my gaze, his bloodshot eyes are shiny. "I— that's her." I take my phone back as he turns to address the men with him. "Tell everyone to stand down. We can't fire on sight.

Anyone does, and I kill them myself, understand?" He waits until they both nod, then he says, "Go."

They leave us, and Creed spins around. "What's your plan?"

"We don't have one. We don't even know if she has the microfiche. I don't know if she's still alive." I try my damndest to keep my emotions out of my tone, but a curious glance from Creed tells me he thinks something is off.

Lennox takes a step toward us to add to my information. "They took her when we were on our way back here. We think it was a fluke they found her. One of my guys was shot in the process. The last we saw of her, Ratchet pulled her off Leon after she gave him her phone."

"And he knew she was alive?" Creed looks gutted. "I'm going to kill him," he promises under his breath before returning to his conversation with Lennox. "What was on her phone?"

"Nothing. It's broken. It hasn't turned on since the plane went down."

I pull it out of my pocket to show him and he takes it, running his fingers across it and opening the empty compartment on the back. I don't tell him what it once held. This isn't the time.

"My little sister was smart. Like wicked smart. She was never one to do something without good reason behind it." He waves the phone between us, catching my attention. "She was always exceptionally analytical and quick on her feet. Why would she go out of her way to leave you something you can't use?"

Creed's accurate assessment of Nyla sparks a thought at the back of my mind.

Nyla held on to her phone for so long because it held Vaughn's photo, but she had given me the photo the night before. She knew her photo wasn't in her phone, but it was still the one thing she risked running to give to Leon.

I put myself in her situation. If I was about to be taken because someone thought I had information that they needed, I would only get rid of something I was holding if—

"Shit. Let me see that." I take her phone from Creed and try the power button again. It still doesn't turn on.

Of course it doesn't.

I open the compartment knowing it's empty, but I'm angry anyway when I see that it still is.

"What are you thinking?" Ryder asks, reminding me that all my brothers are here with me.

"She was so protective of this phone when we were out there. At first I thought it was because—" I pause for only a second. This has to come out. "I thought it was because she didn't want me to find the picture of her daughter."

"She has a daughter?" I've never seen Creed like this.

An emotional Creed is more terrifying than the cold bastard we all know.

"We have a daughter."

"WHAT?!?"

"Not now." Outwardly, I take charge. I had a thought, and I need to stick with it. Internally, I want to shit myself knowing Creed has probably killed men for less. "The photo wasn't in her phone when she went out of her way to give it to Leon. It was a conscious action," I say, as I tap my finger on the inside of the compartment.

Then I realize there is one more place I could hide something, and I brace my thumbs on the back of her phone and peel off the case.

My breath hitches when the flimsy item falls out into my hand.

With shaky fingers, I hold it up between us, and the men around me whisper profanities.

"It's the microfiche."

Creed takes it and holds it up to the light, but the file is too small to make anything out, and our time has just run out.

I grab the microfiche back.

"We need to trade it for Nyla." I draw everyone's attention with my comment, and tensions pull tight once more.

"We need to know who that is." Creed points at the microfiche in my hand.

I try to reason with him. "If Nyla is alive, it's because Ratchet thinks she has this. If we have it, it means she doesn't, and he'll have no use for her. He'll use her as a human shield as he takes us out."

Creed reaches for the microfiche once more, but I stand my ground and pull it back from him. He levels me with a threatening scowl, and I keep talking.

"Look, so what if Ratchet gets this? You have people close to him. We'll find out who it is, we just won't know first." As I speak, I realize we've already covered our bases. There are only two people we know who could be Lucciano's missing male heir because of the birth month and year. Ryder is with us, and if it turns out it's Grayson, no one knows Henry is his son, so we are in the clear. "Our time is almost up. We need to contact him and offer the trade. We all know that once the shooting starts, none of this will matter, and I won't lose her." I threaten Creed right back.

He looks like he's about to explode, like his skin is barely containing years' worth of rage, but he restrains his ire when he grits his teeth and says, "I'll set it up."

The tension dissipates enough that I roll out the muscles in my shoulders, and Lennox steps to my side, clapping his hand on my back. "We'll get her back."

Cole steps over to James and draws him away from our group to talk to him while we wait for Creed to rejoin us. Ratchet should be hitting the outskirts of Vancouver by now.

The only thing I want right now is to see her. I need to know she's still alive. I will face Creed's wrath, and I will fight for her, but I just need to see her face.

The door creaks, and Creed walks quickly toward us.

"It's done." He glances at me begrudgingly. "She's alive." Then he speaks to all of us. "This ends today."

37

NYLA

We're driving through the first suburb leading into Vancouver when Ratchet's phone rings.

He speaks in clipped sentences, giving nothing away to the rest of us in the car. Then he disconnects and stares out the passenger window in a tense silence for a few minutes.

When he speaks again, it is with an eerie restraint. It feels as though Ratchet needed those minutes to reel in his emotions.

"You lied to me." He doesn't turn his head, but it's clear to everyone in the car who he's speaking to.

I'm not stupid enough to play into his games, so I don't respond until he tells me what this is about.

Still without turning around, he says, "You told me you destroyed the microfiche."

I notice the small, nuanced changes in his men. Lackey grips the wheel a little tighter, his eyes traveling up to the rearview mirror to steal a glance at me in the back seat. Bootlicker leans his body away from mine, almost pushing himself into the door beside him, as if he's distancing himself from my indiscretions.

"I did"—I'm too scared to lie to Ratchet a second time, and I correct myself—"tell you that."

He keeps his head forward, looking out the side window as he taps his phone against his chin in pensive thought.

"Well, someone tells me they have it, and they want to make a trade—for you."

My mind spins with this information, and hope brews in my heart, but I keep it all hidden behind an apathetic countenance, and I lower my gaze demurely to my lap.

Dagen found the microfiche in my phone, and he's looking for me.

As Ratchet shifts in his seat, slowly twisting to look at me, I fortify my expression so that when he sees it, I am unreadable and as amenable as possible.

Along the edges of my peripheral vision, Bootlicker turns his head away from the stare-down Ratchet is leveling on me and looks out his window.

Ratchet is a ball of conflicting emotions. I know he's happy he is getting what he wants, but the disgust on his face tells me the fact that someone wants to trade it for me is eating away at him.

I want to ask him why he hates me so much, but there's an air of volatility around him I'm worried about setting a match to.

Finally, he turns around, facing forward, and I suck in a slow and steady breath of air, hoping I'm not making a sound.

He doesn't say another word to me for the rest of the drive.

Shipping containers and unmarked warehouses surround us when the vehicle finally stops, and the three of them get out, leaving me inside.

Minutes pass while Ratchet speaks to both of them, and Lackey raises his hand. It looks like he's volunteering for something.

When they return to pull me out of the back seat, Ratchet steps back and allows both of his men to handle me.

I don't fight them.

We walk in a row of three into the nearest building, and they kneel me on the ground as Ratchet follows behind. Pebbles dig in to my knees through my pants, and I shift, lifting my leg to brush the dirt away and earning another scowl from Ratchet.

When his phone rings, I watch as he checks the display, then straightens before answering it.

His tone turns deferential.

There's a stark difference between the way he is handling this caller and the way he speaks to those on his crew. It's a reverence he hasn't shown anyone since he grabbed me off the street yesterday.

"Yes, sir. We're ready. As soon as we have it, we'll get it done. Thank you, sir."

When he hangs up, he addresses the one I like the best. "You know what to do. Get back to me with the microfiche as soon as you get it." Lackey nods his understanding, but when Ratchet turns his back, he sneaks a glimpse of me with an odd look on his face.

"You stay on her until it's done." Pointing his finger in my direction, he speaks to Bootlicker, who sits nearby on a wooden table as the other two leave without another word to me.

In one way or another, this should be our parting words, and there is nothing.

I can't imagine what happened to Jonah and Carson to make them like this.

Tears escape my eyes, and I sniffle, rubbing my sleeve along my face. Bootlicker offers no tissue like his partner did in the car.

I shift to get blood flowing to my feet, and I'm met with another empty warning of not to try anything stupid *or else.*

I use the time to plan my escape.

If this guy gets close enough to me, I can fight for my life.

I'm confident he doesn't think I have it in me from what he's seen over the last day.

I've been submissive and docile. I've allowed them to lead me, and I've followed their orders.

But I'm no meek puppet.

I test my binds, and they are tight, but I have my hands tied in front of me, so I have a chance.

Contrary to how I want this to play out, the guy stays seated with his gun trained on me from a distance for the next fifteen minutes.

When I tell him I need to use a bathroom, I'm met with the order to hold it or go where I am.

Excitement bubbles up from my gut when he stands to walk behind me, but he only tells me to keep my eyes straight ahead, and he takes his seat.

From this position, I can't see him. I can't tell what he's doing or prepare myself to fight if I have to.

I'm certain he still has his gun on me.

If Dagen is coming, I don't want to give this guy any reason to shoot me before he gets here.

Until an opportunity presents itself, I have no choice but to sit here.

I go to my happy place in my head, where Vaughn is always waiting for me. Her laughter energizes my spirit, and her love gives my life meaning, but now Dagen is here too, and I desperately want to see them again. I want them to see each other.

Ratchet's voice breaks into the room. "We're making the trade. Stand by."

I glance over my shoulder to see the guy looking at a walkie-talkie. His head shoots up to me. "Eyes forward."

I return to my position.

The longest ten minutes of my life passes as adrenaline slowly seeps through my veins, making everything feel terribly real.

My mind wanders to the thought: If they are planning on trading me, why is this guy still here? Why wouldn't they just tie me to a spot on the wall and leave me to be found? Wouldn't he want to be far away from this place when Dagen comes to get me?

The high-pitched feed from the receiver sends a chill up my spine. Then I hear my brother's detached voice.

"We have it. Kill her."

No.

That wasn't the agreement.

I push myself up from my kneeling position and stumble, but Bootlicker moves faster than I do.

I'm robbed of my fight when a familiar pinch in my neck, followed by a rough shove to the ground, stops me.

I should have expected the sedation.

In the distance, gunshots ring out, and I worry for Dagen. Has he been hit?

My hands, still bound, are trapped under the weight of my body, and Bootlicker leans over me, pinning me in place with his knee on my back.

A scream tears from my lips as I sob against the cold, dirty floor, and my limbs turn heavy as I try to kick my legs out around me.

Bootlicker stands, releasing his hold on me, but it doesn't matter.

Exhaustion clouds my thoughts, washing away my fiery

defiance. All that remains is sadness, and I cry as my body shuts down on me.

"Please." My whispered plea kicks up a puff of dust from the ground in front of me.

"It's not personal," the guy says from behind me, as though this will grant him absolution from what he's about to do. "I have my orders, but you don't need to suffer."

I want to tell him I am suffering.

I almost had everything I wanted.

I was so close, and now Vaughn will grow up without me. Time will distort everything, and she won't know how proud I will always be of her. She won't remember that I love her.

She'll forget me.

Darkness creeps in from the edges of my vision, and my body grows numb as a pair of black shoes stops in front of me. I roll my body as best as I can and glance up his pant leg, stopping at the barrel of a gun pointed at my head.

I don't have it in me to give a shit.

The drugs have taken my fucks away.

I close my heavy eyelids to blink again, and I swear I hear the click of a gun before everything goes black.

38

DAGEN

She's alive.

I've been holding on to those words since Creed said them, using them to fuel my determination and hold my focus on my only task.

Protect Nyla and bring her home.

Home.

I want her home with me, but I haven't had my own home for so long. I've moved around; I have apartments in different cities. My home has always been where my brothers are, but now I want home to be something more.

I want more.

When I asked Nyla why she didn't leave as soon as she completed her job five years ago, she told me she wanted more, and now I understand this in my soul.

The microfiche sits in the middle of a small table with eight of us standing around it. We've been organizing our approach as best as we can, but there are still too many holes in our plan.

Now it's time to decide who goes.

"I'll go," James says, and both Cole and Creed say no in unison.

Before anyone else has the chance, I speak up.

"I'm making the trade." This isn't up for discussion. When everyone looks at me, I lay it out. "The whole point of getting the microfiche is to oust Creed as the new leader. All Ratchet needs to do to accomplish that is shoot him. Nyla doesn't trust anyone else, and I don't want to spook her."

Their silence tells me they know I'm right.

We are down to the last five minutes before we need to leave for the meeting point, and Creed's men break away from our group with their orders.

"I'll be with my men." Creed nods toward James, who joins him in heading to the door. "I want to know as soon as you have her."

When the outside door shuts us in, Lennox turns to me. "You don't have to go. Let me go in your place. What if they shoot you as soon as you hand it over?"

"How is that different than if they shoot you?" I square myself on Lennox. "You are no more disposable than any of us." I point between myself and my younger brothers. "We're grateful you took charge of us when we were younger, but you can't keep stepping in front of the bullets meant for us until one finally kills you." Ryder and Cole stay silent, nodding their agreement. "Now, I'm going in, but I'm not doing it alone. I don't give a fuck what they said. You will all be nearby. Lennox, you are the best shooter out of all of us. I need you watching my back. Cole, you'll drive but stay nearby, and Ryder, I need you on the ground, hidden somewhere in case anything goes wrong."

I'm going in without a gun, so I need my brothers close by in case Ratchet decides to cross us—and we expect him to.

The three-minute drive is quiet, with only Cole running through different scenarios.

Lennox has been silent since I told him he wasn't going in my place. It's a conversation we should have had sooner. I should have told him how much we all appreciated the sacrifices he made to keep us together, but it's over now, and we want our brother back.

There was just never a good time, and now I'm sure it came out wrong. Or maybe it didn't, and he's trying to process where we go from here.

Cole stops the car. Lennox is the first out, carrying a few guns with him as he disappears behind a shipping container.

The next is Ryder, who opens the door to an attached building and slips inside.

"Fuck, man," Cole mutters as he drives again.

Above everything, I've always been able to joke around with my brother, with the exception of a few instances that I can think of off the top of my head. The first being when Amara was taken. The second is when Harlow went after James.

And now.

"I know."

The space between the shipping containers narrows too much for our SUV to drive through, and Cole stops the car.

I step out, giving Cole one final nod before I leave him, and walk the rest of the way.

The rendezvous point is just up ahead in a covered area between the containers. A breeze off the water gusts through the open spaces between the large metal containers.

The door to the small, makeshift building creaks on its hinges as I open it, catching the attention of the only man standing in the room. He turns to face me as I join him.

He crosses his arms. "You have the microfiche?"

I tense when I don't see what I want.

"Where is she?"

This has double cross written all over it, and I watch his movements for signs that he's going for a hidden gun, but the guy stays relaxed.

"When you hand over the microfiche, I'll hand over her location." He holds up a piece of paper before tucking it into his pocket.

"That's not what we agreed on."

I wish we had more time to set this up. Ratchet is using everyone's confusion and lack of time to his advantage.

The guy shrugs. "Not my problem. Either I walk out of here with the microfiche and you go get the girl, or I walk out of here without it and they kill her." He taps his wristwatch. "They won't wait forever."

I have no choice.

I reach into my pocket and hold out the microfiche, and the guy takes a step toward me to take it.

Turning it over in his hands, he holds it up to the light like every single one of us did, hoping to see something.

When he doesn't, he reaches into his pocket and pulls out the piece of paper, and I reach out to take it.

His grip tightens around it for a second, drawing my attention from the paper to his face. The guy's jaw ticks as he sizes me up, then lets the paper go.

He lowers his voice. "She's not there."

The blood drains from my face. They were never going to hand her over.

Is she even alive after all?

I must look like I'm about to strangle him because he continues, "He's planning on killing her no matter what, and—it's not right. I looked at the paper. That isn't the building we left her in." He takes a cautious step toward me as I unfold the paper. He lifts it out of my hands and turns the sheet so it's facing the same direction we are. Then, pointing to a small building in the opposite direction, he says, "She's there. Tell Creed: Warrick says we're even. You have until I get to the car and hand him the microfiche. Then he'll call in the order to kill her. You need to move."

I take one last look at the map and calculate the distance before stuffing it in my pocket. She's far away, and I won't make it back to the car to get Cole in time.

I'm on my own, and I need to make a run for her.

The guy points to a door at the back of the room, and I sprint, pushing it open and bursting through into the morning sun.

I have no idea if any of my brothers can see me, but I have no time to call them. Pumping my arms, I get up to my full speed and keep my eyes on the building at the end of the rows of containers.

Over my shoulder, voices carry on the wind, and yelling in the distance alerts me just before the first shot is fired. It came from behind me, so I have hope Nyla is still okay.

She has to be.

There is no path forward in this life without her, and I won't accept anything else.

Air burns into my throat and lungs, mixing with my fear and making me sick to my stomach, but I don't slow down.

Another shot from behind me, and a body falls to the ground from atop a stack of shipping containers twenty feet in front of me.

Then the shooting sounds from all sides, and my stomach lurches into my throat as I close in on the building and all hell breaks loose around me.

If the shooting has started, the order must have been sent, and the world around me goes dark.

I recognize yelling from close behind me. It vaguely sounds like my brothers, but I can't afford to lose any time. Through my tunnel vision, all I see is the door in front of me.

My chest aches and my eyes burn for Vaughn and Nyla. I've only just found them, and I won't let either of them go.

Rage boils my blood.

I am vengeance, and I will kill anyone on the other side of this door who dares to keep me from what is mine.

I don't slow to test the door to see if it's unlocked.

I ram through it, and the sight before me seals the fate of everyone in the room.

Nyla is on the ground, unmoving as a man stands above her with a gun pointed at her head. I didn't hear a gunshot come from in here, but that could be the shock.

I run right at the guy.

Before he is able to lift the gun and fully aim it at me, I reach him. The gun goes off, just missing my side as I slam into him, tackling him to the ground, wailing on him as we go down.

Peeling myself off the floor, I put all of my strength behind my targeted punch, aiming for the base of his throat.

I strike.

His windpipe crunches under my knuckles, and his eyes go wide as his larynx collapses.

When he drops his gun to clutch at his neck, desperate for air he'll never get, I kick it away. He's no threat to me now, and I leave him to get to Nyla.

Ryder already has her in his lap. His fingers are on her throat to check her pulse when he says, "She's alive."

Cole holds up a syringe on the ground beside her listless body. "She's just out. She should be okay."

I hurry to Ryder's side, replacing his body with my own as I pull her onto my lap and fold my body around hers.

When she doesn't hug me back, I pull her into me harder.

Her smell breaks me, and I hug her body to mine, rocking the both of us as I whisper words of comfort into her hair, alternating between kissing her and hugging her some more.

When I look back to my brothers, it is through watery eyes, and neither of them say a thing.

They've both come close to losing the one they love, and I never fully understood the soul-crushing anguish they felt.

Not until now.

I'm not sure when the fighting outside died down, but it sounds quiet.

The door opens, and my brothers huddle in front of me, protecting both of us and ready to fight our intruder. They straighten and step away as Lennox crouches at my side, scanning everything around us before standing and walking away with Cole. Their hushed voices recap what happened after I ran out of the building.

Lennox pulls his phone out of his pocket. "I'm calling Creed. We need to regroup."

He opens the door, glancing outside as he puts the phone to his ear, and I sit with a sleeping Nyla, refusing to let her go.

I'll never let her go again.

The occasional gun fires in the distance while we wait.

Lennox pockets his phone. "Ratchet got away. Creed is coming to us."

I exchange a grim glance with Ryder.

We all know what this means.

If Ratchet got away with the microfiche, then it's only a matter of time before we learn who the heir is, and I'm not sure any of us are prepared for what's coming.

39

NYLA

I groan against the throbbing pain behind my eyes when I finally open them again.

My dire situation shocks my senses, and I return to the last instinct I had before I passed out.

I try to fight.

I push my limbs out when strong arms clamp around my upper body, and Dagen's low tone hushes me.

"It's me. You're okay. I've got you."

I break away to look up at him. My eyes pause on a wet spot on his shirt where I must have drooled all over him, and I lift my hands to wipe the spit off my face.

When I meet Dagen's eyes, his lips thin into a tight smile.

"I-I thought I was—dead."

Crushing his mouth against mine, his lips demand I submit to him and open, and I do, tasting his kiss—it's salty.

He tastes like tears.

When he breaks away he says, "So did I."

A low chuckle from across the room catches my attention,

and my eyes land on a man with light hair and a beard. Standing, he walks over to the two of us. "I don't think he's going to let you out of his sight ever again, Sunshine."

Dagen hugs me tighter to prove him right and introduces the man as his brother, Cole.

Cole smiles before excusing himself and leaving the room. "I'll let them know she's awake. We're heading out soon."

"Where are we?" I pinch the bridge of my nose then rub my eyes, hoping to ease some of the pressure building behind them.

The soft bedding around me is a direct contrast to the dirty warehouse I was held in.

"We're on private property outside of Vancouver."

The memory of the two people Ratchet killed so he could use their home surfaces. "Whose property?"

"It belongs to Creed's organization."

What?

"What's wrong, Nyla? You just went stiff as a board." Dagen draws little circles on my arm before cupping my face and lifting my eyes to his.

"I don't understand. Carson—I mean, Ratchet told me that Creed was after me too."

"Nyla, Ratchet lied to you. Creed was looking for the microfiche, but he had no idea you had it. He didn't know you were alive until I told him, and he agreed to trade it for you. He tore apart half of the Mexican Mafia while I was trying to get to you."

"He's, um—he's my brother."

Dagen's low chuckle holds little humor. "I know."

"Where is he?"

"He had to get to Portland. He said he'll see you again as soon as he can get away. My brothers are driving back this afternoon." Dagen lifts his ass and pulls the covers out from on top of him, sliding under the sheets with me. "You and I are here for a few days while you recover and until we can get a copy of your passport so we can cross the border like law-abiding citizens." He nuzzles his face into the curve of my neck, tickling me as he growls against my skin. "What should we do to pass the time?"

We're interrupted by a knock on the door, and Dagen groans.

"Bad timing!" he yells to the person on the other side. "Go away."

The door opens anyway, and Lennox walks in as Dagen mutters "cock block" under his breath.

Lennox smiles when I pull myself into a sitting position.

"I just spoke to Leon. He's going to be okay. He asked me to tell you it wasn't your fault."

I flash back to kneeling at his side in the middle of the parking lot while I cried and told him over and over again how sorry I was before Ratchet yanked me off him by my hair.

"Thank you."

"We're heading out now." Lennox returns to the door. "We'll be in touch once we're in Seattle."

When Dagen gets up to see Lennox out, I pull the covers back and swing my legs off the bed.

"Where do you think you're going?"

"Me? Oh, um, I was going to say goodbye."

Dagen circles the bed, crowding me back into the covers and boxing me against the mattress. "You'll stay here and rest. You'll get the chance to properly meet my family another time. I'll be back in a minute to take care of you."

He kisses my nose, and my cheeks warm.

When I open my eyes again, I'm sleeping on Dagen, and his arms are wrapped tight around me. His breathing is even, his eyes are closed—and we're both naked.

I'm not sure how I slept through the removal of every piece of clothing on me, yet here we are.

The fluffy bedding swallows us whole, reminding me it has only been a few short days since we shared one sleeping bag and fought our way out of the wilderness.

There's a gap of a few hours between when I blacked out in the warehouse and when I opened my eyes here.

"You're supposed to be napping." Dagen's chest rumbles under my cheek with his words. His hold relaxes, and he brushes the tips of his fingers up the length of my spine.

"What's he like?" I ask.

Dagen chuckles. "We're naked, Jensen. You really want to ask me about another man right now?"

I snort-giggle and try to cover it up by clearing my throat as Dagen peels me back from him, looking me in the eyes.

"Your brother is a good man, Nyla." He brushes a stray strand out of my eyes, and I lay my head on the pillow. I'm eye level with him as he turns on his side.

His hand doesn't leave my body.

When I take too long to consider his words, he continues, "I'm not going to lie. I am shit-terrified of only a few people. Creed is one of them. Never tell Lennox this, but he is another. I don't fear them because they are horrible men; I fear them because they are fair. They are true leaders, and I respect them, and if they are ever coming for me, it means I will absolutely be deserving of their wrath."

"But I thought Elia Lucciano was corrupt."

I was bitter when my brothers left our family. Our parents aren't rich, but we never went without anything we needed. I was sure my childhood was happy, and they both left. They chose a gang, and they turned their backs on our love.

"Well, that requires a little context. My father grew up alongside Elia when they started making names for themselves. It was all racketeering, none of it legal, and they were taking over the town. I'm going to make a long story short because I want to get in between these thighs."

Licking his lips, his hand disappears below the covers, cupping my mound and rubbing. The hint of discomfort makes me groan. It turns out I like it when he is rough with me.

"My father claimed Seattle; Elia took Portland. When Elia's second died, Creed filled that spot. We are a product of who we allow to influence us, and Creed slowly showed Elia a different path. It isn't all legal, but it is better than it was, and it's why my brothers and I stayed in business with their organization. Our father, though, is a different story. He pitted my brothers and I against each other. At one point, we were all so hungry for his approval that it almost broke us. He wanted each of us loyal only to him. It haunts me what kind of man I would have become if it wasn't for Lennox."

Lifting my hand, I cup his cheek and angle his face until his eyes meet mine. "You are all good men, Dagen. I wouldn't pick another father for Vaughn even if I could."

I feel his smile in my heart.

"I want us to go get Vaughn—together—as soon as we can. We'll figure it all out. Do you think she'd like to—" His voice breaks apart, showing little signs of uncertainty creeping in.

We haven't discussed any of this, but being together and having her with us feels like the only option that makes any sense.

"I know she'd love to, and we will. My cousin will have to bring her to us though. Only a few people know where they are."

His eyebrows pull together as he eyes me curiously. "What did you say your cousin did?"

I wink at him. "I didn't."

He squeezes my folds together once more in retaliation before abandoning my core and moving up to circle my breast, but he doesn't push the subject, so I change it. "You said there are a few people you are terrified of. Who else makes that list?"

"You and Vaughn." He pinches my nipple, sending little shockwaves to my pussy and stoking my arousal.

"Why us?"

He looks at me for a long time, his lighthearted smile morphing into something more profound. "Because you hold everything I am in your hands. I will topple worlds to protect you, or I will die trying, and that is both terrifying and liberating all at once."

When he rolls over me to kiss me, I surrender, following his lead.

He wedges himself between my legs, his muscular thighs spreading my legs around him, his fingers combing into the back of my hair, then fisting.

I crave the little sting when my hair pulls, and my mouth opens on a gasp he swallows whole.

"You taste like everything I didn't know I needed, and I'm going to fuck you into this mattress until you pass out. Then I'm going to carry you into the four-person party tub in the other room and take care of you."

He drops his head, and his lips caress the bandaged spot where I was stabbed. A shiver runs through me, making me shudder in his arms.

His wicked eyes watch my reaction before he lowers his head and does it again.

"You're going to be so much fun." He takes a reluctant

breath. "First though, you need to eat. Have you had anything since yesterday?"

I shake my head. "Only some bread." Then the last twenty-four hours crashes into me. "Ratchet held me in someone's home. He killed them."

"I'll have Cole monitor the news and let you know what I find," he growls against my skin before putting some space between us and sitting up. "You need to eat. Nonnegotiable."

Standing to his full height, he hides nothing from me, and my eyes lower, then zero in on his junk.

"Okay," I sigh as I lean over the side of the bed, looking for my clothes.

His dark chuckle settles into my bones, making me wish the whole eating thing was negotiable. "You only get these." He tosses my panties into my lap. "And it's only because I want to peel something off of you later."

I sigh wistfully as I pull them on. Then, turning onto my hands and knees, I turn myself on the bed, showing him my bottom while glancing at him over my shoulder.

"Hold that thought. We're eating first. Tempt me again, and I'll spank that ass while I decide if it's time to fuck it."

"Promises, promises," I giggle, and his eyes turn dark.

He steps closer to the bed, and his cock stiffens as he skims his fingers over the cotton covering my ass before pulling his hand back and slapping it down on my skin.

Heat floods my body.

His fingers return to drawing lines along the seams of my panties. "You like that?"

"Yes." My answer is carried out on a lusty breath.

He smirks, pulling his hand away.

The bed dips as he climbs over me, the tip of his shaft nudging into my hip. Folding himself around me, he wraps his arms around my front, squeezing my breast in one hand while his other tickles lightly over my panties.

He lines up his lips with my ear.

His voice deepens an octave when he whispers, "Good. Now get up like a good girl and join me for lunch, or you don't get any more today."

He breaks his hold and nudges me forward. I fall onto the bed, groaning my mutiny into the mattress before pushing myself up.

"Fine. If I must eat."

He tangles his fingers into mine, leading me from the room, and I pause when the rest of the home comes into view.

The modern rustic cottage has an open floor plan and a giant fireplace in the middle of the area. Floor-to-ceiling windows look out on a mountain range.

"A girl could get used to this." I follow behind Dagen as he leads me to an island in the kitchen.

"Good. We'll be here for a couple of days until Ryder can fast-track your passport and get it to us." Dagen opens the fridge, pulling out some cheese and grabbing a loaf of artisan bread off the counter.

"Is there a computer I can access while you do this? I'd like to see if my messages were received and close my contract with my buyer. I think they should know I don't have their microfiche anymore."

Dagen considers my request while he slices into the crusty loaf, and a fresh bread smell hits my nose, making my mouth water.

"I think you should warn them. We're ready if it's Ryder or Grayson. If someone is trying to stay hidden, then they should be given the chance to remain that way. It's over there." He points to a credenza nestled into a tiny nook by the patio doors to the deck.

I spend close to ten minutes online, updating Dagen over my shoulder.

My team checked in yesterday, and everyone is okay.

From their words, it sounds as though everyone is looking forward to retiring from our line of work. This last scare was just a little too real for all of us.

I told Dagen that I scanned the microfiche when we were in Hazelton and sent it over to my team to see if they could extract what he needs, but that it was a long shot.

It turns out they were able to retrieve the image from the microfiche. They're trying to blow it up as best as they can, and they'll send over anything they recover, but it might take some time.

Signing in for my contract was straightforward. I updated my communication to tell them a group within the Lucciano organization is now in possession of the microfiche, then I closed my job and suspended my account. I have no plans to take any further work, and the sooner I bury myself, the safer Vaughn will be.

Dagen watches me hungrily, his eyes lowering to my breasts as I return to the kitchen.

I reach for a piece of cheese when he stops me.

"We're eating out there." He tilts his head toward the deck. "Grab the knit blankets by the door."

He lifts a tray of food and walks ahead of me, leaving me to follow his fine ass out the door. I cuddle into a chair as he sets the food down and tells me to get started while he pours our water.

The property around the home is vast. From my spot on the deck, I can't see another building. The cool breeze carries the notion of fall, and I wrap a blanket around me. After a few minutes, the sun warms my little cocoon while the soft knit cover blocks the wind.

Dagen takes a gulp of his water and points to the plate of food on the table in front of me with wicked intent in his eyes.

"Get your strength up, Nyla. I want a do-over of us fucking outdoors that doesn't end in me getting cuffed to a tree."

40

DAGEN

There are few moments in life that can truly be defined as perfection.

This is one of them.

I will never get enough of hearing Nyla scream my name while her legs grip me tight and her pussy pulses around me as she comes all over my cock.

My heart thunders into my rib cage, not only from the exertion, but from the connection of making her mine, from reminding her who she belongs to over and over again.

Nyla is a formidable partner in all ways.

"I want to try that thing again where you lift up my legs really high and spread them out before you do that other thing with your fingers." She swirls two fingers around before scissoring them. "That was a good time. Maybe we should call that move the Helicopter Mom."

I chuckle into her sweaty hair.

She is absolutely my better half.

"I think the next thing you need is a bath, dirty girl." My

cock perks up at the mental image of cleaning her up just so I can make her messy all over again.

"Mmm. I like smelling like you. Can I stay like this a little longer?" She lifts her eyebrows and pouts her face as she asks the question.

Fuck. My primal side loves the sound of that.

"It's getting cool. Why don't we get some clothes on, and I'll open a bottle of wine. We can soak in the tub while we watch the sun set later."

I explored the house while Nyla was sleeping earlier and found the attached bathroom with floor-to-ceiling windows in front of the extra-large soaker tub, and I've been fantasizing about soaping her up and sliding all over her body ever since.

"That sounds amazing." Her smile goes all the way up to her eyes.

When Nyla tries to sit up from our place on the chair outside, I pull her into me, cradling her in my arms and carrying her through the house to the bedroom before I let her take a step on her own.

I grab a bag by the door and empty its contents onto the bed before she puts her old clothes on.

"What's this?" She eyes the clothes on the bed.

"Creed ordered his guys to stop in town and pick up our groceries. He also tasked them with buying you some new clothes." I point at the pile of fabric. "This is what two middle-aged bikers with too much money and no fashion sense came up with."

She returns her attention to the bed and grins, thumbing the thin black sweater on top before holding it up. "They did pretty good."

When she pulls it over her head, I have to agree with her. It fits her tits nice and tight, and it shows off everything that's mine.

"So what happens now?" she asks. When I lick my lips in anticipation of what I want to happen now, she clarifies, "I mean, now that Ratchet has the microfiche."

"Once he knows who the heir is, he'll get in touch with my father, and they'll hunt him down. Right now, Elia's organization is split because there is a challenge for leadership. Creed has the respect of most of Elia's men, but the majority of their group will follow Elia's heir, and it's the quickest way to end the war."

"What if the heir says no? I mean, someone is going to great lengths to protect their identity, so it stands to reason that he wants no part of it."

I lean my weight into the dresser behind me, resting the heel of my palms against the surface. "Then they better hope Creed finds them first. My father has tried to kill all of his sons at one time or another. He isn't above torturing a random stranger into submission to take over an empire."

Nyla's face twists into disgust. "I still can't believe your father tried to kill you."

"He tried to kill you too when he posted the hit on us. He's the one who is challenging Creed for control. Ratchet is just his puppet, a lapdog doing his bidding."

She half sits, half falls onto the bed in disbelief as she mutters "Jesus" on an exasperated breath.

Finally, she says, "Well, there's no point in sitting around here crying over spilled coffee."

I glare at Nyla.

Her apathetic expression is not giving anything away.

"It's 'crying over spilled milk,'" I correct her.

"Why would I cry over spilled milk?" She makes a barfing face. "I hate milk. I wouldn't cry. I'd be happy if milk spilled."

"Well, yeah, I mean, I'm lactose intolerant so—wait. That's

beside the point." Crossing my arms, I level her with a wary look. "Nyla?" I say her name using my stern voice.

Lowering her head, she lifts her eyes, batting her lashes. "Yes, Dagen."

"Are you fucking with me?"

She bites her lip, then offers me a culpable smirk.

"If I admit I am, do I get a spanking?" Her voice turns throaty when she says the last word.

I imagine if I shoved my hand down the front of her brand-new pants, I'd find a telltale wet spot growing between her pretty thighs.

Closing the distance, I stop in front of her and ease my fingers into the hair at the back of her head.

I fist a handful and tilt her face up to meet mine.

"You're getting one anyway, you little hellcat." I bend over, licking along her bottom lip before claiming another kiss.

Her mouth is tied with one other body part for the place on her body I most like to kiss.

When I pull back from her, she takes a deep breath.

Her deep brown eyes take on a golden hue when she's aroused.

Noted.

"I've been fucking with you," she admits.

I knew it.

"Well then, I'll be returning the favor tonight, after our bath."

"What favor?"

"You fuck with me, I fuck with you—harder."

I give her a peck on the lips. She opens her mouth to take more, but I stand and hold out my hand. My cheeks stretch into a wolfish grin I can't contain.

"Why don't you check to see if your team has pulled

anything from the microfiche image, then we'll curl up with some wine and talk some more before we move on to the fun stuff."

In truth, I want a few minutes to check my phone for updates.

My brothers should be crossing the border if they haven't already.

I won't be able to focus on Nyla if I'm worrying about them.

I leave her to the computer in the main area and check my phone, which I left on the kitchen counter.

Sure enough, I have a few missed calls and texts.

The last is from Lennox, threatening to turn the car around and come back if I don't respond. I send him a quick text to let him know we're fine, and my phone rings a few seconds later.

Cole is laughing on the line when I answer. "He was totally going to make Ryder turn around and cross back into Canada to come get you. I told him you were busy schtupping your baby mommy. You're on speaker. Go ahead, tell me I'm wrong."

"Fuck off."

They all laugh.

It's clear, since he's using the same nickname for Nyla that Lennox used, that they've been using their time driving home to discuss our relationship.

I hear Lennox in the background. "Tell him about the contract."

"Oh yeah. Hey, the hit on you and Nyla has been canceled," Cole says.

"Really? Why would he do that?"

"Well, it's not good news. We think it's because Dad knows who the heir is, and killing you is no longer necessary for him to take what he wants."

I go quiet while I think about what he's saying.

If our father is successful, he will fight to control all of our businesses, and that includes the companies we've been trying to hold on to.

I pull a bottle of red out of the cupboard and start searching for a corkscrew. "Where are you guys now?"

"We crossed the border about ten minutes ago. We're stopping for gas, then we should be home in a couple of hours."

I look over at Nyla, who is tapping away at the keyboard, then pour us each a glass.

"Message us to let us know you're home, but give me a break if I don't respond right away, yeah?"

There are more chuckles before Cole says goodbye and ends the call.

I watch Nyla work for a few minutes in silence.

When Ryder found Amara, and when Cole found Harlow, everything about adding them to our group felt right and natural.

Now I feel the same about Nyla.

Our father may have fractured our foundation, but we're claiming our new family, and it is stronger than it was before.

We also have more to lose.

Nyla jumps to her feet, sending her chair back a couple of feet and snapping me out of my reverie.

My skin prickles at the sight of her ashen face as she points to the screen with worry in her wide eyes.

"Dagen, everyone made a mistake." There is a slight shake in her hand as I round the counter and walk toward her.

"What do you mean?"

"My team pulled the birth certificate from the microfiche. Elia's heir—"

Nyla points to one spot on the screen, and I close the distance between us as she clasps her hands to her mouth, looking too shocked to say the name out loud.

I scan over the birth certificate. I first see a birthdate that I know isn't Ryder's. I travel further down until I land on a name I never thought I would see.

The heir isn't a male after all.

"It's Sloane."

Now I'm a pawn in a game with no rules, and I refuse to play the part I've been handed. The only way to win is to be the queen and I'm taking the throne to protect my son.

To stay alive, I have to make a deal with the devil and hope it's the lesser of all the evils that surround me.

I've lost too much and I've had enough.

I will burn this vicious empire to the ground, and from its ashes, I will rise.

ACKNOWLEDGMENTS

Wow...book three is done already. I want to thank you for sticking with me through this series. Your words of support are fuel for my next stories so thank you to everyone who reads and also to those who take the time to send a note or leave a review for a future reader who may be a good fit for my writing.

I want to thank everyone who helped me bring this book to life:

Cover design: Kirsty Still (Pretty Little Design Co.)
Editor: Caroline Knecht (Reedsy)
Photographer: Wander Aguiar
Cover Model: Zakk Davis

And, always, my family. I want to thank them for their encouragement, interest and support.

Until next time...

ABOUT THE AUTHOR

Luna Kayne is a multi-genre romance author located in Canada. She writes dark, explicit, romantic suspense with a hint of humor and angst. Her men are dominant and often stubborn, and her women are usually underestimated. As for tropes and sub-genres, nothing is off the table.

In 2021, she won an IPPY (Independent Publisher Book Awards) award with her novel, *Step Darkly* which earned a bronze medal.

Luna Kayne is the pen name of author *Sheri Landry* who writes non-romance action thrillers and has won awards for her writing under both names.

You can learn more at LunaKayne.com.

facebook.com/LunaKayne

twitter.com/LunaKayne

instagram.com/LunaKayne

tiktok.com/@luna.kayne

bookbub.com/profile/luna-kayne